the Libertine

Also available from
Saskia Walker
and Harlequin HQN

THE HARLOT

From Spice Books

RAMPANT

And coming soon, more Taskill adventures unfold in
THE JEZEBEL

The Libertine

SASKIA WALKER

HARLEQUIN® HQN™

Recycling programs
for this product may
not exist in your area.

ISBN-13: 978-0-373-77739-6

THE LIBERTINE

Copyright © 2013 by Saskia Walker

This edition published by arrangement with Harlequin Books S.A.

For questions and comments about the quality of this book, please contact us
at CustomerService@Harlequin.com.

Printed in U.S.A.

For my wonderful agent, Roberta Brown.
For my exceptionally talented editor, Susan Swinwood.
For my rock, the man who supports me every step of the way, Mark Walker.

chapter One

Saint Andrews, Scotland
1715.

Even as she urged her mount through the forest, Chloris Keavey questioned her judgment and sanity, for the place she sought was an ominous, gaunt dwelling where those who practiced witchcraft gathered under the protection of their leader. It was a dangerous undertaking, and when she caught sight of the building a shiver ran through her. Stone built and covered in ivy, the house merged into its setting as wild and foreboding as the forest itself.

"I pray that my quest is not ill-fated," she murmured, steeling herself for what she might encounter. Chloris approached with a mixture of wariness and determination, for it was both a last resort and a terrible risk. The people who gathered there practiced forbidden magic, despite the threat of persecution and death that hung over their kind. Who was most insane—those who defied the law laid down by King James VI of Scotland over a hundred years earlier, or her for willingly seeking them out?

A breeze swept up around her, stirring the tall trees that surrounded the dwelling. Early spring leaves and blossoms were more abundant at this spot, which meant the trees cast the building in shadows as they swayed in the breeze. Evening was on its way. A candle set in a small window to one side of the heavy wooden door was the only welcoming sign she saw.

Dismounting, she looped her horse's reins around the branch of a tree then approached the house. Now that she was closer she saw the barns and wooden outhouses beyond, nestled deeper in the trees. It was there that the commerce was undertaken, the cart and carriage construction. The work that proved a respectable mask for the other practices that went on there. Over the door she saw that a word had been carved into the wooden plinth. *Somerled.* It did not sound like a warning, but neither was she clear on its meaning.

When she rapped on the door a young woman appeared. The woman lifted the candlestick from the window, held it aloft and eyed Chloris with caution. "What or who is it that you are seeking?"

Was she a servant, or was she one of them? Chloris wondered. There was no cap covering the woman's head and her hair was hanging loose about her shoulders. Her eyes were unusual, being a misty-gray color. In all other respects she appeared none other than a normal young woman.

"I have been advised that a…" *Witch.* Chloris paused. She knew she must avoid saying the word. "…that a knowledgeable one abides here. Someone who might be able to advise me on an intimate matter."

"What intimate matter might that be?" The young woman looked beyond Chloris, as if checking she was alone.

Chloris had been told she would have to state her cause to gain entry, so she was prepared. It was hard to voice the nature of her problem, however, especially to a stranger. The sense of discomfort she felt was great, and yet the woman before her scarcely blinked when she said it aloud. "I've been told that your leader can influence a woman's…fertility."

"Who told you this?"

"Maura Dunbar."

Mention of her contact by name drew a nod from the woman. She stood back and ushered Chloris into the hallway. "Wait here a moment and I will announce you."

Chloris stood in silence and then looked back at the door. Evening was already closing in. She would have to be back at Torquil House in time for dinner or her absence would raise suspicion. It was still possible to leave, to disappear into the encroaching evening and return to the safety of her cousin's home. *No. I need to be here. They might be able to help me.* The risk was great, but her options were few. Anything, absolutely anything, was worth an attempt, and Chloris Keavey, wife of Gavin Meldrum of Edinburgh, was determined to be a brave soul.

Before she had the chance to think on it any longer the young woman returned, nodded and led her into a parlor. Chloris followed, warily. Once inside she discovered it was far from what she might have expected, being both pleasantly furnished and warm, with the fragrant aroma of a peat fire filling the room.

Apart from the fire there was only one candle, the one that was held by her escort. The young woman nodded beyond the fireplace. "I'll leave you to your dealings."

She was gone inside a blink, taking her candle with her.

As the door clicked shut Chloris looked about the room. With only the glowing embers in the grate to see by, it took a few moments for her eyes to adjust. Then she noticed that the parlor was comfortable, with solid wooden chairs arranged around the fire and a well-stacked bookshelf at the nearside of the hearth. On the far side she spied a generous stack of peat. The flagstones in front of the fireplace had been well polished and glinted in the firelight.

Almost immediately she knew she was not alone.

There was someone sitting in the gloomy shadows beyond the fireplace. It was the feeling of being watched that alerted her to the presence. Shrouded in darkness as the seat was, she could not discern the person, nor did the person make it easy on her by revealing themselves. Instead they remained hidden, watching her.

Chloris clasped her hands together so that they did not tremble. Never let them know you are afraid, her father had taught her when she was a bairn. She swallowed, reminding herself that she was not easily frightened. Despite the lurid tales she'd heard told about the nature of witches, the house indicated some level of sophistication. Grandeur, even. Perhaps the old woman would be kindly. Something had kept her and her coven safe for a number of years, after all. Chloris could only guess at what it might be. She had come here with little information other than what she'd overheard the servant girls discussing. When she'd taken Maura aside and asked for the whereabouts of the local coven and its leader, she did so out of desperation. Now that she was here, the stories she'd heard about witches over the years came to mind and made her uneasy. Chloris did not want to be afraid. She'd made the decision to come here and she stood by that.

She coughed aloud and took several paces forward, closing on the fireplace. Peering into the gloom, she tried to discern features of the person sitting in the armchair. "Good evening," she said, her voice faltering.

The figure moved in response, long booted legs stretching across the floor toward her.

Chloris peered in disbelief. It was a man. *How could this be?*

She had expected a mature woman who could aid her with her problem, or at least speak with knowledge about women and the problems of their sex. Instead it was a man who sat before her, languid—yet poised as a nobleman.

She struggled to maintain her composure, but her heart beat erratically. This was so far from what she had expected, and she had thought on it at length. Chloris was practical by nature, and whilst she had her doubts about how much their forbidden craft could achieve, she'd felt sure an older woman would have some sage words about fertility.

"Good evening." His voice was deep and resonant.

It sent a shiver through her, because she could not see his features clearly in the gloom. In his hand she saw that he nursed a crystal glass half-full with dark wine.

"Please take a seat and speak with me about your concerns." The man leaned forward in his chair.

Chloris inhaled sharply. The firelight cast his face in stark relief. There was a wild look to him for he had harsh, angular features and dark winged eyebrows that barely shaded the brilliance of his strange blue eyes. The firm outline of his mouth and the rakish look in his eye were evidence of a sensual nature. That left her in no doubt the rumors she'd heard about the carnal nature of those who practiced witchcraft were indeed true. On a woman she might have been able to ignore any blatant signs of her wanton ways, not so this man. She was scarcely able to look away, though, despite the fact that she felt the urge to run. "Forgive me, sire. I have made a mistake in coming here."

Frowning, he rose from his chair. "Why so?"

Chloris stepped back into the shadows.

His eyelids flickered and he scrutinized her more intensely.

Chloris attempted to lower her gaze, but still found herself compelled to consider his impressive personage. He was built large and wore a skirted coat in dark red, with a fitted waistcoat beneath. The lace at his cuffs was well made but not overly extravagant. His knee breeches emphasized his build, tightly fitted about the thighs as they were, and his woolen stockings and buckled boots also displayed his stature. His clothes were finely made and stylish, but he wore no wig and his dark hair was loose and hung to his shoulders. In sum, he was dangerously attractive.

She mustered a response, forcing her gaze back to his. "On reflection I am not sure you are the right person to help me."

A knowing smile passed over his handsome mouth. He stepped after her. "If a soul calls to me I am obligated to assist, if it is within my power to do so. In coming here, you have already called to me."

"No." The more she backed away the closer he seemed to be, looming over her, bright eyed and determined.

"Why not?" His manner was blatant to the point of rudeness. He swigged from his glass, draining it, and set it down on a nearby table. Devilment shone in his eyes. It was almost as if he was aware of her discomfort and its cause.

"I do not wish to discuss my intimate matters with a man." A man who was several years younger than her, by the looks of him.

"We are equally able to help you, man or woman. I will

treat you no different for being a woman, if you treat me no different for being a man." Humor danced in his eyes. "We are equal in our humanity, are we not?"

His statement shocked her. It went against the rebellious ways she expected of his sort, and it was certainly nothing she ever expected to hear a man say. In her experience men were all too ready to demean a woman for their own aggrandizement, not elevate her to their own status. Shocking her was, no doubt, his purpose.

He circled her as he continued to speak, eyeing her from head to toe, his gaze lingering particularly on her double-breasted riding jacket as if he was able to discern her figure beneath. "I am aware of the matter that has brought you here. You described your problem to Ailsa, did you not?"

Chloris felt her face heat. Presumably Ailsa was the woman who had opened the door, and she had gone into the parlor to announce the visitor. That meant he was already fully informed of her problem. That and his bold inquisitive stare as he circled her, looking her up and down with total candor, made her situation verge on humiliation. She was desperate for help. Nevertheless she could not discuss matters of her marital bed with a young man, a man who some would say was in league with dark forces.

It was a mistake. She regretted coming and turned away, heading for the door.

He closed on the door quickly, striding over to bar her way.

Chloris drew to a halt. Her breath was trapped in her lungs. Cornered as she was, she defended herself. "Aren't you afraid that someone will reveal the presence of your coven here, so close to the royal burgh of Saint Andrews?"

It had been an attempt to divert the nature of the exchange

on her part, but it only seemed to amuse him. A lazy smile passed over his handsome face. "Coven?" He gestured around the room, where he was her only host. "What coven?"

The man's manner was infuriating. "I know that people come to you for assistance," she explained, "for your knowledge of…" *Magic.*

"The old ways." He grew serious for a moment and she caught sight of a weary look in his expression. "What we believe in and practice are simply old ways, passed down from mother to child." His eyes darkened. "It is time for the Church and its slaves to cease the persecution of those who differ from them."

Chloris felt oddly moved by his comments, and her mood leveled. "But I have heard that people like you are still hunted down. Surely you take a risk every time someone comes into your home for help."

He considered her thoughtfully. "Those who come to us in earnest have little cause to be angry and oust us. Is that your intention?"

Remembering her own need and its intimate nature, she shook her head in shame. "No, I…"

He cocked his head to one side, as if considering her comment. "You think I should be more cautious than allowing a strange woman into my home?"

Somewhat affronted, she rounded her eyes at him.

He laughed softly then bowed his head. "Perhaps you are right. Perhaps I should be more cautious. It was Maura Dunbar who advised you to come here. I do not recognize you. In what way are you an acquaintance of Maura?"

Chloris immediately regretted her comments, for they had

drawn her into a deeper conversation. "She is a servant at the home of a friend of mine."

More accurately, Maura was the servant of her cousin Tamhas Keavey, with whom she was visiting. Chloris was unwilling to draw her cousin into it. Tamhas was a prominent landowner and a member of the town council of Saint Andrews. He would be appalled to know she was here with people who he thought should be strung up for their beliefs and practices.

The man studied her then nodded thoughtfully. "Intriguing." His eyes glittered darkly. "As you are known to Maura I will choose to trust you to stay a while longer in my home."

Again Chloris's face heated. She had the feeling he was more than a little amused by their exchange. Before she could respond he moved, quick as lightning, and reached for her hand. His action took her by surprise and she was unable to react before he unfastened her kid glove, tugged it off and touched her bared hand.

"You wear a wedding band, I see."

"Yes, I—"

He rested her glove over the doorknob.

Chloris stared at it. She knew what it signified. He no longer barred the door. If she picked up the glove she would be on her way.

"Tell me," he continued, "do you wish to be with child, or to avoid that situation?"

Still he held her hand, keeping her close to him. She should have been affronted by his forthright questioning, and yet he was so strangely compelling that she whispered her response. "I wish to…to be with…" It was his stare, so bold and suggestive, that made her falter. Pulling her faculties together, she braced herself. "I wish to fall pregnant with my husband's child."

He considered her at length. All the while he stroked the tender skin on the inside of her wrist with one finger, softly, drawing her to him.

Try as she might, she could not summon the will to pull her hand free.

"Tell me your name." His voice was so melodic, so seductive.

She swayed.

When she did not respond he inclined his head. "Your given name will suffice."

"Chloris," she whispered.

"Chloris." He repeated it as if exploring the word that drew her attention, learning it inside and out. "Chloris." He said it even slower, rolling the word around his mouth as if tasting it—as if tasting her.

Her legs went weak under her.

He reached his free hand out.

She flinched, thinking he was about to touch her face.

He paused, then pulled a spring blossom from her hair. Chloris realized it must have been trapped in the loose tendrils that had escaped her lace cap during her hasty ride. What surprised her most of all was his actions. First he examined the small bud as if it were of great importance, and then he slipped it into his pocket. "You have no child."

"No. I am barren."

"I doubt that." His comment was glibly stated.

She pulled her hand free of his and snatched her glove from the place he had rested it. "You seem to revel in being forthright to the point of rudeness, sire." Moreover, his words only made the pain worsen. It also made her doubt his skills. "What would you know of my life? My husband's first wife carried a child. Alas they both perished. He married again to sire an heir. Eight years we have been married without issue and now my husband is ready to disown me."

Regret swamped her immediately. She'd blurted it out and now she was embarrassed by her confession. Only she and Gavin knew about her shame over this private matter. A man such as Gavin Meldrum, with a sizable fortune and numerous commercial interests, wanted a son. She had proven to be a failure in his eyes. Nevertheless her pride made this difficult for her. She rarely spoke of it, even to her closest friends, although she suspected many friends and acquaintances in Edinburgh whispered about her sorry state of affairs, and some of her friends had even suggested ways in which she might fall pregnant, many of them quite immoral and totally unacceptable to her.

Tugging on her glove, she made ready to leave.

"Why do you attempt to turn away now? Now, when you have finally summoned the will to come here?"

It unnerved her that he knew that it had been a dilemma for her. Of course he did. In all likelihood, she surmised, it was a dilemma for anyone who came here.

They practiced witchcraft, after all.

"The hardest part is over," he added.

She met his gaze, determined not to be cowed by him, no matter how striking his presence. "Maura said she saw an older woman when she came here last week. I thought it would be the same for me."

"Ah, so it really is because I am a man that you reject my potential assistance in this matter."

She opened her mouth to ask why else, and then thought better of it. Everything she said only seemed to mire her deeper in this awkward discussion.

"I was not here last week." A shadow passed through his eyes. "I am often away on…family concerns." There was a mysterious, secretive edge to his expression and it made her wonder about the nature of his family concerns. "But I returned less than an hour ago and I was here for your visit. That is because fate has deemed it so."

Chloris stared at him. Fate. Could it be true?

Moreover, how could it be that she was so strangely intrigued by the man, when she balked at the idea of discussing her intimate matters with him? He was no more than twenty-five years of age in her estimation, and yet he was so strangely age-old, even though he was also rebellious in his ways. She was about to turn thirty years, and she was afraid to be alone with him. It was his air of questionable morals. He was unruly, a wolf in sheep's clothing. He was also overly frank while he referenced her malady without stricture or concern.

"You are skittish and wary, Mistress Chloris. I understand why. However it is a shame because I sense you truly believe I have the power to help you." Once again he spoke bluntly, but this time it was somewhat more serious and sympathetic.

She nodded. "Yes, I did believe that you might be able to help me. I know little of your ways," she added cautiously, aware that many would think her insane walking into the house such as this, "however, as a child I had a nursemaid who had some skills as a healer. She used to take me for walks along the shore and in the meadows, and she would tell me about the plants and herbs and what ailments they could be used for. She was very fond of me, and I of her."

The man's curiosity seemed baited. "Tell me something of her ways."

Chloris thought back to those times. "She wore scarlet ribbons around her wrists. She told me it was to ward off rheumatism."

"She believed?"

"Yes, she said it eased the pain. Others said that the ribbons were a sign of her..." her voice dropped to a whisper "...her bond with the Devil."

When she grew quiet he nodded. "You were not afraid of her, though, and that is what has made you brave enough to come here."

"My need is what made me brave enough. There is no other path available to me." She lifted her chin. She was not used to sharing such intimate details about herself. "However, it is because of my Eithne, my nursemaid, that I believed it might be worthwhile coming."

He studied her carefully. "Tell me, what became of your nursemaid?"

Chloris inhaled. It was not what she expected him to ask, for it was the part of the story she would rather not have shared. His gaze held hers, though, refusing to let her ignore the question, demanding the truth. It was obvious that if she denied him any knowledge that he asked for, he would refuse to help her.

She took a deep breath. "A dreadful illness took most of my family, the cough. Some say she protected me from it because she favored me. Others said she was unwilling to help the rest of my family by healing them." She paused. "Eithne was turned out by my guardian."

Eithne had been turned out by her cousin Tamhas Keavey,

with whom she now visited, but that was not the point. At the time she'd been a child and Tamhas's ward. He'd been a man in his early twenties and the only one willing to take her in when her parents perished.

The man stared at her, assessing her. "You did not believe she was responsible?"

"No, I didn't. The ability to cure the illness was beyond Eithne. But she knew things and she whispered for me in her prayers, using words that I didn't understand." Seeing the interest in his eyes she went on. "She told me I would be protected from the cough."

It was so much more than a cough, but she knew they called it that in order to force its darkness back, to stand up to it. Chloris stemmed the other painful memories. Memories of the way her cousin and guardian had called Eithne a slave to the Devil while he cast her out. Chloris had been plagued with doubts, respecting him as she did, but she had never been able to believe it.

Drawn back to the moment, she lifted her head. When she met the man's stare she had the eerie suspicion he knew what she was thinking. "I was always happy when she held my hand."

"She was a woman who respected the old ways." He spoke softly.

Chloris felt comforted. Had he moved closer? His knees were pressed against her full skirts, but she had not been aware of him moving. "What do you mean when you say that, 'old ways'?"

"Some call us pagans, heathen, because we believe in the power inherent in the natural world and we seek it in our rituals. Many Christians have benefited, and they will not speak out against us. However, they cannot defend us because they would be in danger of being called out themselves." He shrugged. "We are forced to live a secretive existence."

His tone had turned embittered, and Chloris felt he had shared something that was fundamental to his character. There was a brooding, almost angry look at the back of his eyes.

In a blink, it was gone.

He smiled, briefly. "Enough of that. We understand each other a little more now." He inclined his head. "There are rituals that we undertake to increase both virility and fertility." His gaze raked over her. "If you are willing I will perform the rituals myself, in order to help you."

He was so close she felt the heat of his body, yet the whispered nature of their conversation suited her more than the blatant words he had delivered before. "What would these rituals entail?"

"I would need to lay my hands upon you."

She knew by his expression that he meant more than holding her ungloved hand. Could she allow this compelling young man that liberty?

She needed to know more. "Why do you need to do that?"

"To evoke the essence of spring and direct it inside you."

His whispered words affected her oddly. She felt suddenly hot, her limbs heavy.

His eyes burned more brightly. Was it the reflection of the glowing embers in the hearth?

"By drawing on the essence of something from the natural world we harness the gift of birth and rebirth." He lifted his hand and opened it to her. It gleamed, as if he held sunlight right there in his palm.

Gasping aloud, she saw what he intended—to demonstrate.

A moment later he spoke again, but his words made no sense. He repeated the phrase several times beneath his breath. Chloris could not look away, so intense was his gaze.

Heat swelled in the pit of her belly. Glancing down, she saw that he now held his palm open in front of her skirts. It was directly above the spot where she burned, and when his hand moved and he whispered those strange words, the heat roiled and gathered within her. Her thighs shuddered, her core tingling.

It was so carnal a sensation and so utterly unexpected that she swayed and her head dropped back. *I might faint.*

Then he blew across the bare skin of her exposed neck. A gentle breath it was, and yet it felt like the wind through the trees to Chloris. Heavily scented, as if carrying blossoms like the one he had plucked from her hair.

Beneath her corset her chest felt constricted. Panic rushed in on her.

Recoiling, she whispered, "No. No, I cannot—"

"Hush."

He stepped away, breaking the connection. When he looked back his eyes were normal once again. "Take your leave. Think on what has been said and done here."

There was no doubt she would think on it, at length, if only she could get away and gather her faculties. She could scarcely function due to the wild throbbing in her loins.

Fumbling for the door handle, she could do no more than mumble her thanks to him in response, rendered speechless as she was by his demonstration of magical power.

Mercifully, the door clicked open.

"Mistress Chloris?"

With her breath captured in her chest, she forced herself to meet his eyes. "Yes?"

"You asked if I could trust you. My instinct told me yes, and once I had touched you...I knew without doubt that I could trust you. That's why I took off your glove."

That was why. Her palm tingled in response to his comment, and at the very same moment she knew that he was informing her of something much deeper than the issue of trust between them. What was it—that he could connect with her intimately that way, perhaps read her thoughts and gain the measure of her, by running his fingertips over her skin?

When she responded, she could hear the tremble in her own voice. "I see."

"A great deal can be learned and achieved through touch," he continued, and his voice was low and heavy with suggestion, "and through laying my hands on you, I could ensure that all your desires could be fulfilled."

Desires? Flustered, she tried to muster an appropriate response.

One corner of his mouth lifted. "You know where to find me."

chapter Two

As the door closed Lennox breathed her in, savoring the woman for several long moments after she'd taken her leave. How tempted he'd been to clasp her wrist, to wrap his free hand around her waist and hold her still to the spot. It was only the magic that made her want to run. She'd wrenched the door open as if her life depended on it but she'd been convinced, earlier. Desire held sway with her, too. It was only a matter of time until he had a taste of her, of that Lennox was sure. Moments longer and she would have submitted willingly, but Lennox relished giving her freedom when she was so ready to capitulate. It guaranteed a return that would be worth the wait.

Who was she? She'd been introduced to them by Maura Dunbar, which indicated a connection with Tamhas Keavey, who was Maura's employer. Lennox and Tamhas held old grievances, and the opportunity to rattle Keavey was always tempting.

The woman was as enticing as a rose coming into bloom, her pale skin like its petals—blushing, soft and inviting to the fingertips—her eyes wide and imploring with bold determination. She was quite a riddle, for she was mature and brave— and just wary enough to tease his interest—yet she was also a woman who had not been fully awakened, of that he was quite sure. That combination was something he found rather intoxicating. He'd become jaded perhaps.

Women who sought him out were either lusty sorts who were all too ready to lie on their backs for him, or they feared him so badly he found it disagreeable to be in their company for long. Not so Mistress Chloris. Whilst she was measured and cautious, she spoke and acted with a level of courage that impressed him. It was quite obvious to him she was embold-ening herself in order to attain her goal.

How sweet it would be to help her fulfill that goal. His thoughts ran to bedding her himself, and the prospect was quite delicious. It would be even more pleasurable if she were to need it beyond measure. Lennox poured himself another half glass of claret as he contemplated it. He wasn't altogether convinced that she was barren. The fact that she seemed con-vinced of it was important. It made him curious about her circumstances. Was her caution toward the ritual driven by what others might think of her coming to Somerled, or gen-uine trepidation about magic and carnal matters? He knew with certainty that he would discover more about her. What he saw in her was a woman who had not yet truly awoken to her essential nature. That was an abomination.

She was a pretty woman, too, with hair the color of hay in summer sunshine and hazel eyes spun with green flecks. When she had stated the nature of her concern he'd felt her growing shame. It disturbed him that she was fretting on the issue so, when so many women who came to see him had the opposite complaint, the fear of being saddled with an unwanted bairn that they could not support. Yet he also saw what a fine mother she would make, and how she longed to hold her own child.

Ultimately it was her attempted resistance to him that convinced him she was worth his time. There was a mutual draw between them, it was instinctive and immediate, and he had relished it. He couldn't help himself. Toying with her was pleasurable, especially so the startled look in her eyes when she became aroused by him. It would be pleasing to watch her unravel while he seduced her.

Their encounter had lifted his mood, which was a mercy. He'd been sour to his people on his return that afternoon, and they did not deserve that. It was often the way. Whenever he heard talk of witchcraft he'd follow the trail of whispers and accusations, hoping it would lead him to his lost kin, his sisters, Jessie and Maisie. Years had passed since they'd been parted. He was always hunting for them, and along the way he'd witnessed too much suffering and pain amongst those who practiced the craft. If the timing was right he was often able to assist the accused, breaking several free before they were put to death. But he was yet to find his sisters, and that meant he returned to Somerled with a heavy heart. Ailsa's smile disappeared when he returned alone. They all wanted him to find his kin, knowing it was what drove him. Once he did, they would all depart the Lowlands, where the persecution of witches had gone on too long.

He'd been brooding on it in the gloom of the parlor when a timely distraction had arrived in the form of Mistress Chloris. The woman had brought a breath of spring with her. He fished the small hawthorn blossom out of his pocket and turned it in his fingers, once more savoring the woman's essence. It was not yet the end of April, and the hawthorn didn't usually come into blossom until May. Most normal folk held suspicions about hawthorn being an unlucky bloom, but Lennox's people used it in their healing. The fact that Mistress Chloris had unwittingly arrived with it in her hair endeared her to him.

Abandoning his glass and pocketing the hawthorn, he left the parlor and followed the sound of voices and laughter into the scullery beyond. When he opened the door he saw Nathan and Lachlan seated at the large table at the heart of the house, deep in conversation, the crumbs of a hearty repast scattered on the oak table, their ale mugs near empty.

Ailsa hovered nearby, ale jug in her hand. She looked his way as soon as he entered the room, as if she had been awaiting his appearance. By her side Glenna, Lachlan's wife and the oldest member of the coven, worked at a mixing bowl.

"Ladies." He nodded his head their way.

Glenna lifted her mixing bowl from the table and held it against her waist with one hand, stirring its contents with the other. She did not answer, but she observed him with an air of disapproval. At her side, Ailsa looked sullen.

He could tell by the set of them that they had something to say.

Nathan waved his way eagerly, interrupting the ominous presence of women with something on their minds. "The carriage for Master MacDougal is near done. He'll be pleased with the craftsmanship, I warrant. I have studded the velvet seats myself today, and his wife will look as fine as a queen when she rides in it."

Lennox strolled over, squeezed Nathan on the shoulder, then lifted the ale jug from Ailsa's hand, using it to refill Nathan's and Lachie's mugs. "Good work. It will pay to have the head of the town council and his wife sitting comfortably in such a fine carriage."

Lachie grinned at Lennox. Nathan was a young and eager

craftsman and his pride lay in his work, but Lachie was older and understood more of Lennox's intent—to gain the approval of the burghers of Saint Andrews.

Lennox chatted on the subject of commissions awhile with the men, but the weight of the women's stares on him forced his attention back.

When he glanced over his shoulder at them Ailsa nudged Glenna. "Shall I tell him, or will you?"

"Tell me what?" He turned fully to them.

Glenna carried on with her tasks, turning out clootie dumpling mix from her mixing bowl into a damp square of muslin, as if it was imperative to make haste with her work and therefore ignore him. She tied the fabric in a knot and carried it to the pot hanging over the fire to steam.

Lennox withheld a sigh. "Glenna, spit out your thoughts."

"You take too many risks and you put me in fear of our lives." She spoke sternly as she worked. "This is a dangerous folly indeed. That woman, you should have turned her away. She is Tamhas Keavey's cousin, visiting from Edinburgh these past few weeks."

Lennox smiled. He'd suspected something of that order for she was clearly wellborn. Because Tamhas Keavey and Lennox were all but daggers drawn on each other, this news made the evening's events so much more interesting. Tamhas Keavey would spew bile if he knew that another of his womenfolk had all but offered herself into Lennox's hands. The confirmation of kinship with Keavey only sealed his commitment to the task on offer. The seduction of Mistress Chloris would be just the thing to bring ill fortune to Keavey's household. The very thought of it made him more keen, for it amused him mightily.

That, however, was not Glenna's intention.

He laughed softly, strolled over and reached in to run his finger around the mixing bowl she had left on the table. "The recommendation to come here did not come from Keavey, I wager."

Lennox sucked the sweet treacle dough from his finger as he contemplated it some more, relishing the opportunity.

Glenna shook her head at him. "It is boredom that drives you to these things."

Lennox laughed, but there was some truth in her observation. His life was divided between the hunt for his lost siblings and the need to validate his people. When he failed to move forward with either cause he grew restless. Often enough he sought minor amusements to temper that. But he was angry, angry at those who persecuted his kind. When one of their women willingly offered herself to him it was a way for him to give the menfolk a taste of the destruction and loss he and his siblings had experienced. Because the affair always came out, one way or the other. The woman would tell a friend who told another, who told the husband. Reputations were ruined, hearts were broken and shame rained down. It was a drop in the ocean compared to what he and his kin had endured, and he would never take a woman unless she was willing, but when it had happened before he found perverse release in the repercussions.

Glenna muttered on. She wasn't afraid of him, and nor should she be. They spoke their minds to each other, and he could see he was about to get another piece of hers now. She peered at him. "It's as if you have a death wish, Lennox Taskill."

Lennox's mood altered quickly. Glenna only used his family name when she wanted him to heed her words. Locally he went by the name of Lennox Fingal, and he did not appreciate his real name being said aloud when Keavey's cousin had only just left. Her comment scraped harshly along his bones, for every day he wished that he had been the one to be stoned and burned in place of his poor mother, who had been put to death for witchcraft when he was a lad. Craving his own demise was the only power he had over the painful memories, but hearing it spoken aloud was not easy for him, even after all these years.

"Hold your tongue," he snapped.

A chair shifted loudly at the table. Nathan bade them goodnight and left.

Lachie stayed, observing the conversation with a frown.

Glenna waved her hand dismissively. "You spend so much of your time trying to make us welcome in the burgh and yet when a temptation comes along..." She shook her head disapprovingly. "You are wayward and reckless."

It was time to set her straight. "You are wrong there. I do not do anything without a thought. Tamhas Keavey is our barrier to a better life, that is why I admitted her. I realized the woman was somehow connected to him. If it were not for Keavey, the ministers from the Kirk would not be watching us, and the council of Saint Andrews would not be suspicious every time I tried to present matters of commerce to them. It is Keavey who puts the bad look on our ability to heal."

"Is it worth seeking their approval?" Glenna demanded. "They will accept us while it suits them, but as soon as someone points the finger it all unravels. I've lived long enough to see it happen, just as you have. Young witches put to death on the whim of an enemy."

Lennox felt the old pain building again. "I will protect you."

Glenna cast her eyes to the left, to the place where her husband sat working a bit of wood, as was his way. The slender branch Lachlan had chosen to work upon was set between his thighs and he whittled with one hand, his left. His right arm was useless, strapped to his chest where it was secured by a stitch in his sleeve to the front of his coat. It was down to Tamhas Keavey that Lachlan has lost the use of his arm. Keavey had witnessed Lachie collecting forage from the riverside and called him out. Lachie had resisted, and Keavey had urged his mount to trample the old man where he knelt on the ground. Though they had gathered and pooled their restorative powers, Lachie had refused to be fully healed by his coven in order not to draw more suspicion upon them. When Lennox confronted Keavey, Keavey claimed he'd lost control of his mount. However, he also alluded to the fact the old man seemed to be collecting poisonous leaves. Keavey warned him he was watching and seeking evidence. Lennox denied his accusation, but he knew that if they took one step wrong it would not stop at a useless arm.

It only served to frustrate Lennox all the more. The fact that he could not always protect his people reminded him of his failure to protect his mother, and his sisters. If he went ahead with a plan to get at Keavey through the woman, it would mean going against his coven. Then he recalled Mistress Chloris's upturned face, her vulnerability as she requested his assistance. He would have to tread carefully, and in secret, but he wouldn't relinquish the opportunity. Have her he would. "Perhaps you're right," he said to Glenna, keen to put an end to her meddling. "Turn Mistress Chloris away if she comes back here."

Ailsa sidled over and embraced him, clinging to his arm and warming him through. Glenna continued to work. It indicated the extent of her frustration for she would often busy herself with extra tasks when she was brooding upon something.

"We should be on our way," Glenna said eventually. "We should leave these parts. You told us that you grew up without censure, with total acceptance, in the Highlands."

That was hard for her, he knew, for she had been born here in the Lowlands.

"Lennox, I am only angry with you because I feel the clouds rolling in." She met his gaze then looked away, wiping her hands on her apron.

Lennox took note, for she was gifted with some level of foresight, or at least foreboding. Unease built in Lennox. The people who made up his coven were growing restless. He'd tried to make it different, to free them of the fear of persecution suffered by hundreds before. The country was on the cusp of change, he felt it, but he was still haunted by the ghosts of those who had died for their beliefs, for their power to heal and create magic.

"You're a strong master," Glenna continued, "and you've guided us well, but we came together as a coven because we saw wisdom in your words. If we do not find acceptance, we leave. I hoped…but I don't believe full acceptance is possible. We should go north and soon, before the worst happens."

Ailsa squeezed his arm. "How pleasant it would be, to roam free and gather herbs without looking back over my shoulder, fearing I will soon feel the hangman's noose around my neck."

Lennox sighed and wrapped his arm around her shoulder, drawing her in against him. Obligation weighed him down. Obligation to the past, the present and the future. "Hush now.

You will see the Highlands soon, I promise." *After I have found my sisters.*

Ailsa's head lifted, the troubled look in her expression vanishing.

That was pleasing. He slapped her on the rump. "Away up and warm my bed, wench."

Ailsa beamed then trailed her fingers down his arm invitingly before she followed his instruction. He gave a wry smile. At least he was able to keep one of his coven happy, if only in matters of a basic nature.

Once she'd gone, he turned back to Glenna and Lachlan. "When there is no hope of finding my sisters, then we'll be gone. I would understand if you wish to be on your way ahead of me. Something holds me to this place. It is the simple wish that I will be reunited with my kin here."

"Aye, we understand that." Glenna's expression softened. "And we have bound ourselves to you. You are our guide in these difficult times. We trust you to make the right decision should they come after one of our own."

Lachie, who rarely offered his opinion, nodded. "We only comment on your actions when we have concerns." He worried at his jaw with his good hand, as he did when he was unsure whether to speak out or not. "Sometimes you are a mite hotheaded."

"It is a family trait, and it is the reason I fear for my sisters, both pure born witches."

Glenna tapped his arm. "You will find them, mark my words."

"In the meantime," Lachie said, "we have to comment if we think you're putting yourself at risk, and that cousin of Keavey's is an attractive sort."

"And why were you looking?" Glenna asked.

"No crime in looking," Lachie retorted with a chuckle.

The fraught mood had been broken, but Lennox still brooded on their comments. Glenna was correct, to some extent. Boredom drove him to be reckless, or something of that nature. Frustration drove him, too. Finding his siblings and keeping them safe had been his goal since they'd been parted as young ones, and when he was thwarted in his searches he directed his frustration toward those who sought the ruination of his kind. Keavey was set on keeping Lennox and his commerce out of the Royal Burgh of Saint Andrews. Others he did trade with supported the legitimacy of Lennox's interest in affairs of the burgh, whereas Keavey spread rumor and suspicion.

And now Keavey's pretty cousin had offered herself into his hands.

Risky or no, Mistress Chloris was far too tempting a spoil for him to ignore.

chapter Three

"Are you well this morning, cousin?"

Chloris set her fork down in order to respond. She forced herself to smile across the table at her cousin Tamhas and his wife, Jean. "Much better, thank you."

Tamhas observed her briefly before returning his attention to his plate of bannocks and eggs.

Chloris was relieved. She wasn't sure how much amiable conversation she could offer. The night before she'd been unable to attend dinner as planned. After her visit to the house in the woods her emotions were in complete disarray and she knew she would be unable to act sociably. Claiming a dizzy spell after her ride, she had excused herself and gone to her bedchamber. Jean had the cook prepare a gentle broth, but Chloris could scarcely even manage that, so preoccupied was she by the strange events of the evening. Even now, the morning after, she did not feel fully in charge of herself, and if she did not order her thoughts and maintain her composure her host would notice and question it.

However, the man at the house in the woods was not easily dismissed from her thoughts. Distance did not lessen the connection he'd made with her, or her curiosity.

It was only as she mounted her horse, driven by the urgent

need to turn back toward her cousin's house, that she realized she did not even know the man's name.

It was likely that he withheld his name for self-protection, she decided. Even though he'd been somewhat discourteous and had touched her and alluded to more acts in that vein, he was as charming and well mannered as any polite man in society when he chose to be. Yet his fundamental nature was very different to her own—wild, unruly and decadent.

Even though she knew he was at risk of being called out for what he did, Chloris couldn't actually imagine anyone attempting to challenge him. There was a sense of power about the man that was astonishing. Something borne of his witchcraft, no doubt. Deep down she recognized there were men out there who would indeed challenge him, because he did not swear allegiance to king or kirk but to some other, forbidden law.

She'd all but run from the place the evening before, but she'd lain awake thinking about everything he'd said to her. Her mind and body had been filled with the experience, not only the potential of what he'd said, but the odd thrill there had been in it, despite the danger of consulting with those who practiced dark, perhaps even evil ways.

There was also a devastating allure about the man and when she had eventually drifted into a fitful sleep her dreams were restless and filled with images of him. The fact he had been so eager to help her, so interested in her, made her wonder if he planted those images in her mind. Was he capable of such things? She had no idea, but she'd never before spent every moment recalling each word of a conversation with relish, reliving every moment—every glance, every touch—in her mind.

She was afraid of him, but also fascinated. That he was a

compelling personage was unquestionable, but still she wondered at the effect he'd had on her. Moreover, she still couldn't decide if it was wise or foolish to return and partake of his ritual. Hope and curiosity made her want to try it. Wariness and fear battled the desire to do so.

As she attempted to eat her breakfast, she questioned whether she could put herself wholly in his hands, open to him and trust him to undertake this act—this ungodly, heathen act—to save her marriage, to redeem her in her husband's eyes. She had yearned for a child all these years, and now it had become a matter of life and death. A tide of doubt had forced her to pull free from his spell, for his intimate actions not only made her believe in his abilities, they also made her aware of his potential power over her. She remembered the way it had felt. A wave of arousal assailed her.

Flustered, she raised her hand to her throat. The heated physical reaction to her own thoughts shocked her. That a man could affect her so intensely was beyond her experience, and he had done so when she was alone with him as well as in mere memories. She had escaped and she knew she should be glad of that, turning away from a dangerous situation that she shouldn't have entered into in the first place. Instead, she was craving something entirely different, more of the same. It was as if she were being pulled in by the mystery, by the promise and the thrill.

A moment later her dangerous thoughts were interrupted. The nursemaid entered the room with young Rab and Tam, Tamhas and Jean's twin sons, dressed and ready for their morning in the nursery. Chloris was grateful. She always warmed at the sight of them. Barely three years old and adorable little men they were already. They always appeared somber and serious when presented to their parents, but Chloris had also observed them running amok in the gardens and it was those times she enjoyed the most. Often she would join them, taking a seat to observe and encourage their games.

Jean kissed both boys on the forehead and straightened their neckties and collars. When the boys turned to face their father, Tamhas mopped his mouth with a handkerchief, then nodded at the nursemaid and waved his hand, dismissing them. Rab and young Tam bowed their heads to their mother and then to Chloris, and then the nursemaid ushered them out. Chloris observed the family scene wistfully.

Jean caught Chloris's eye when she turned back to her breakfast and nodded over. "I warrant you are missing Gavin."

"Yes, I am." It was the necessary response of a dutiful wife. In truth she felt strangely adrift. She'd been born in Saint Andrews but her place was in Edinburgh now. Besides, she was not sure Jean was entirely comfortable with her staying with them at Torquil House on such an extended visit.

Mention of her husband also made Chloris feel an all too familiar sense of failure. Gavin had sent her to the country to make her health more robust, so that she could bear him a child. It was his sole desire these days, which meant her role in his life went unfulfilled. Anger and frustration often characterized his mood toward her, whereas they'd been friends at first. He'd never been an affectionate man, but more often than not she saw disapproval in his eyes when he looked at her now. It haunted her. More so since she had left Edinburgh for Saint Andrews, because Gavin's final words had been terrifying, more threatening than anything he had said or done before, and that set her on this outlandish path of action where she was willing to try anything to make it happen.

"I have to sit for the town council today," Tamhas informed them as he rose to his feet. "I will send the carriage back for you if you wish to visit the market."

"Yes, we shall." Jean's expression brightened considerably.

Chloris's heart sank. She would be expected to accompany Jean, when what she longed for was some time alone to unravel her thoughts.

Jean was speaking again, and Chloris forced her attention back.

"I am in need of lace to trim a new gown. I want to look at it myself, and my dressmaker informs me that there is a good selection available from a new merchant. He imports the best Flemish samples and brings his wares to the market." Jean looked at Chloris expectantly. "Will you help me in my selection?"

"That would be most enjoyable." Perhaps the distraction would help her muddled thoughts, and Jean was making an effort toward her. There had been some awkwardness from them initially, for Chloris had been Tamhas's ward before he'd met Jean.

Within the hour the carriage had returned and the two women had readied themselves for the outing. As the coachman set off and the carriage jolted along the lane in the direction of Saint Andrews, Chloris noticed that Jean seemed much enlivened by the prospect of visiting the town. Wisps of her chestnut hair escaped her bonnet as she turned her face eagerly to the carriage window. With one hand she held back the curtain for a better view, while the other toyed with the brooch that fastened her cloak at her collarbone neck. Her eyes were bright, and the pale pink glow on her skin was most becoming. It made Chloris smile, for she, too, had found the Keavey household oppressive as a young woman. Not so now, when her life situation had changed drastically. Torquil House was akin to a refuge. Jean was younger than Chloris and appeared to struggle with her role as mistress of the house. She had been married to Tamhas for over four years and had quickly fallen pregnant with twin boys. Chloris did not feel jealousy. It was a kind of wistful sadness she experienced, because she could not fulfill her female obligation to her husband in the same way.

Jean caught her smiling and returned it. "I am enjoying your company, cousin," she said, projecting her voice over the rattles and creaks of the carriage. "It is not often that we have visitors."

It seemed to be an offering of friendship, for which Chloris was grateful. "And I yours. I appreciate you allowing me to visit."

Her comments seemed to put Jean at ease. Was that what she needed, to feel it was her choice to have Chloris as visitor?

Jean brushed her cloak with her hand, apparently busying herself. "It was difficult for me at first," she continued. "Tamhas speaks most fondly about you, and I know you were close after the demise of your family."

Chloris attempted to hide her surprise. Had Jean made a deliberately provocative statement in order to gain an honest response, to get the truth? Jean looked quite sincere. "It was a challenge for him, taking responsibility for a grieving young woman. And it was most kind of him to do so, and to find me a respectable match when the time came."

Jean's eyebrows lifted. Apparently that was not what she'd expected to hear. It made Chloris curious. She did not want to pursue it lest it upset Jean. They had only just found common ground. Chloris did not want to lose that.

Was it true, though, that Tamhas spoke fondly of her? It was far from her experience. When she had been foisted on him as his ward, there were many difficult times. When she grieved her loved ones, he became annoyed. He ignored her and traveled abroad, leaving her to her books and memories. When Tamhas eventually returned, he was sure of himself and ambitious. He assumed control of her, then expected things she could not agree to. He began to hint at their union—first, a union of the flesh. If she pleased him, he might wed her. The pressure of such a proposition for an innocent, grieving woman with no guiding female in her life was immense. Tamhas gave her time, determined, it seemed, to have her. Ultimately Chloris could not warm to the terms, or to him. When his initial plan for her failed, Tamhas treated her as a pawn that he could barter with in order to gain prestige and power. By then she was already beyond the ideal age to wed and it took a while longer before he struck an agreement with Gavin Meldrum of Edinburgh. It was with relief that Chloris accepted Gavin's proposal, unaware that the situation she would encounter in Edinburgh would be even worse than what she had known at Torquil.

It was because of her past relationship with Tamhas that Chloris had not visited Torquil before. Not until Gavin had insisted. However, Chloris found her cousin to be a more mellow master of the house, now that he was older and married. His ambition still drove him, but in matters of the household he seemed content to leave that to his wife.

As the carriage progressed toward the long-established heart of Saint Andrews Chloris observed the familiar streets. Thankfully they did not pass the house where she'd been born and lived, until the dreadful illness came upon her parents and many of their servants. Chloris had not been back to the place since then.

Jean pointed out the households she knew of, merchants and traders who Tamhas engaged with. As the streets grew more narrow so they grew busier, with farmers driving sheep and goats alongside the path. They grew closer to the sea, the air becoming sharper, and Chloris breathed the aroma in. It took her back to her childhood, to the fonder, earlier memories when she would be taken down to see the sea.

The coachman pulled up at a stable yard and secured their carriage there. Then he assisted the two women as they stepped down and he walked ahead of them at some distance, clearing a path.

Gulls wheeled overhead, their distinctive cries drawing her attention to their flight. How they soared as they observed the activity below, eager for pickings amongst the traders' carts and wares. Chloris chuckled when Jean pointed out a brazen gull that flew low over the stalls, scouting. Jean's mood must have reached her, for Chloris felt more alive than she had done in some time.

Or was there some other reason for it? The question flitted through her mind as memories of her illicit endeavor the night before crept up on her again. Now that she had put some distance between her and Torquil House she felt more at ease recalling her impetuous visit to the abode in the woods called Somerled. The whole experience had invigorated her. Safely away from the place, there was a thrill in remembering how brazen she'd been, how daring. Even if she did not pursue the purchase of a magic favor, she knew she would never forget her strange encounter with the master of Somerled. The intrigue and excitement she felt when recalling his actions were foreign emotions, and yet she knew it was the furthest thing from what she should have felt. How could she hold her head up in front of the minister on Sunday, knowing that she had sought out persons who were considered evil—no better than vermin—by good, God-fearing folk?

By her side, Jean was making observations on the chaos of the market.

Chloris nodded. "I do not recall Market Street being as busy as this. It appears Saint Andrews flourishes under the union with England?"

"You would do better to ask Tamhas, for he speaks a lot on the subject and comments frequently that we would do well to look at ways in which Scotland might prosper from the union, instead of raving about independence and civil war." She leaned in and whispered to Chloris conspiratorially, linking her arm. "The truth of the matter is that the burgh is not what it was," she added, "but Tamhas works with the council to bring more trade here."

"It seems their efforts are proving fruitful."

Jean nodded. "I must confess, I find such talk of politics and trade tedious, but do not tell Tamhas I've said that."

"I promise your secret is safe with me." Chloris smiled, but she secretly wished her own husband would talk with her about such matters. As a landlord in Edinburgh, Gavin was much ingratiated with politicians and men of commerce, but he refused to discuss any such matters with her because she was a woman. Tamhas did share those things with Jean, but apparently Jean only feigned interest to please him.

The shared confidence bonded them somewhat and as they wended their way through the busy market, Jean continued to link arms with Chloris. The coachman was always ten paces away, in case they needed assistance. Jean chattered busily at Chloris's side. They passed that way happily for half the length of Market Street, then Jean grasped Chloris's forearm. "There, the lace merchant."

The merchant swept a low bow when he saw them approach. "The finest Flemish lace for your perusal today."

He gestured to the selection of garments and samples he had laid out on a trestle table. Jean examined each and every one, or so it seemed. It was a task Chloris trusted her own dressmaker to fulfill, but for Jean it was a pleasure. Chloris encouraged her and soon they had made purchase of a delicate lace cap as well as placing an order for a length of lace suitable for Jean's dressmaker's use.

When they set off, Jean was in high spirits, but then she froze and gestured to the other side of the cobbled path. "Quickly, there is someone we must avoid at all costs."

Chloris did as instructed but glanced back, her curiosity aroused. When she saw that it was the man from the house in the woods, she inhaled sharply.

By firelight he had appeared attractive. In the light of day he made an even more striking figure than he had the night before. His presence was startling. From the top of his felt tricorne hat to the polished, buckled boots he wore, he was devastatingly handsome. Moreover, he cut a path through the crowd, standing a good head higher than most of those who passed.

Many of those he passed greeted him, which made it seem quite rude of Jean to move out of his path. Perhaps it was better that they had not encountered him directly, though, Chloris reflected, for she would not be able to acknowledge that she knew who he was.

As if aware of the scrutiny he turned his head her way.

His gaze locked on hers. He inclined his head.

Stumbling on the cobbles, she drew to a halt.

"Hold tight to me," Jean advised. "The stones are uneven."

Chloris could do no more than nod in response. From under her lashes she could see that the man continued to observe them, making no pretence about doing otherwise. His gaze flickered over them, as if he was eager to determine the nature of their friendship and the purpose of their outing. When he saw that Jean was guiding her away to the other side of the street while casting black looks back at him, his sensuous mouth moved. Apparently he was amused by that.

Inside her glove Chloris's palm tingled. The sensitive skin there, where he had caressed her, seemed to be stimulated by a sensual memory at the sight of him. It was oddly seductive, and it made her senses rush. It also made her wish he was touching her again. Shocked at her own reaction to the sight of the man, she asked herself how it could be. His nature, was that why? His curious powers and his wild ways? Flustered, she turned away, reminding herself that it was imperative Jean did not see her exchanging glances with the local Witch Master. However, his nearby presence and the nature of the situation meant she was quite unable to stop herself playing the innocent in order to question her cousin's wife. "Who is it that we must avoid?"

"That man, Lennox Fingal. A questionable man if ever there was one." Jean scowled.

Lennox. His name whispered around her mind. How well it suited him—strong, direct and memorable. She feigned confusion, hoping for more information. "Questionable?"

Jean leaned closer, lowering her voice. "They say he dabbles in witchcraft. There are a bunch of them around him and all are suspected of wrongdoings. Tamhas has been watching him."

Chloris was not only startled by the vehemence with which Jean spoke, but also by the information she imparted. Tamhas was watching the man from the house in the forest? He'd often spoken out against witchcraft, and he'd been vehement about Eithne leaving, all those years ago. She hadn't, however, been aware that he currently had suspicions about the people who met in the house in the forest. If she had known, she would never have ventured there. "He does not appear as I might have expected a witch to appear," she said, giving her honest reaction.

"That is half the trickery. The man is a rogue, and even if it is not true about his evil ways…" She paused, and Chloris could see Jean wasn't sure, or else didn't want to believe it. "Even if it isn't true, he lives a wild life up there in that house of his. He's a handsome devil and many women are eager to be in his bed."

Jean flushed and cleared her throat, as if stating the information would somehow tarnish her by association. Chloris had to suppress her amusement for she had the distinct feeling Jean wondered what it might be like to be in bed with a man such as Lennox.

"They say a woman is helpless under his spell, if he chooses to seduce her," Jean said, blurting out the words. She wriggled her shoulders as if in distress, but Chloris noticed Jean kept glancing back for another look at him. "The shameless libertine," she added, disapprovingly.

Chloris was not in a position to pass comment.

Across the shifting crowd Lennox lifted his hat and inclined his head at Jean, then at Chloris. His attention lingered on Chloris, and his gaze made her blood heat. *He's a handsome devil, and many women are eager to be in his bed.* Jean had warned her, and those words stayed with her. It was wise that she'd left his house when she did. *They say a woman is helpless under his spell, if he chooses to seduce her.*

Nevertheless, Chloris couldn't help herself, because this Lennox Fingal was now looking across the crowd at her and her alone, and it affected her oddly. He was staring into her eyes and beyond and she felt as if she should have been disturbed by that. For some reason she found her senses wildly aroused.

His eyes glittered oddly.

Beneath her clothing her skin grew hot. She felt restless, flooded by self-awareness as she was under his gaze.

Jean rattled on at her side, but Chloris could scarcely take the words in. "Just look at him, staring at us so rudely."

He was indeed staring, pure, candid interest in his expression.

Chloris lowered her head, but she could not keep the smile from her lips, unbridled pleasure swelling in her. Then the crowded street seemed to grow busier still and a fearful noise sounded to their right-hand side. The dense crowd stopped moving.

Half a dozen chickens had escaped their coop and darted about in front of Jean, clucking loudly. Jean screeched, lifted her skirts and took flight, as if to pass by the chicken seller. When she did, she bumped against the owner of the chickens, who was trying to shoo them back toward their enclosure with one hand. In the chaos, Jean dislodged the basket of eggs the owner of the chickens had clasped in her other hand. The basket was dropped and several eggs were broken.

An argument broke out.

Chloris watched in dismay. Jean scolded the woman who was selling the eggs and refused to pay her for the broken ones, insisting that it was her fault for letting the chickens run free. The coachman was now at her side. Then the crowd thickened again and Chloris found herself isolated from her cousin's wife by the flow of people, many of whom were gathering in front of her to observe the argument about the eggs.

That's when she became aware of his stare, the man Jean had called Lennox, the Witch Master. He stood off to her left and he looked only at her, his smile lingering.

It struck her oddly. Did he have something to do with it? Surely not. But what if it were true about his abilities to effect change? She tried to shake the thought from her head, but as she stared at him in wonder she saw a remnant of that strange light flashing in his eyes. For the briefest moment it seemed as if those eyes of his were even more luminous, as if they reflected the sunlight itself. That couldn't possibly be the case, for clouds flitted across the sun and his eyes were well shaded beneath his hat.

Chloris shivered.

Then it was gone.

He raised an eyebrow, making a connection with her.

It felt as if he were reminding her of their previous encounter, where—as he so rightly pointed out—she had sought him out. To her right side waves of laughter and jeering emanated from the area of the argument, the onlookers relishing the entertainment. Flustered and guilty, Chloris tried to catch sight of her cousin's wife, her heart racing while Jean's word of warning flitted through her mind—his notorious reputation with women, his dissolute ways, the rumors about dark beliefs.

When she looked back again, he was gone.

How did he disappear from view so quickly? While Chloris wondered on it she felt something tickle across the back of her neck. Instinctively, she reached back to brush the loose strands of hair away from her nape. Her body tensed. It wasn't her hair. It was him. His breath on her, followed by the briefest touch of his mouth on her skin.

Even before she glanced over her shoulder, she knew it was him.

A hand rested briefly on her waist, as if to reassure her.

His face was so close to hers that when she looked back at him, her legs grew weak. Dangerously handsome and so willful, he was all but pressed against her back.

"Careful," he whispered close to her ear. "Look toward your hostess while I speak to you."

From the corner of her eye she saw that he nodded over at Jean. Chloris did as he said, her senses reeling from his presence so close against her back. It made her entire body tingle, her skin racing, her nerves alive and chaotic.

"You look very beautiful today, Mistress Chloris. If I might be so bold to mention it."

Him making bold enough to comment on her appearance? Chloris withheld a smile. The man was bold in every way. A whispered comment was the least of it. But his hand remained on her waist, and it felt as if he was claiming her through that simple touch. She almost felt him scooping her up, walking away with her in his arms while everyone stared the other way. The wild notion shocked her. Where had it come from, and why did it make her want it to happen? Her vision blurred.

She blinked, forcing herself to look as if she were watching the squabble unfolding before them. It was difficult because she could feel him, his hand at her waist, his legs against her skirts and his breath on her skin.

"Have you thought about our discussion?"

She had thought of little else, but she couldn't admit that. To tell a man like him such a thing would empower him. Yet Chloris could not deny the arousing charge she experienced with him so close at her back, whispering to her, while all around were oblivious to their secret connection. It was madness but it was a delicious diversion all the same.

She turned her head slightly, to be sure he heard her whispered reply. "I have. However, I am afraid it is not wise for me to come to you again, because my hosts would disapprove."

"Your cousin Tamhas Keavey?" He gave a low chuckle.

She pursed her lips. She had not stated her family name the night before, yet he knew it. A man like him would have ways of finding out exactly who she was, she supposed.

"If you are afraid to come to Somerled," he continued, "I could come to you in secret. It would be less dangerous for you."

Chloris was astonished by his suggestion. "How? At Torquil House?"

That sounded even more dangerous. Perhaps that was his way, though—to court danger to amuse himself.

"I could easily come to you in the night. I know the lay of the place. It would be possible."

Chloris felt light-headed. An image of him in her private chamber drifted through her mind. Him, approaching her. Him, touching her again. Her grasp on her surroundings was slipping away as she considered his words. "For the ritual you described?" she murmured.

"Of course. Why else?"

Was that amusement she heard in his voice again?

"You would be more comfortable in your quarters," he added. He ran one finger down her spine from her hairline to where her gown began, reminding her of what he had said about laying hands on her.

Her head lolled back in reaction to his touch. It made her bones melt and filled her mind with thoughts she could scarcely believe she was having. Imagining herself turned in his hands she recalled that magical heat he had conjured in her very center, and she felt dizzy.

"I will call upon the rich vitality of the earth and the power of the seasons to flourish inside you."

The seductive tone of his voice as he said those intimate words made her body heat, rapidly. More images assailed her, shocking her. She saw their two forms entwined while he imbued her body with magical prowess. She saw him hold her, set her alight. She swayed. Then she felt him begin to draw away.

An immense sense of loss swamped her.

"Your hostess is about to return," he warned. "Give me a sign and I will come to you at midnight tonight."

Shocked, she looked at where the crowd was breaking apart—where the Keavey coachman was counting coins into the chicken keeper's hand, and where Jean turned on her heel and flounced away.

There was no time to think on it. Jean's warnings flitted through her mind, but she had to know more. Her body wavered momentarily but when she looked ahead she saw that Jean was striding back to her, the coachman in tow. It was dangerous, but she had to know. She had to pursue it, or forever regret that she had not taken this chance.

Once again his breath was warm at her ear. "Give me a sign and I will be gone. They will not even notice that we have spoken."

He truly was prepared to wait for her to respond, even though Jean was almost upon them. Jean who had warned her against him moments before. Chloris should have felt panic, she knew it. All she felt was his presence, as if the encounter had sped the entire burgh away and only the two of them existed in this place. She slipped her hand behind her back and reached for him. His fingers entwined with hers, setting alive a chaotic thread of arousal in her. She squeezed his hand.

"Tonight," she responded, whispering the word that he had whispered to her. Doing so made her feel even more lightheaded.

His fingers slid from hers, and her eyelids lowered in relief. Then he was gone.

Breathing deep to steady her nerves, she suddenly realized she'd agreed to his ultimatum. He would come to her, at midnight. In Tamhas's house? The dangerous nature of the proposal became all too clear, as if her clarity of mind had returned on his departure. Her thoughts reeled.

What have I done?

chapter Four

Tamhas Keavey slipped on his formal cloak and took his seat in the town council chambers. As he did, he nodded his greetings at the men gathered, surveying them all with an eye to allegiances. The prominent townsmen and civic leaders were there, landowners such as himself, as well as those who represented their guilds—the head of the bakers, the craftsmen and merchants. A representative of the university was also present, the illustrious academic trophy that Saint Andrews held in pride, for it brought them attention and prestige, drawing many of the great learned minds of Europe.

The murmured conversations around the table desisted, and a quick glance assured him that everyone was present.

Master MacDougal, the head of the council, rose to his feet and welcomed them, moving on quickly. "As council members we are here today to progress our membership. For many hundreds of years Saint Andrews has been the religious and intellectual center of Scotland, the jewel in its crown. The situation has changed since the union with England." His expression grew overcast. "It is our duty to protect and build the reputation of our town. On our previous meeting we discussed ways in which we might achieve this, and we agreed that opening the council to more guildsmen would strengthen it." Master

MacDougal smiled. "Word had scarcely been put about and noble craftsmen stepped forward to represent their guilds."

A murmur of approval went around the table.

MacDougal gestured to the usher by the door, who opened it.

Tamhas craned his neck to see. A gentleman entered. He stated that he owned a printing press associated with the university. Somewhat nervous, the gentleman explained that the press was well established under the university's protection, and their wish for the future was to become more involved in town matters.

Tamhas found the gentleman's account of how the printing press might be expanded quite tedious, for it was not an area of interest to him. The council voted and all present accepted the gentleman to represent his guild.

The printer took up a seat at the table.

The following discussion was quite long-winded, and Tamhas was surprised to see that a second application had been put forward and was being heard that day. His interest lifted, for he had not seen anything of personal interest or gain in the previous gentleman. On MacDougal's word the usher again went to the door.

Tamhas, together with most of the gathering, turned to see who had arrived. The man stepped swiftly into the chambers and bowed his head toward the head of the council.

Tamhas frowned heavily. It was Lennox Fingal. What in God's name was that heathen doing here?

Surprisingly, MacDougal seemed pleased to see the interloper. "Master Fingal, welcome." He turned to address the assembled men. "Master Fingal is here today to present the case for his wainwrights to be recognized as the official cart and carriage makers of Saint Andrews."

Tamhas's blood boiled. He was so outraged at the idea of Lennox Fingal joining the town council that he scarcely heard a word the man said about his trade and his craftsmen. Fingal was a dubious character at best. There were rumors that he indulged in all manner of heathen acts up at that house in the woods, and his reputation as a shameless libertine amongst the women of the town was well-founded. That was the least of it as far as Tamhas Keavey was concerned. Witchcraft was at the heart of it all, he was sure of it.

When the time came to vote, Tamhas voted against, as did one other. When pressed for the reason, the other man stated that the wainwright trade had not been long in Saint Andrews and was not well enough known, despite the quality of their wares. He suggested that Master Fingal present himself again the following year.

When Tamhas was asked for his opinion, he urged himself to be cautious. He could see the querying look in Master MacDougal's eyes. Fingal stared at him openly, one corner of his mouth lifted. Was he doing favors for the leader of the council in order to receive a good response to his application?

Drumming his fingers on the table he proceeded with caution. "I am concerned because Master Fingal's origins are not known to us. In addition, many of us in the burgh are wary of those who are not churchgoers." *Those who are detestable slaves of the Devil instead.*

MacDougal frowned. "A compromise can be reached, I am sure." He thought on it awhile then addressed Lennox Fingal. "We will offer you a seat on the council, not as a guildsman but as a town member."

Tamhas clenched his jaw lest he shout out in rage. The compromise meant Lennox Fingal would have less say in matters of commerce, but if he got his foot in the door there might be no stopping him.

MacDougal proceeded. "Assuming your comments are well received and of benefit to Saint Andrews, we will once again consider the application for your guild to be officially recognized. Once accepted, each guild is given a tenure of one year as a trial. If your craftsmen become an established part of the burgh in that time and you have contributed well to the council, that arrangement will be made permanent."

Fingal bowed. "I am most grateful for the opportunity to prove our worth."

Tamhas rose to his feet, pushing his chair back noisily. He exited the chamber without further comment, his fury building. It was shameful. Depositing his formal cloak in the adjacent chamber, he made his way down the corridor.

"I trust that I will gain a more genial acceptance from you in time."

Tamhas froze. Turning his head, he saw that Lennox Fingal had sauntered down the corridor after him. "I doubt that very much."

Tamhas refused even to look directly at the man, for something was there in his eyes. Witchcraft was at the back of it. Tamhas was sure the good council leader had been swayed. A favor had been granted, of that he was almost certain. The blackguard must have wheedled his way into MacDougal's good graces by dubious means. He intended to find out what it was, too. He would soon set them all to rights, and take his rightful place as head of the council.

"That is a shame," Fingal said, "for we are almost neighbors."

"You are no neighbor of mine, and I'll have you know I've sent your kind running from Saint Andrews before, and I'll do it again."

"My kind?" He raised an eyebrow. "Fair-minded members of the burgh?"

"You jest."

"I don't." He smiled, seemingly at ease. "Oh," he added, "I meant to compliment you on your taste in women. Your wife and your pretty cousin were looking most fetching when I saw them in Market Street this morning."

Tamhas's hands fisted at his side. "Your attempts to rile me only make me more determined to obtain the evidence I need to see you and your people put to death for your evil doings."

To his annoyance, his adversary only laughed softly. Standing his ground, he gave a shallow bow. "Farewell, Master Keavey."

Tamhas had no choice but to leave. He stormed out of the council chambers and elbowed his way through the crowded streets outside, furious that Lennox Fingal had gained a foothold within the burgh. He would have to pay closer attention to the man's activities. He needed evidence to oust him. The man had the ability to sway opinion, and that was dangerous. He was able to enchant people with favors and charm, but Keavey saw past that and he would make sure others did, too.

The insinuation that Fingal could get close to his womenfolk nagged at Tamhas, for Fingal was widely known as a man who could charm any woman into his bed. Had he spoken to them in the market? Had he dripped his evil charm on them?

Tamhas decided that he would have to question them on it.

chapter Five

"Did you fare well in Saint Andrews today, ladies?" Tamhas addressed them both from the head of the table.

Chloris forced a nod when he looked at her. "It was most reviving."

She concentrated on her food. The suckling pig was quite delicious but Chloris could eat only a small amount of the dinner. When she thought of the events of the day she could scarcely manage a morsel, fretting as she was about the illicit rendezvous she had somehow agreed to. Here in the rather splendid dining room she could hardly believe the arrangement she had made. It was one of the most sumptuous rooms in Torquil House, with a long and heavy table and bulrush chairs. The fireplace was large and expensive carpet covered the stone floor on the area from the door to the table. Tamhas lived like a laird, and at his bequest dinner was always a grand occasion. It was his way. He wore fine wigs and expensive clothing, for it was important to him that his wealth and position were visible to all.

"It was a most pleasant outing and Chloris and I enjoyed the market," Jean replied, "until we saw that Lennox Fingal prowling about the place as if he owned it."

Chloris reached for her wineglass, her heart tripping.

Tamhas's expression altered, a scowl developing. "The heathen had the audacity to present himself to council."

Chloris took a swig of claret. Her situation felt strangely dreamlike. Earlier that day she'd been compelled to question her cousin's wife about her comments regarding Master Lennox, but now she had a sense of foreboding that made her very uncomfortable about the rendezvous that had been arranged for that night. It was not only her own misgivings that made her uneasy. Now she feared for Master Lennox, who apparently intended to secret himself inside the house where he was despised, in order to assist her. Never in her life had she been in such a strange situation, but there was no way out of it now.

Jean shifted in her seat and looked at her husband aghast. "I am most surprised that the council received him."

Tamhas continued to observe them both closely as he spoke. "The council would not have received him if I had been in charge of proceedings."

He pressed his lips together and looked at Chloris.

It was necessary to say something. She struggled with it. The nature of the conversation was so unsettling, given that the man they spoke of had said he would come to her that very night. "I'm afraid I did not recognize the man's name. Is he a newcomer to Saint Andrews?"

Tamhas nodded. "He first appeared in Saint Andrews after you married and went to Edinburgh. He is a bad sort, and it ails me to know he is abiding so close by my land."

Tamhas returned his attention to his wife, who was still looking indignant on his behalf. "Tell me, did he speak to you directly?"

"No," she said, eyes rounding. "We crossed the street as soon as I saw him."

Mercifully Tamhas did not ask Chloris the same question. Nevertheless it brought about an immense sense of unease about her secret negotiations. She could not begin to imagine how she would respond if Tamhas asked her.

"If he even looks at you," Tamhas told his wife, "look away. There is witchcraft in those eyes of his and no woman is safe when he is around."

Tamhas looked Chloris's way again, obviously expecting a reaction to his comment.

Chloris put down her cutlery. "Witchcraft?"

"The things that go on, cousin dear…" Tamhas narrowed his eyes.

Was he thinking about Eithne? Chloris wondered.

His mood was dark. Tamhas was a distinguished-looking man and could be quite charming at times, but he also had a temper on him and Chloris had experienced it early on in life. As a result she was always a little tense in his presence— always ready to stand up to him, if necessary.

Jean shook her head disapprovingly then gestured at the serving girl who was standing by waiting to take the plates, indicating that she was finished. The girl moved around the table, causing a minor distraction for which Chloris was grateful.

After the serving girl had gone, Jean leaned closer to her husband. "You fear for his influence over women? Do you think it is true, what they say about them…when they gather together as a coven?"

There was a distinct look of curiosity in her eyes. Chloris wondered if Jean was as eager to know what exactly went on when these people came together as she was.

"Their activities obey no rules," Tamhas replied, "no decent bounds."

Jean dabbed her neck with her handkerchief, her cheeks flushing.

"No respect for the rules of the king or Church," Tamhas continued, his thoughts clearly deeply occupied. "They are heathens, no better than animals."

Chloris's thoughts reeled. Could she stop Master Lennox coming?

I have to go through with it, everything depends upon it.

Her belief in his powers had grown solid and she had to concentrate on his ability, not his dubious reputation. If she thought about the potential result she could be brave. Yet there was no guarantee the ritual he described would engender any change in her, and she risked great disapproval from her cousin—who had allowed her to visit these past weeks, when her husband was on the brink of casting her into the streets with nothing but the clothes she stood up in.

"You would be wise to quell your curiosity about them," Tamhas told his wife. "Let the men deal with these vermin. The fair sex should mind their doors and be wary."

Everything he said only made Chloris more uncomfortable about the arrangement she had made for that night. Why had she been foolish enough to allow him to come to the house?

Tamhas still pontificated on the matter, including Chloris in the conversation. "You would not remember our grandfather, Lucas, but when I was a wee lad he took me to see a witch burning."

Jean looked astonished. Her attention was all his. "Oh, Tamhas, you never told me."

"It was disturbing, that is why, but it never left my mind,

just as Lucas planned. My grandfather was protecting his family for generations to come by teaching us what to look out for. I'd already seen good Christian folk in their coffins, at peace. There is no peace for those who worship the Devil." He paused to shake his head in disgust. "Kicking and screaming and cursing us all they were, as they were led to their end."

Was it guilt, fear or injustice that made them do that? Chloris wondered.

"It must have been quite a sight." Jean looked enthralled.

"Three of them there were, two women and a man. One of the women, she was wickedness incarnate. She cursed everyone there, cursed their cattle and harvests and offspring."

Jean crossed herself. "Did they hang them?"

Tamhas nodded. "The rope first, then they lit the kindling that had been built at their feet. They burned the bodies to be sure the demons were gone. It is necessary, you see, this double death. We thought they would be dead after the hanging, but one of the women was so evil that the Devil kept his slave alive and put breath in her lungs, and when the flames lit her gown, a terrible scream issued from her. Even while she burned, she seemed to live on until she was burned to bone and ashes."

Chloris took her serviette to her mouth and then dabbed her forehead quickly, for she felt quite ill at her cousin's lurid description.

"Their flesh melted like wax candles. I will never forget the stench. Inhuman they were."

Jean frowned. "Wouldn't any person smell bad on burning?"

Tamhas, who seemed to relish sharing this sorry tale, glared at his wife. "Not like this, this was a smell only demons would carry."

When Jean didn't look convinced, he avoided her question—a question that appeared to be quite sensible, to Chloris—and hurried on. "My grandfather, he told me what to look out for, and I see it amongst those who are gathered around Lennox Fingal. They hunt for strange leaves in the forest and they gather in numbers, but when you come upon them they split so that you cannot count how many there are. If only I could catch sight of thirteen of them at once then I would have the evidence to oust them."

It shocked Chloris that he was so deeply driven on the matter. She already knew he didn't approve of anything that might be construed as witchcraft—she had known that when she went to Somerled—but she didn't know his goal for Lennox and his kind was prosecution and death.

"They're not family," he continued, "all those people that gather in the woods with him. No, they are similarly afflicted by servitude to the Devil. No good Christian should have to live with such creatures practically on the doorstep."

The fraught nature of the situation she had agreed to made Chloris want to run from the room, and as soon as the servant appeared again she bade Tamhas and Jean good-night and took her leave.

Alone in her chamber, she paced back and forth, checking the clock on the mantel every few moments. Leaving their company only gave her more time to fret upon it, and now her doubts were manifold. Tamhas had said they were no better than animals. Was it true?

Chloris reflected on the image of Lennox. There was a wildness about him. That was undeniable. There was a noble air about him, too, something in his posture and his manner that showed he would fear no man. That was where the dark thrill lay, she suspected, the rebellion she saw in his eyes. She'd never known anyone like that. The men in her life, her husband and her cousin Tamhas, were powerful because of what they owned and the ability they had to supply others with shelter or food, or not, as they chose. Lennox was not a wealthy man, and yet there was something almost regal about him. It was little wonder that he attracted women.

I must be cautious. Once again she warned herself to think about her goal, to fulfill her obligation to her husband by having a child. It was wrong to think upon the man's looks and his bearing and his potential to woo women when she was about to let him undertake some mysterious, unchristian ritual on her. Besides, he might not even appear.

When the chambermaid came to turn down her covers and offered to assist her disrobing, Chloris declined. It wouldn't be seen as odd, because Chloris seldom accepted assistance. The girl looked at her with sympathy as if she assumed Chloris was reserved, which suited Chloris. Her servants in Edinburgh were used to her ways and no longer offered. For reasons she kept private Chloris had learned to deal with the task of undressing—managing all manner of hooks and ribbons and layers of fabric—alone.

The serving girl stoked the fire, then left.

Once she was gone Chloris took a deep breath. The serving girl was, in all likelihood, the last person she would see that night and she would not have to deal with Master Lennox. He would forget or have second thoughts perhaps. That should have been a relief. It did little to quell her emotions. The truth of the matter was that she would wait up all night, hoping for the chance to partake of the magic he offered. If he did not come, that would be more painful still.

The hands on the clock neared the midnight hour and she lingered by the window, peeping out from behind the curtains. As the clock chimed, she saw him pacing across the lawn in the moonlight. She clutched at the curtains, staring down in disbelief. Several times over she wondered if she'd imagined his promise. What man in his right mind would enter the home of someone set on having him and his people persecuted?

He paused and lifted his head, apparently looking up at the windows. What a startling figure he made, so tall and sure of himself. He was as much at ease prowling in the moonlight as he was stalking about in the busy market earlier that day. It should have made her wary. It only made her curious, eager to know more about him.

Swallowing hard, she opened the curtains wide and showed herself. When he lifted his hand in acknowledgment, she dropped the curtain and paced back and forth again.

What would happen should he be discovered entering the house? He might not even make it as far as her room. Part of her wished that he wouldn't. The rest of her was ready to run to the door and open it for him if he knocked.

How would he even know which room was hers?

The thought sent a shiver through her. She had no idea of the extent of his powers. She'd heard tales, of course, dark stories about the dreadful things that accused witches had done. Was Master Lennox as powerful and unruly as the ministers said when they warned of those who indulged in witchcraft? If he was, he could do many things.

Therefore he could enable her to have a child. *Salvation.*

She darted over to the door and listened, straining for any sound that would indicate the household had been alerted to the presence of an intruder. Silence was all she heard. Would he enter by means of magic? That had not occurred to her, but when she thought on it she supposed he might. Doubts assailed her. Magic, work of the Devil? What had she agreed to? She stepped over to the mantel shelf over the fireplace and clutched at it to steady her.

A moment later the door clicked and she saw a sliver of light by the doorway.

The candle on the mantelshelf flickered.

The sliver of light vanished and stillness descended again.

Chloris wondered if she had imagined it, so imperceptible was the movement, but then she discerned the outline of a tall, dark figure standing in the gloom by the doorway.

He was here. The Witch Master was now inside the room.

Her fingers clutched tighter to the shelf. Her blood had already been racing, but when she sensed his presence—so brooding and so mysterious—here in her private chamber, her heart thumped against the wall of her chest. They were alone. She took a deep breath, attempting to keep her thoughts in order. It was difficult to do so. Her chest was constricted, her corset and bodice unbearably tight.

Once again she wondered if she'd gone insane, agreeing to have him come here. It was bad enough that she had sought his kind out. Why had she succumbed to his offer in the marketplace? His presence here in her private quarters was outrageous, and it flustered her immensely, even more than she had imagined it would.

Then he stepped closer, into the light by the fireplace, and those questions faded into the background. She was captured by the look of him. Unruly, yet poised and elegant. He had the quality of a sleek parlor hound that could turn into a wild hunter at whim. When he looked at her with those intense eyes, her reason faltered.

"Good evening, Mistress Chloris." He bowed his head.

"Sire." Her voice wavered. She knew she must press on, and quickly. She'd readied her words and forced them out. "You have risked much coming here, thank you."

A shadow of a smile passed over his lips. "You asked for my help, but you were wary of being seen coming to my home. That is understandable. We can talk here in privacy."

She nodded, but somehow felt safer not meeting his piercing gaze. Instead she risked only fleeting glances in his direction, remembering what Tamhas had said about his eyes, and what she thought she had seen in the market. Was it true? She meant to proceed quickly, lest they be discovered conversing in secret in the midnight hour. However, curiosity had its hold on her. "You seem to know your way about the place. You found my chamber quickly."

"Aye, I have been inside the house before. Not that Tamhas Keavey knows of it, I warrant. Your cousin's wife invited me here, secretly." He observed her as he spoke, almost as if he wanted to study her reaction. "It was shortly after she became mistress of the house."

Chloris was startled on several accounts and found herself unable to respond with an appropriate answer. It appeared that he'd known all along that Tamhas was her cousin. It would not take much investigation, she supposed. Perhaps she had even given it away the night before. She'd been taken by surprise on meeting him and had not thought clearly. The fact that there was some previous involvement between him and Jean made her unbearably curious. It went some way in explaining Jean's response to him in the marketplace that morning. Most of all it unnerved Chloris that Jean had apparently invited him here, just as she had. Why?

Unbidden, Jean's words of warning ran through her mind again—her comments about his immoral nature, his ability to seduce. Chloris's face heated as she recalled Jean's flustered state while she explained why they had to avoid him. She'd said it was because of his reputation. Was there more to it? Had Jean herself been involved with him?

Her visitor gave a soft laugh, as if he sensed his statement had confused her. "Mistress Jean is a kindly woman, but somewhat gullible. As a young bride," he continued, sidling closer as he spoke, "Mistress Jean was convinced of a ghostly presence in the west wing. She asked me here to seek it out and send it on its way. Alas, it was a wasted visit, for I could not discern any such presence."

"Ah, yes." Chloris nodded, relieved to get to a reason for his previous visitation. "The illusive wandering spirit, there has always been talk of it amongst the servants. As my cousin's ward I spent several years living here at Torquil House, before I left for Edinburgh, and there were no sightings while I was resident. I suspected it was a fanciful tale woven by one of the servants."

He did not seem surprised. "Oftentimes we are called upon when there is no real reason for our intervention."

The way he said it—with careful emphasis—made her wonder.

"Superstition, hearsay, fear, mistaken assumptions...all of these things bring troubled ones to us." He gave a wry smile. He had drawn to a halt an arm's length away from her. "And the very same things are often turned and used against us." There was a bitter undercurrent to his tone, but he quickly gestured with his hands, breaking the tension. "So, you have given thought to our discussion?"

Questions still flitted through her mind. Making haste was imperative, though. The threat of discovery made her uncomfortable. Especially now that she knew the real reason for Jean's concern. Jean had kept a secret from Tamhas all these years, and his mood at dinner was some indication why. "I have made my decision. I want you to undertake the ritual tonight."

He cocked his head on one side, considering her. "I'm surprised. I wasn't expecting you to agree so soon."

For a moment she felt he was disappointed by her eagerness. Every time he spoke, he surprised her.

"I thought I might have to convince you," he added. He looked her over with an appreciative glance.

The way he studied her made her feel unsteady. The man was a force of nature, to be sure. "I considered your words carefully, and although I am somewhat nervous about the ritual itself, I want to proceed."

He quirked an eyebrow.

Apparently it was necessary to give him just cause. Her gaze lowered. "I would not have come to you if I had not been convinced of my need for help. I have long since known that I am flawed, as a woman."

She paused in order to swallow down the shame she felt. It was not in her nature to discuss her problems openly with a man, let alone a stranger. She was a proud woman and this had taken some effort on her behalf. "If you can help me I would be most grateful."

"No one is perfect, Mistress Chloris. Keep that in mind." His mouth twitched in amusement. "We each strive to be more able and useful. It was brave of you to come to us, under the circumstances."

She lifted her chin, meeting his gaze directly. "And it was brave of you to come here to this house."

Once the comment was out, the exchange affected her oddly. Was it because they considered each other silently? A moment of mutual respect, she assumed. Chloris wasn't used to a man like him, one who could so easily control a situation—either by mastery, seductive magic or surprising moments of respect. As a woman, she rarely encountered any of those things in her husband, who was an altogether different type of man.

Why am I even thinking like this, comparing them? It was wrong of her and she clutched her fisted hand to her breastbone, ashamed of her wayward thoughts.

She turned away and picked up the pouch of coins she had readied, offering it to him. "Please, tell me if this is enough for your fee."

He weighed the pouch in his hand and then set it back down on the table without looking inside or counting the coins. "I suggest you determine how much the fee should be when we complete our endeavor. If you are pleased with the results, you can decide the amount."

Was that because he was so sure of his magic? "If that is what you would prefer."

He nodded.

His poise was breathtaking. The way he stood, so still yet so apparently ready to pounce into action, made her feel restless. "And now we begin?"

She asked the question and yet she did not know what she was doing.

His mouth lifted at one corner. "The ideal situation would be to perform the ritual in nature's bower, at first dawn or shortly afterward, when we could engage with the ebb and flow of the natural world more readily. But we can initiate it here, now."

Her level of concern rose. "Initiate?"

"It may need more than one meeting."

"Oh, I had not realized." Chloris was set on it, but she had hoped it would be done that night. She could not risk her hosts discovering her actions. Doubts assailed her. What if the nature of his ritual was disturbing to her? Would she be able to continue?

"Trust me, Mistress Chloris." His eyes glinted. "The power we invoke is only that which is around us at all times, the cycle of the seasons, the power of nature to flourish and multiply. I will call upon the spirit of spring, when the land is most fertile, and I will draw her vitality into you."

His words alone made her feel aroused. She had never heard such things, and his knowledge was compelling. As was his presence.

"I must, however, warn you. If we were outside, the magical forces I engender would dissipate into the air around us, but here, in this space, it may linger."

Breathlessly, she queried his meaning. "Linger?"

"You may feel…stimulated." His gaze covered her, as if he relished the idea of seeing it. "I thought it fair to warn you."

Chloris was fairly sure he could tell she was already stimulated. Was he teasing her with his warning? Objection parted her lips, but before she had a chance to speak he turned away and removed his coat.

Chloris stared, disbelievingly, as he slung it over a nearby chair, revealing broad shoulders under the fine linen of his shirt. He wore no waistcoat, and the shirt fell from his shoulders loosely. When he turned to face her again Chloris attempted to avert her eyes. She could not. His powerful chest was exposed through the soft material—the opening at his neck showing bare skin. She glanced beyond him, at the door, dreading what might happen if he was discovered here.

"You are cautious," he commented, "which I can understand. You are a proud woman, but I sense you are mistrustful, too, for some reason."

"Oh. I—"

"For the ritual to take hold, you must believe, you must trust."

"It is not you that I am mistrustful of." She shook her head quickly. "Forgive me. I am wary because I am afraid for both of us, meeting here. My host would not approve. Perhaps I should not have let you come."

"Fear not." He smiled, and that smile seemed to warm her from the inside, comforting her deeply.

"I am truly grateful for your efforts." She lowered her eyelids, wishing she had not said that much. She'd blurted out her thoughts because she did not want him to leave.

Stepping closer, until he was right against her, he put his head to one side. "May I remove your pearls?"

Startled, her hand went to her throat, where she wore a triple strand of pearls that had belonged to her mother. Pearls were not as fashionable as they had been in her mother's time, but she often wore them in order to be close to her mother.

"Allow me." He eased her hand away and then stroked his own around the back of her neck, paddling his fingers against the catch.

Her chin lifted. She couldn't help it. His touch was subtle yet so invigorating, like nothing she had ever experienced before.

When her head fell back he gazed down at her exposed neck and the swell of her bosom. He was so blatant. He looked at her indolently and without censure, apparently without concern for manners and the fact that she was a married woman. Nevertheless, she had agreed to this, to whatever contact he would have to make, and the consequences of that contact would just have to be endured. And there were consequences. She felt the tension building inside her all the while, and the air around them seemed heavy with desire, making her feel even more self-aware and shameful.

His gaze sharpened. "Turn your head to the side."

When she looked away, he pressed harder at the back of her neck and the collar at her throat clicked open. When the choker slipped from its place he gathered it in his hand. But his hand remained at the back of her neck, the choker gathered in his fist. "Unfettered, that is much better."

As he took his hand away, he ran the back of one knuckle the length of her throat. "You are very beautiful."

She knew she ought to question his actions and ask what would happen next, for then she would be prepared. But she was unable to.

"If it were up to me," he added in a low suggestive tone, his gaze devouring her, "I would have you completely unfettered, naked and glorious."

Chloris gasped.

He put a finger to her lips, silencing her objection.

"Forgive me. I cannot help admiring you. You are a desirable woman, and I am a man, after all." His mouth pursed in a sensual smile.

A man? Why did that suddenly seem so much more dangerous than him being a witch?

He removed the shawl she had around her shoulders, dropping it onto the ground nearby. "Open your heart and mind to me."

His voice was so low and husky it tugged at her nerves.

Then he pulled the kerchief free from her bosom, casting it aside.

Chloris swayed unsteadily. "Please, you shame me."

"I will need to lay my hands upon you. There is no shame in this. You are a woman, a woman who desires her fulfillment."

Fulfillment. Deep in the pit of her belly a pang of need sprung loose in response to that comment. It was not bearing a child she thought of then, however, but a different kind of fulfillment. He stirred it in her. Was it because she had never heard a man say such things? Or was it because he was there, and he was undeniably alluring?

"Are you ready?"

She nodded.

He circled her and, as he did, he spoke in a tongue that she didn't recognize. Chloris felt the heat in the room build. She turned her head to watch him and saw a man deep in concentration. His eyes were hooded, which only made him look more handsome.

Again he spoke, his tone growing more forceful.

The fire crackled, flames leaping high in the grate.

He moved closer to her. Dropping to his knees before her, he bent to place a kiss on her slippered feet, first the right, then the left.

Chloris stared down at him, astonished. All the while he chanted beneath his breath. A strange draft moved through the room and on it the scent of damp earth and sap. Instinctively, Chloris glanced over at the window, thinking it open. It was not.

Lennox lifted her skirts and kissed her knees, first the right, and then the left.

Mortified at the sudden exposure of her stockings and legs, Chloris's hand went to her throat. "This is so untoward."

Then her limbs tingled and heat pulsed through her.

"Close your eyes," he instructed, looking up at her, eyes luminous, "allow yourself to be taken by the spell."

It took a moment, for she was captured by the sight of him, but she did as he said. As soon as her eyes were closed she heard him chant again. Her skin tingled. Her head dropped back, her hair tumbling loose over her shoulders.

"What do you feel?"

Chloris struggled to find the right words. "A surge, as if something is rising up inside me."

Lennox pressed his mouth to her belly through her skirts.

Like a rising tide inside her, she felt gloriously vital. She drew a deep breath and lifted her arms, twining her fingers together over her head.

"Oh, yes, you are like a young sapling reaching for the sky." He rose, but as he did, he embraced her around the waist with both hands and bent to kiss the swell of her breasts at the edge of her gown.

Her eyes flashed open. Her breasts swelled against the confines of her corset and bodice, nipples chaffing. She trembled with the immense rush of sensation within her.

He stood before her, watching her. "I must kiss your mouth to complete the ritual, do I have your permission?"

The twinkle in his eyes made her pause. Struggling to make sense of myriad sensations she felt, and doubting the need for the kiss, she was about to query him. Then she looked at his mouth—so handsome, so lush and firm—and she wanted him to kiss her. She wanted to know what it would be like.

Her head tipped back as she offered her mouth to him.

When his lips touched hers she froze, suddenly afraid, but he held her to him with one hand against the small of her back. *Am I doing this because of his magic?* she thought vaguely, but the question wisped away on the spring breeze he had conjured.

His mouth was firm and warm and persuasive.

Closing her eyes, she let it happen, too aroused to think clearly and too entranced to refuse herself this. When she melted and moved against him, his kiss became more provocative. He parted her lips with his. Exploring her, he kissed her mouth until her body arched against his, and then he demanded more by thrusting his tongue between her parting lips. The action was so suggestive that she tingled wildly at her center, the heat between her thighs building by the moment.

Pressed body to body, she responded by grasping his shoulders, and as she did, a hidden part of her blossomed inside. She gasped against his mouth as the strange feeling grew, becoming intense, and she felt dizzy with pleasure. Her entire body vibrated with the need for more. Her intimate flesh grew damper by the moment, her breasts aching for contact.

Lennox drew back, but kept his hands locked around her waist.

Chloris was glad he anchored her that way, for she felt as if she might swoon. Her body truly had warmed and blossomed after his strange actions, but the state it left her in was no easy burden. "You have made me…"

She inhaled deeply, but that only seemed to increase her agitated state.

He cocked his head to one side, a predatory smile on his lips.

Had he done that on purpose? Frustration and objection swelled in her. "You have put me in a state of…need."

His hands roved lower, around the curve of her hips. "I warned you, did I not?"

"I did not know it would be like this." It was the strangest experience, for his proximity alone had stimulated her before the intimate contact. Her breathing was increasingly constricted and she felt dizzy, as if her garments were too tightly laced.

"You have not felt this way before?"

There was no doubt he was being provocative. She pressed her lips together.

"It will pass, try to breathe steadily." His actions contradicted his soothing words, for he drew her in against him, resting her head against his chest, which only made her situation worse.

It was akin to being embraced, and the hard bulk of his chest beneath his shirt only served to convey the kind of masculine virility that could slake her current needs. What had he done to her with his magic? Surely, if he had put her in this state, he could end it? Touching her forehead with one hand, she looked up and gave him a pleading glance. "Please, can you help me?"

With a nod he bent and lifted her in his arms and took her to the bed. Being held that way—totally enclosed and easily carried in his strong arms—only made her state worsen. Before she had a chance to object, he bent over her and began to loose the ribbons on her bodice, deftly untying them and tugging them open. Astonished, Chloris tried to stop him. "Please, sire, no."

Arching an eyebrow, he gave her an amused glance. "Hush, you are in danger of fainting, I am only assisting."

He wore a dark smile, though, a smile that only seemed to confirm his ability to seduce her.

Chloris whimpered. Then his hand brushed the swell of her bosom and, as her bodice was loosed, made fleeting contact with her left breast. "Oh, lord, you are making it worse."

He leaned right over her and captured her chin in his hand, forcing her to meet his gaze.

Chloris stared up at him, taking in the self-assured look in his eyes. He knew the effect he was having on her, and he was about to kiss her.

Her lips parted.

With a sigh of admiration, he brushed his fingers over the swell of her breasts again and then ducked his head and rested a kiss in her cleavage.

The contact made her melt into the bed. Her emotions soared. Never before had she been touched with such persuasive hands. Torn, she knew she should feel this was wrong, allowing this man so close to her bed. But it didn't feel wrong, it felt good, and she wanted more. *Have I lost my sense of reason?*

"You are most desirable. Perhaps I should not confess this, Mistress Chloris, but you have made me crave a taste of you." Mischief glinted in his eyes, the candlelight picking it up as he turned his head.

She shook her head.

"Why do you fight it?" He breathed against her collarbone as he rested a kiss there. "This is what you wanted, to be a woman who is fecund and rich in possibility."

His words were so suggestive, so flagrantly outrageous. Yet it made her entire body throb in response.

"You are all of that and more." Whispering the words close against her ear, he captured the lobe between his teeth and tugged at it gently. "What man could resist?"

"But I…"

"Don't fight it. This is what you came to me for."

Was it? She wasn't sure anymore. He was a wild one, living by his own rules. Why did that intrigue her so?

Brusquely, he undid the remaining ribbons on her bodice, and then tugged her shift down, exposing her nipples where they rose up and breached the top of her corset. Unruly fire built in his eyes as he looked down at her.

He ran his thumb over her peaked nipple. "Take your pleasure from my touch, it will serve to bed down the magic of the ritual."

He lowered his head and kissed her nipple. It was gentle, barely a breath of a touch, but it drew the heat inside her up and to him, linking them together somehow, swelling the vitality inside her.

Even in the peculiar heated state she found herself in—adrift on the sensations he introduced into her—she tensed in his grip. Decorum forced her reaction. She was shocked at his intimacy. She drew back. "Master Lennox, please…"

Don't.

Please don't. That's what she had intended to say, but she stumbled on the words.

He swooped, kissed her other nipple, this time fiercely.

"Please, Master Lennox, I cannot bear it."

He lifted his head, but his expression had turned serious. "I cannot help but wonder at this," he said gruffly, and she realized his whole body was tense with withheld passion.

She stared at him, unable to believe that this man wanted her. It was there in his eyes, though, in every touch and action. "Wonder?"

He sat alongside her on the edge of her bed. "This, it seems so unnecessary, for you are a desirable woman, Mistress Chloris. As lush as a ripe fruit and just as tempting."

The man was every bit the seducer Jean had suggested, and Chloris leveled her gaze at him, battling to control her senses, for they were driven wild by him.

"I do not sense that you are barren," he added.

Reference to her malady made her emotions tumble. "It is almost certain. I have seen a physician in Edinburgh, the best of his profession. But you're attempting to distract me from what just occurred."

His eyes narrowed. "Perhaps it is your husband who is barren."

"No." She shook her head. His comments did nothing to quell the tension she felt.

"If you were to take a lover, it would prove the matter," he added.

Chloris expected to find mischief in his eyes, but his expression was quite serious. She sighed. "How convenient to have a man in my bed, should I feel your suggestion was appropriate."

That made him smile. "I take it you do not have a lover, or have you?"

"No." It was a suggestion she'd heard many times before,

though, from her friends and acquaintances in Edinburgh. She'd even been offered the opportunity of an introduction to a suitable man who would be willing to undertake the task. "If I were to take a lover…I would not do it to prove my husband was at fault. I am loyal to Gavin. That's why I…" She beseeched him, searching his eyes for understanding.

His eyebrows gathered. "Loyal, through love?"

Duty.

His question was too much, worse than the intimate touch, the heated kiss. She forced herself to nod and then turned away. "I fear I am and always will be a failure to my husband."

Leaning closer, he stroked her hair back from her forehead with a tender touch. "Is that what burdens you so?"

Why was it she was compelled to share her thoughts with him, to be honest about things she had never told anyone? "It disappoints me greatly, I cannot deny it." She pursed her lips a moment. "I am, however, not prone to melodrama over such things."

Once again, he smiled. "But you do carry a secret burden, something you have shared with no one, not friends or kin."

Tensing, she shook her head.

"I sense it in you. If you tell me what it is, I will be more able to help you." There was a firm, commanding tone to his voice.

"You're my last chance."

"And we have made progress. It is that important to you?"

"Would I have put myself at risk with a stranger if that were not the case?" She turned her face away.

"What is it?" Grasping her by the chin he forced her to meet his gaze.

Chloris felt something turn in her chest and her will to keep her private matters private weakened. "I must fall pregnant with my husband's heir."

He cocked his head as if waiting for her to say more. Expecting it.

The truth knotted in her chest, but the dark secret she carried—that which filled her with shame—was being drawn out as surely as if he had it harnessed by a thread of magic and tugged gently, drawing from her.

Her lips parted, but she said it unwillingly. "I fear my life depends on it."

chapter Six

My life depends on it? Lennox studied the woman, attempting to read the turmoil he saw there at the back of her eyes.

Prior to that moment of confession she was all but ready to surrender herself to him completely—and he was more than ready to lose himself between her soft thighs. His intentions, at first, had been almost wholly selfish. There was a twisted pleasure in entering Tamhas Keavey's house while he slumbered unaware. There was also great pleasure in dallying with his cousin. Her tender beauty called to him. She would be soft and supple beneath him, and he craved the clasp of her body on his hardened cock as he entered her. During the ritual she had responded so readily, and that only increased his desire.

How sweet it was to enjoy her, with the certain knowledge that Keavey would be horrified when the tale came out. The nature of the situation had changed, however. She'd drawn back a curtain and showed him her secret fears. An instinctive need to know more came over him. He regretted the interruption, but there were times when discovering the truth overwhelmed his cause. It was because he hated to see fear in a woman's eyes. Desire was good. Fear was not. It was always the way because of what he'd seen happen to his own womenfolk, as a youth.

"Your life?" he queried.

Her eyelids remained lowered, the patches of color on her cheeks high. "I should not have said that."

The tug of resistance was more than he would expect in a well-to-do woman who had lowered herself to seek help of the local witches. There were the basic fears—that they would be discovered together, that she would be mocked by her hosts for indulging her whims with the demonic Witch Master. Beyond that there was a deep fear, something that had forced her footsteps to his door. She wanted a child, and yet that wasn't the only thing pushing her footsteps on. The need in her was something far deeper, rooted in obligation and mired in a situation from which she felt she had no escape.

"Come now." He stroked her face, urging her to tell him more. There were so many intriguing things about this woman. She was a wellborn lady, and yet she was suggesting that she had suffered. "You have said it, and you have lowered a barrier between us."

"Please." She looked at him from under her lashes. "My comment was overly dramatic in the heat of the moment." She swallowed. "I meant only that my husband would be so much happier if I were to have a child."

Lennox took a lingering glance at her breasts, so voluptuous spilling from her loosed bodice, her peaked nipples a telltale sign of her state of readiness for lovemaking. How he would enjoy disrobing her completely, pleasuring her until she cried out for him. It would happen. He had commenced her seduction in order to make Keavey suffer. Now that he saw the humility in her, and he felt the vital spark of her burgeoning arousal in response to him, his opinion on where to take matters was divided. He shrugged it off, disposing of the moment of doubt. He could have her, embolden her in carnal ways, bring her to an understanding of her perceived lack of womanhood, and still it would annoy Keavey.

In the candlelight he could see the pulse beating at the base of her throat and the swell of her breast rose and fell rapidly. Stimulating her had been easy enough, stepping away was going to be harder for him. She was ready, and the startled expression in her eyes convinced him that she was not familiar with being in the state of readiness for passion. How interesting it would be to lead her further along that path.

The pressing need to find release himself played its own part. The way she'd looked at him when he began to weave his spell turned him hard. Those eyes of hers, so open, so honest. The way her lips parted when she found her senses stimulated. It made him want to enter her, to satisfy the desire that had been brought about in them both. He had not expected to be so readily stimulated, but the moment he entered her chamber he began thinking about how pleasant it might be to lie between her legs.

Advances had been made to his satisfaction.

Now, to be sure she would meet him again.

He traced his fingers across her collarbone and down into the shadowy dip between her breasts. Hooking his finger over the bodice of her gown, he tugged at it, freeing her breasts entirely. Her head pressed back into the pillows, her eyelids fluttering down as the soft globes of her breasts were fully revealed. Her body undulated against the bedcovers. She reached for him and her hands fisted on his shirt.

There was no doubt in his mind that she was ready to capitulate, to allow him to take what he wanted. However, that wasn't enough. He wanted her to need him so desperately that she pursued him and begged for her release at his hands. Only then would he accept that he had done his job well enough. Knowing that she had flaunted herself, offered—nay—given herself to him, she would hang her head in shame when Keavey asked her if it was the truth, if she had sullied herself at the hands of the local Witch Master.

He had made it easier for her tonight, traveling to meet her here. She had needed that, however. The night before there had been regret in her eyes. Now the new fear that she exhibited was that he would not take this further.

It was time to test her a little. How far was she prepared to go?

He rose to his feet. "We have done well tonight, and now I must take my leave."

Her head lifted from the pillows, seeking him out. "But you…you have put me in such a state. I do not know how I will rest." Round-eyed and delightfully innocent-looking, she continued, "Is there no way you can alleviate the condition you have put me in?"

Lennox attempted to keep his manner serious. In truth it amused him immensely to think how outraged Tamhas Keavey would be if he knew the despised coven master was in his home, making his pretty cousin swoon after mere moments of preliminary lovemaking. Lusty thoughts filled his mind and it took some effort to ignore the state of his cock when he stood upright. Her whispered pleas and protestations did not help to quell his state of readiness. "I cannot risk staying longer. I have not forgotten your honor is at stake, nor do I want to."

She sat back against the pillows and rested her hand against her forehead, her expression apparently startled to the point of dismay by his imminent departure.

Lennox observed the depth of her need. Unleashing her passions—when the time came—would be most pleasurable indeed.

"But I… Is it done? I mean, have we achieved our goal?" There was a demanding expression in those wide eyes of hers. "I have seen your magic but I do not know if it has changed me. At least—" she put her hand to her throat "—not in the way I meant it to."

Her honesty was startling.

Did she truly not believe it, or was it the fact that she was left aroused and bewildered that brought about that reaction? Lennox pulled on his coat. "The ritual will need to be repeated and reinforced."

He quelled his smile. Tapping his finger against his bottom lip thoughtfully, eager to see her plead with him some more.

She peered up at him, so pleasingly oblivious to her disheveled state—her breasts on display, her hair escaping from her lace cap to tumble down past her shoulders, so fetching—as she awaited his words.

"I believe you rode to Somerled last night, is that correct?"
She nodded.
"Tell me, do you ever take an early-morning canter?"
"No, I haven't."
"Would you do so, in order to pursue your…desire?"
Her cheekbones colored.
"Your *heart's* desire," he clarified, amused.
Her eyes flickered. "Would it be helpful?"
It was clearly against her better judgment, but she was responsive all the same.

He half turned away lest she see his smile. "As I mentioned earlier, the ritual would be better performed in the early morning, when the spring blossoms open and nature is at her most fertile and inviting."

It was another boundary that he was suggesting she cross to reach her goal.

Her pretty mouth pursed.

How she liked to assess the danger, he noticed, watching her eyes flicker. She was not as easily led as he initially thought. When she had walked into Somerled he had assumed she had come there on a whim. Now he realized she had probably considered it at great length.

He did not wait any longer. "Do you know the place where the lane forks on the way to Saint Andrews, where there is an old oak with a broken limb that reaches down to the earth and beckons like a hand."

She stiffened, turning her surprised gaze to him.

"Ah, I see you do." He nodded his head. "I will meet you there when the sun tips over the treetops."

With that parting instruction he took his leave, not allowing her time to respond or think on it any more before he was gone. With luck that would create a sense of obligation in her and she would have to attend, no matter how hard she fought her desire to submit to him in the full light of day.

At the door he paused briefly, turned back and bowed in her direction.

Heady female arousal swelled from the place where she half sat on the bed.

Lennox breathed it in, allowing it to fire his loins—allowing her vitality to infuse him and fuel his craft. As he stepped out of her room and shut the door, he cloaked himself by means of magic. If anyone sensed a presence and emerged from one of the many doorways in the corridor, they would see only a shadow.

Lennox left her in such a state of arousal that Chloris had to pace her bedchamber for a long while before it began to pass. Plumping the pillows into shape, she undressed and put on her nightgown. Then she assumed a reposed position on the bed and closed her eyes.

When she did, she felt as if he were still there, arched over her, whispering his seductive words as his warm breath teased over her skin. Turning on her side, she pounded her pillow again and pulled the covers higher, attempting to block out the thoughts. Then she realized that she would be readying to meet him in just a few hours, and that sent her further into a spin. Could she even begin to consider it?

It has to be done. If she felt this disturbed after the next stage of the ritual, then she would have to reconsider. She'd come this far, and she did feel different. There was no doubt about that. The stable boys began work at dawn, and she would ask them to saddle a suitable mount for a morning ride.

When she eventually fell into a restless sleep, Chloris dreamed of the Witch Master. The Witch Master, holding her with his hands about her waist—holding her steady, despite the unruly magic he unleashed around her. Somehow, that soothed her, and she drifted on the sensation until she awoke suddenly at dawn, gasping for breath—awoke from a much more frightening image: *Gavin.*

Gavin with his hands wrapped around her throat.

chapter Seven

The gnarled old tree beckoned to Chloris from the woods, its broken limb eerily reaching out of the forest to where the earth was trodden by foot and hoof. It had occurred to her that she might have misheard the details of the meeting point, but mention of the old oak tree had pinned it in her thoughts, despite her befuddled state of mind and body the night before. The urge to turn back was fierce, and yet she'd had to come.

Now that she had initiated this endeavor she had to see it through. Not least because the restless forces within her demanded it. Doubt hampered her every move, however. Why, she asked herself most of all, did she have this simple, hankering need to see the man again? Her purpose was to take the ritual magic further in order to achieve her goal. Why did she crane her neck so, eager for sight of him?

She dismounted as she looked about.

Alas, there was no sign of the Witch Master.

The sky was clear and the sun well risen, but the early spring air was a little chilly and fresh. Dew still glistened in the shaded spots of moss beneath the canopy of leaves overhead. Birds twittering nearby encouraged her. She stepped closer to the tree.

As she did, Master Lennox emerged from behind it. Silent, stealthy and sudden.

The sight of him made her footsteps falter to a halt.

"Mistress Chloris." He nodded her way.

Taken aback by his appearance, she gripped her mount's reins tighter and prayed for good sense to prevail in her dealings with him. It would not be easy. The only saving grace of the night before was that they were hidden away. Even so, she'd had to continually remind herself they were conducting a healing venture and not conversing on her bed for any more dubious purpose. This morning he had come out with no coat at all, no necktie. His waistcoat was undone, too, and his loose shirt hung open at the neck revealing his broad, powerful chest.

Seemingly at one with his wild surroundings, he rested one hand up against the rough-hewn tree trunk and gazed over at her with an assessing eye. "The morning light becomes you."

Taking a deep breath, Chloris attempted to deflect his remark. "Compliments are not necessary for our transaction, sire."

"No. It must be said." The twinkle in his eye was wickedly suggestive. "Your pale beauty is most appealing. Something has put color in your cheeks. The morning ride, perhaps?" His tone insinuated something entirely different.

Chloris gave him a wry smile. "You are well aware that your ritual magic of last night has left me in a…delicate state. You warned me of it, therefore you likely expected the result to linger."

His gaze raked over her as he stepped closer. "Unleashing your deepest carnal desires may help your quest for fertility."

With the help of the clear light of day and a fortified will, she lifted her chin, determined to keep a hold on her wayward emotions this time. "Is it true what they say about your kind...that you see no shame in seeking carnal gratification?"

His mouth curled.

Damn the man. He was amused by her provocation. Not only that, but his humor made him look more roguish. That had the unfortunate effect of making him even more attractive to her.

Chloris turned her face away. This was a dangerous situation and she regretted voicing her question so directly. She'd meant to be bold—to show him she was strong and not easily played. She'd come in to this with a goal, but she was aware he was deriving more than his fee from it, and he seemed to be enjoying her discomfort. She would not play this dangerous game with doubts in her mind as to his purpose, therefore it was better to let him know she was aware of his nature. Or, at least that is what she had determined as she tried to decide whether or not to attend the meeting he suggested.

"It is true, yes. Because there is nothing more powerful than the life force exchanged by lovers, and we believe that nature's way should be revered, respected and harvested."

Chloris wished she hadn't asked. The honesty and forthright manner in which he spoke about matters of physical congress left her speechless. It seemed that whenever she presented him with a question, his response was so direct and lacking in shame that she felt somehow raw and exposed.

His eyelids flickered and he reached out and grasped her hand.

Chloris resisted when he attempted to draw her nearer to him.

A warning flashed in his eyes. "Make haste, I hear a carriage."

Startled into action, Chloris hastened alongside him. When she glanced back she saw that her mount followed them, which was a great relief.

"Here, shelter here." He drew her in behind a large oak.

With her back to the tree she was completely hidden from view. Master Lennox faced her, one arm protectively raised against the tree trunk to shield her. Concern marked his expression. It struck her oddly. He appeared to care.

Moments later a carriage trundled by.

"Thank you," she whispered when it had gone.

The light was behind his head and the shadows made his features appear even more dramatic. Chloris felt light-headed and found herself unable to do anything other than stare up at him.

"Come, we'll go deeper into the forest." His voice was low, and he moved his hand to the small of her back, encouraging her to move.

That touch made her feel self-aware. Her feet were strangely leaden as if she were unable to step out. She looked back for her horse. The mare was grazing.

"She has found a sweet patch of grass," he said. "She won't wander."

Chloris stared at him. How could he be sure? Was he that in tune with their surroundings? Then he smiled at her, and she believed.

Mustering herself, she returned his smile and stepped alongside him.

"It is a good time," he said, looking up at the canopy of leaves overhead. "The sunlight will fall across a patch of bluebells soon, yonder." He nodded his head deeper into the woods.

Something about the way he spoke made her feel his deep bond with the place. How strange it was, when he could so easily appear to be a fine, cultured gentleman. Now, here in the wilds, he seemed even more at ease.

His lip curled at one corner. "I believe it is the perfect place for you to blossom."

Blossom. Yes, I believe I will.

"Fear not, Mistress Chloris. I will look after you." He reached out and lifted her gloved hand to his lips. Even through the kid leather she felt his heat.

The smell of fern and blossom intensified.

Affected by his concern for her rather than his charm, she felt disarmed. He spoke in such persuasive tones, and when he met her gaze it was with certainty and reassurance. Chloris believed he truly wanted her to flourish in that way. It struck her that he took pride in his task, despite his outlandish and forbidden nature.

As he led the way, he took her hand. "The path is uneven, allow me to guide you."

With her hand in his, her senses heightened. The twitter of the birds in the branches overhead seemed more musical, more resonant. The smell of the undergrowth became even more intense. It was him, she realized. His craft, his magic. She was all but seeing through his eyes. It was startling. Her determination to remain levelheaded was slipping away. *I'm falling under his spell.*

When he looked her way, the steady warmth he conveyed only confirmed it.

"There." He gestured beyond.

Between the trees she saw it, a hidden glen, the floor of

which was covered in bluebells. The glen was sheltered, the breeze only shifting the highest leaves overhead. Sunlight glinted through the leaves and dappled across the flowers. It made the ground seem almost as if it was a moving, living, breathing thing. Chloris was awestruck by the sight. "Oh, Master Lennox, it truly is a beautiful place."

"Please, my given name will suffice."

"Lennox," she whispered, enjoying the implied intimacy.

"Are you ready?"

She nodded, breathless with anticipation. If her experience was anything like the night before and it happened here in this beautiful place, so hidden and precious, she knew instinctively that it would be magical.

He led her again, through the bluebells to the very center of the carpeted spot. Her riding skirt was tugged by the thick foliage, and as they carved a narrow path through the blooms the scent permeated the air around them, stimulating her to inhale deeply.

When Lennox drew to a halt, he touched her on the shoulders to still her. Then he began to chant in that secret language of his, moving around her while she stood still.

Chloris blinked, swept up quickly into the moment.

The more he stepped around her, the more bound up in him and his strange chant she became. The stir of the breeze through the treetops sounded louder, too, as did the distant birdsong. The scent of the flowers grew stronger and the moss grew denser, and her pulse raced, her skin tingling with excitement. This time she did not fight it, she embraced it.

Vitality plumed inside her, rising like a vapor to warm every part of her.

Losing herself, she looked up through the canopy of leaves and felt the sun on her face. Sinking and rising all at once, she felt as if she had joined with the forest around her and breathed as one with it. Then she felt his fingers in her hair, loosing it.

Lennox. Craving him, desire beat an urgent rhythm in her blood.

His eyes were bright and lust-filled. She stared up at him, transfixed. It had affected him, too, she could see that. Trembling wildly she clutched at his shirt. Her knees went weak under her. She faltered. Lennox caught her in his arms.

"Lie down," he instructed, his tone low and suggestive.

She wanted to lie down, lie with him. When she nodded, he lowered her safely to the ground. She sank down gratefully.

"Rest back, I'll hold you."

His voice was reassuring and she gave in to it readily, resting on the bed of succulent bluebells. The fleshy stems and petals around her seemed a bed too blissful, their musk too inviting. Then he was lying alongside her and when she turned to him their gazes locked.

She reached out, touched his jaw with her hand. "Do you need to kiss me again, to make it work?"

"Aye, that I do." The look he gave her—pleasured and brooding all at once—made her ache for more.

Moving over her, his mouth covered hers, his hard body pressing against hers, heightening her need. His kiss was hungry and Chloris answered in kind. She held tight to him, her body moving under his, her hips arching up. When she felt his hard length pressed against her thigh, she moaned with longing. At her center she clutched as if reaching for him, reaching for that part of him that could join them.

He lifted up onto his arms, looking down at her, but he did not move away.

Nor did she ask him to.

Between her thighs a riotous pulse beat, her folds growing slick and humid with desire. The need for relief was overwhelming. The sunlight was behind his head and Chloris stared up at his shadowed face, wanting more, wanting him. All she could think of was what it might feel like to have that hard length of his driving inside her.

"You are such a temptation," he whispered.

She had to battle the urge to lift her skirts and beg him to take her. Gathering the fabric in her fisted hands, she wondered where such a wild notion had come from. His spell?

His eyes glinted. Did he know that was what she wanted to do?

"Confide in me. Tell me if you feel a change manifest."

"A change, yes, but it is…it is desire that I feel." Overwhelmed, she stared up at him. "It is fertility I seek, and now I begin to question this…lust."

"Question it?" He leaned closer still, his hand on her waist. "Why would you question it? I can see the vitality in your eyes and the color in your cheeks. Your essential womanly nature is flourishing." He shifted his hand, moving it, so that it lay over her lower belly.

Even through her skirts she felt it, as if she were being branded by his touch. She moaned aloud, for the proximity of his hand to the place she currently craved him sent her closer to madness. "I should never have come. I was warned against you."

He lifted an eyebrow. "Were you? And yet you came anyway, putting yourself at risk of the very thing you have been warned about."

She could not speak, because all she wanted to do was writhe beneath him and it was taking all her efforts not to do so.

He gave her a lingering glance and she saw her own hunger reflected in his eyes. Mutual desire. It struck her fiercely, for it was something she had never known before and it felt right and true and powerful.

"The arousal," he continued, "it is part of opening the deepest secret part of you to flourish and receive your lovers freely...here."

Chloris moaned aloud because he applied pressure through her skirts as he spoke, and his hand was directly over her intimate places. She felt herself grow damper still between her thighs. Never before had she felt this way. It was him. And she wanted him. Wanted him badly. Turning her face away, she closed her eyes tightly and tried to steady the wild beating of her heart.

"Ah, I see the true nature of your problem, Mistress Chloris."

She turned back.

The provocative smile he wore made her ache with longing.

"Your desire is out of control, perhaps?"

Thoroughly ashamed of her predicament, she managed to nod her head.

His hand moved lower still and he applied a mite more pressure, right over her groin.

"Oh, dear God!" She stared down, her lips parting in objection. But when she saw his hand moving there, where the fabric of her gown dipped into the hollow between her legs, she was so astonished that she could not say more.

Then the pressure he applied met with a response—a pang of bliss melted her center, and she could not pull away. Instead she let him rest his hand there, overawed at the immense pleasure that point of contact gave her.

"There is a pleasurable way to alleviate this tension, I'm sure you know what it is." His smile was wicked, but he kept massaging her in that place and her head dropped back, tears dampening her cheeks.

He was going to make love to her, and she wanted him to. Needed it, badly. Never before had she felt this way. "I do not wish to be unfaithful to my husband."

"I would not invade your husband's territory, not unless you requested I do so." There was a level of gentle sarcasm in his voice that she could not fail to notice, despite the state she was in. "I would not take a woman, married or otherwise, unless she was determined to be mounted and begged for it."

Chloris was so close to doing that very thing, but the fact he'd said it astonished her.

"You are shocked that one such as I has a code of honor?" Humor danced through his eyes.

Chloris was entranced. Every time she thought she gained an understanding of his motives he surprised her anew. His eyelids were half-lowered, but that did not shade the vital spark in his vivid blue eyes. The dark of his lashes seemed only to emphasize the fire she saw there. Could she trust his words? Everything he said seemed to contradict his actions—actions that had put her in such a state of stimulation that she was ready to beg him in the very manner he had suggested.

Again he kneaded her mound in the cup of his hand. "I am merely suggesting a little light relief."

The bulky layers of fabric did nothing to protect her. Her emotions were adrift in a haze of pleasure, the weight of his hand there making ripples spread through her loins. What would it feel like if she were naked? A fresh wave of heat covered her skin as the thought flitted through her mind.

"I will take your silence as agreement." Lifting her skirts he pushed them to her waist and covered her bare mons with his warm palm.

Chloris was about to disagree when his finger moved into her hot folds and stroked. Stroked again. Back and forth, sliding easily against her swollen nub because of her copious juices. It felt so good. Chloris half sat, wrapping her arms around his neck, working her body against his hard fingers as they plied her open.

She was already close to spilling.

Then he eased a finger inside her. "Oh, yes, this is what you needed."

Chloris flashed him a warning glance, and then he pushed deeper and rested his thumb against her nub. Her head went back, and when the release came she rocked her hips and moaned, long and loud.

Lennox kissed her exposed throat, and when her thoughts finally ordered themselves, she pulled away, rolling onto her side and facing away from him, embarrassment swamping her. And still she craved more—craved him. Even though she had come undone, the tension was building again.

"What ails you, mistress? Have I not brought you relief?" He lowered his head to kiss her shoulder, encouraging her to be open to him.

"Yes, but apparently I have grown ever more needful in its wake." She tugged her skirts down over her legs.

"Don't hide yourself, you are beautiful." He lay alongside her back, molding his frame to hers.

"Please, I cannot bear this. I am mortified by my own lusts."

"It was not meant to shame you, I would never do that." She glanced back at him.

"But now that I have seen you like this…" His eyes darkened. "I think it becomes you, and it rouses me immensely." He bent to kiss the side of her face.

Why did that arouse her again? Her body responded to his words as if they were invitations to more pleasure.

When she glanced back, Lennox was looking at her with hungry eyes and she could feel his erection against her behind. He was ready. It made her weak with lust.

"You are making it worse." Her voice faltered.

"Perhaps, but I know I can make you enjoy it."

"I don't doubt that, you are a master seducer." Chloris pursed her lips. She had not meant it to sound like a compliment. Meanwhile, her traitorous body responded to him eagerly. She was a married woman. What was happening to her? She had lost all sense of reason.

Lennox laughed softly, his fingers brushing languorously over her bodice above her nipples. She wriggled and attempted to roll farther away, but found herself hampered. Lennox sighed and ran his hand over the surface of her bodice, down around the outside of one breast, slowly cupping it through her clothing.

He bent to rasp his tongue over her earlobe, where it set alight a wild flickering flame. She couldn't voice the objections that ran through her thoughts, because her body wouldn't allow it. With Lennox toying with her—his large male body pressing so determinedly against hers, his mouth brushing over her skin—she was speechless, helpless, a victim of her own desire.

Pressing close against her back, he stroked his hand under her skirt again, pushing it up. "You are ready to have a man inside you."

"Please do not say that." *Because it's true.*

"I want you, Chloris," he coaxed. "You're so hot, damp." His hand was between her thighs. "I feel your need in the palm of my hand."

With his fingers stroking over her folds she was as weak as a rag doll in his hands. Her heart raced, her body clamoring for him.

"Tell me you don't want this, and I will desist."

She wanted him, wanted him badly. "Lennox, please…"

"This?" He shifted at her back and she felt the hard rod of his erection pressing against her bare thigh.

How good it would feel to writhe on it, to work off her frustration on such a fine weapon. Tipping her head back she invited him closer, relinquishing herself to him, offering no resistance.

Holding her, he reached over to kiss her mouth. But he kept her in that position, on her side. A moment later, his hand returned to the underside of her thigh and he lifted it, parting her legs. The blunt head of his erection pressed into her from behind. It was lewd and shocking, and when he pushed into her, stretching her open, it drew a harsh gasp from her open mouth.

"This is what you needed?" He paused.

"Yes," she cried out. "Yes, yes, yes!"

"Then you shall have it." Thrusting deep and hard, he claimed her.

Chloris panted, her breath caught on the extreme rush of pleasure being filled by him brought about. Then he lifted her upper thigh, drawing it up and toward her chest, grinding deeper still. Her body flamed.

He rode her hard, and her body welcomed it. Dizzy with sensation her emotions soared, her entire body carried on it.

"Oh, yes," he breathed, "your body clutches me in welcome. You could not deny this and I did not want you to."

She pressed her lips together.

He thrust harder and faster, working his way in and out. Her hips moved of their own accord, taking every thrust, meeting him.

Then she felt the head of his cock brushing her center, loosing hot tides of pleasure that reached her womb and beyond. Cries of ecstasy escaped her, and she gulped them back. Her core rippled around his length. It was as if she lifted from the ground, so intense was her pleasure. Hot fluid sluiced the tops of her thighs.

His rod grew harder still and she squirmed, for she was so sensitive it was almost too much. He whispered her name in a tormented tone, pulling free as he spilled his seed.

The power of the shared moment stunned her and Chloris trembled, inside and out. *What have I done?* Once again, she asked herself that question. It was as if she was spinning out of control, as if his spell had led her to the brink of madness and beyond.

But even though she knew the consequences were many, Chloris could not bring herself to regret it—not then, not when his arm stole around her and he held her close, whispering words of affection and praise to her as he caressed her— for it was the closest thing to love that she had ever known.

chapter Eight

Chloris had never known such intense pleasure.

Or such overwhelming guilt.

She sat at breakfast the following day, barely aware of the voices around her until the children came in. Tam and Rab scuffled amongst themselves, until their father lifted his head and peered at them. Chloris watched the two young lads, and their innocent young faces confused her all the more. Remorse filled her. She'd been weak. She had succumbed, even though she had promised herself she wouldn't.

Not only that, but she had agreed to meet Lennox again that very morning. Torn between desire and remorse, she could not go to him. Why not? Wasn't it what her closest friends had suggested she do, take a lover? She had nothing to lose. Chloris Keavey was nothing but a burden to all around her, and that had been the situation since her family was taken by the cough. It weighed heavily upon her, and providing her husband with an heir was the only thing that would make any difference to her life.

Worthless and wretched, she had gone to Lennox in a desperate effort to find her meaning in life. The truth of it was that she was only in Gavin's way, she was stopping him getting what he wanted—someone else. If this magic of Lennox's didn't work she might as well be dead. However, if it did work and she bore Gavin's child, her life would be little better than death. Now she saw that—now she admitted it to herself. Only because she'd been offered a taste of something illicit—passion, unbridled passion, a few precious moments of pleasure—something that she could savor forever to carry her through the bad times.

Perhaps enough ritual had been undertaken, and she would be fertile for Gavin.

Meanwhile, she could not risk succumbing to Master Lennox's charms again.

Resolving to put an end to it and never see him again, she felt more clearheaded. Until a sense of loss quickly assaulted her. Steeling herself, she made plans to send a message with Maura Dunbar, informing Master Lennox that she would no longer be pursuing the matter they had discussed.

Once the boys had been taken away by their nursemaid, Jean cleared her throat. "Husband, cousin, I have some news to share."

Both Chloris and Tamhas looked her way.

"The midwife has confirmed it. I am with child once more. A girl, I hope."

Tamhas patted her hand. "Another son would be better."

"Oh, Tamhas, have pity on me. I need a daughter. Otherwise I will be an old woman alone in a house full of men."

Tamhas mumbled incoherently.

Chloris watched the exchange as if from above or beyond, and for a moment forgot her place. When Jean looked her way expectantly, smiling as she did, Chloris nodded. "That is wonderful news, you are much blessed."

Shortly afterward Tamhas went to his study to receive the

tenants who were due to call on him that day. Once he had gone, Jean pushed back her chair.

"I hope my news does not upset you, cousin." Jean rose from her seat and skirted the table. She pulled Tamhas's abandoned chair closer to Chloris and sat down by her side. "I am aware it might be a sensitive matter, given that you have no child of your own…as yet."

Chloris shook her head. "It is joyous news, I am happy for you."

"Thank you, cousin." Jean rested her hand briefly on Chloris's forearm.

Chloris was plagued by an altogether different question. While Jean chattered on about when the baby might be due to arrive, Chloris studied her. Had she succumbed to the Witch Master's seductive ways? Is that why she was so fertile? The question refused to go away.

"Listen to me rattling on," Jean said, "when I am sure you have more sensible things to occupy your time."

Given Jean's current loquaciousness, Chloris could not keep her curiosity in check. "No, I am interested in every detail. I am also curious, have you ever sought guidance on the subject of falling pregnant?"

Jean looked startled, then smiled. "Oh, I see why you might ask that. No, I have been lucky. You will be lucky, too, soon. God willing."

Chloris noticed that her smile was somewhat trite. The curiosity still lingered. "Can I trust you with a delicate question?"

Jean nodded.

"The man who we saw in the market in Saint Andrews, the one who you said dabbles in witchcraft…"

Without hesitation, Jean answered. "Lennox Fingal."

"Do you know if they, the witches, can influence a woman's fertility?" It was not the question Chloris wanted to ask, but she was edging closer to it.

Jean studied her for a short while before responding. "You must not entertain such a notion. The man is dangerous."

How curious. Yet Chloris knew Lennox had been in the house at Jean's behest. Had he seduced her, too? "How can you be sure that he is dangerous?"

Jean stiffened.

"I am most eager to please Gavin, you see," Chloris added, in explanation, "to provide him with an heir."

Jean considered her comment then leaned closer as if she suspected her servants might overhear the conversation. "That is not the way. Lennox Fingal would prey upon your...womanly needs."

A chill crept over Chloris. It was too close to what had actually happened.

"He would use you and taint you forever if you sought his help."

For a moment Chloris was unable to speak, and then she forced herself on. "Has he done this to you?" When Jean flinched, she added quickly, "Or someone you know?"

Jeans lips tightened. "Thankfully not to me." She sighed deeply. "I confess I came close to falling under his spell a long time ago, but his eyes were set on a much bigger prize." There was bitterness in her response. That alone answered one question—Jean had wanted him, would have given herself to him, but it hadn't happened.

"That woman, however," Jean continued, "never regained

her reputation after she was bedded by him. Nor did her husband for letting her stray."

Never regained her reputation. The comment shouldn't have bothered Chloris, because Lennox had gone to such lengths to keep their meetings secret, but bother her it did. *I must end it. Now.*

Jean frowned. "Promise me you will not consider such a desperate act."

It was hard to force a smile, but force it she did.

Jean's mouth twitched at one corner and for the briefest moment Chloris sensed jealousy in her. Surely not? Jean had so much and seemed happy. Could it be that she was so enamored with Lennox that she begrudged Chloris's ability to seek him out, if she chose to?

"Good. Now I must supervise the household or nothing will get done." Jean rose to her feet, then hesitated. "I hope it is not my own happy news that has set you thinking such wild, desperate thoughts about that rogue and his barbarian ways."

Chloris felt strangely adrift. The conversation had enlightened her, but Jean's parting words were oddly barbed. Barbarian ways? He was wild hearted, that was true, but she had never encountered a man who deserved that slur less than he did. *Am I bewitched?* The wild urge to laugh hit her. Even if he was bewitching her, she still knew charm when she encountered it, and there was no denying the Witch Master's charm. Rising to her feet, she shook her head. "No, it is not your happy news, rest assured."

When Jean left Chloris felt oddly wistful. Had her instincts been in charge she would be running out to the stable to fetch a horse to ride into the forest. Luckily she was keeping a check on those instincts—barely, but she was. Instead she went to her room to fetch her mahogany inlaid writing box. It was time to bring order to her life once more. She carried the box downstairs to the drawing room.

The drawing room desk was conveniently positioned in a bay window overlooking the terraced gardens. She set her writing box on the desk and placed her reticule nearby. Taking up her seat she opened the box—a gift from a dear friend and neighbor at home in Edinburgh—and arranged its contents carefully, opening the ink well and readying the quill. She would write to him immediately, calling an end to their clandestine meetings.

She placed the blotting pad to one side and dusted off the leather-covered writing slope before repositioning the sheet of parchment on it. Turning away, she stared out at the gardens, admiring the luscious shades of green within her field of vision. But as she gazed, she suddenly remembered that it was that very place he had paced across to visit her in secret. Chloris stared out at the gardens, picturing it again. What a striking figure he had made, and how fast it made her blood pump, the sight of him on his way to her.

But it was wrong, and she had to end it.

Write to him and be done with it, she told herself, and forced her quill to the page.

Master Lennox

I write to you first with an apology that I did not attend the meeting you kindly arranged for us this morning. I am most grateful for your efforts regarding my malady. However, I feel I will not be able to pursue the matter further. Therefore I am canceling the ongoing arrangement forthwith.

That you have engendered change in me is undeniable, and I am most grateful. I will remember your efforts to help me most fondly.
Chloris

Chloris stared down at the page and gave a rueful smile.

She would indeed remember his efforts fondly, more than fondly. She had the feeling they would keep her warm on many a cold night. She had attempted to state her case plainly and politely in the brief note. Yet when she read back over it, it sounded like some sort of jest, made so by its understatement about the powerful, unforgettable encounters she'd had with him.

Sighing deeply she put down her quill and reached for the blotter. Pressing the wooden roller firmly over the parchment, she told herself once again it was for the best. And she was grateful, she just could not trust herself to let it go further, especially in the light of Jean's comments. She had already sinned, and now she must force herself back to the more honorable path, no matter how hard it was to resist such an amorous lover who was so readily available to her.

She folded the parchment, sealed it with wax and set it aside.

Outside, a sound drew her attention. She caught sight of young Rab racing down the terrace with Tam close behind. Their nursemaid was also in tow, hitching up her skirts as she attempted to catch them. Chloris smiled then stared down at the letter she had begun to write the day before.

Dearest Gavin.

It was so hard. Every time she tried, her thoughts drifted. First into guilty admission of her infidelity, then further, into breathless remembering of each and every forbidden touch, each kiss, each thrust.

Forcing herself to concentrate on the letter, she reminded herself that this was a small task, one that she had undertaken many times before. Usually she would tell him of her activities, but she could not tell him or anybody of what she had done these past three days. Prior to that she had written to Gavin twice a week since she had come to her cousin's home in Saint Andrews. At first it had been a reasonably pleasant task to reassure him of her increasingly robust health and query after his trade in Edinburgh. Gavin did not reply, but she felt it was part of her wifely duties to keep him informed of her well-being, in order to reassure him of her health and, more specifically, her ability to bear him a child.

It was never an easy task. Any manner of communication with Gavin was fraught, painful and dangerous, but putting ink on the page was easier than sitting through a dinner with him, knowing what would follow.

For some reason she found it harder than ever.

Was it the guilt?

She put down her quill and sat back in the chair. She had allowed a man who was not her husband to be intimate with her, to touch her in ways that would be considered shocking. Her motives had been genuine, and although there had been pleasure in it—pleasure such as she had never known—she had honestly pursued the endeavor for the sake of her marriage.

I do feel guilty, though, because I enjoyed his touch.

Chloris never allowed herself to shy from the truth for long. She did not consider herself brave, but she was honest with herself. She believed her most reliable characteristic was the ability to endure. Her failure as a woman made her more timid than she might have been otherwise. For that she mourned. She saw women who managed their position so much better than she did, but it was her failure to fulfill the basic duty of a wife that crippled her will and her spirit.

Staring at the gardens with unseeing eyes, she considered her position. She had come here to Saint Andrews for a reprieve. That was all it was, in truth. A reprieve from Gavin's torments, so that she could return and face it with more tenacity, willing herself all the while to fulfill her obligations to him. Gavin had suggested it, she was not sure why, but she had grasped the chance for time to heal, to breathe. But distance had only made her more aware of her pitiful existence.

When she'd gone to Somerled she'd hoped for help. The wildest hope had been for some miracle, the more realistic hope had been for some sage advice—perhaps a whispered method of holding her husband's seed inside her long enough that it would bed and flourish. Instead she'd been set on a different, unknown path, and now Chloris felt as if a closed door had been flung open to her, a door she had not even been aware of before.

It does not mean it is right.

No. She was at risk of being disloyal again, and she was dabbling in matters that she did not fully understand, matters that most God-fearing folk would turn away from in fear. Other women had been ruined by him. She knew that now but still she could not force the desire away. Was it hope, foolhardiness or sheer contrariness that pushed her to it?

Witches. She covered her eyes with her hands, but it only took her back to the moment when he had pulled off her glove that first evening, and touched her palm. Thirty years old she was and weary of life, and that simple action on his part had been the most pleasurable, most sensuous thing she had ever experienced. She became vulnerable to him from that moment on and she knew it. She was greatly at risk of falling further under his influence. And she knew his kind were wild.

They had few boundaries when it came to pleasures of the flesh and he had not denied that when she confronted him about it. That was why their knowledge of such things was substantial. It made her want to turn away, to protect her reputation.

What reputation? It was shortly to be destroyed, along with any air of respectability, when her husband threw her out of their home for failing to bring him a child. To successfully carry her husband's child was the nature of her quest. A quest that she had undertaken in desperation after failing to provide him with an heir.

It was their forbidden carnal knowledge and its inherent virility that she had gone there for. There was little doubt she had been well prepared. The rituals she had undergone had left her as supple, willing and eager as a spring sapling. Surely now she could bear her husband's child? If not now, it would be never.

She picked up her quill.

My time in Fife has brought me robust health and I feel our dreams will be fulfilled soon.

She paused.

Why don't you take a lover? Lennox's words echoed through her mind, as they had ever since he had said them.

She was compelled to consider them over again, like some fascination that she could not separate herself from. Why hadn't she taken a lover before? Why had she done so now? She thought herself a loyal wife, despite the difficulties she had

survived under Gavin's will and rule. There had been oppor-
tunities to take a lover in Edinburgh. Several female acquaintances had suggested it to her, in pity, and two men had even
offered their services. Her female friends had informed her
that women often did so when no child had been forthcom-
ing from the marital bed. It was a chance some women took
to redeem themselves. The idea had never been attractive to
Chloris before. Not until she met Lennox Fingal.

"Begging your pardon, mistress."

Chloris started in her seat, sitting bolt upright. Turning,
she saw that Maura was standing just a few paces away. Chloris had been so far away in her thoughts that she had not even
heard the girl enter the room. "Maura, good day."

"Mistress." Maura bobbed a curtsy, then came closer and
lowered her voice. "Did you find Somerled?"

Chloris smiled at the young woman. She was a sweet girl
with hair the color of chestnuts and freckles over her cheeks. "I
did. Thank you, Maura. Your directions were most helpful."

"I hope they were as good to you as they were to me."
Maura ducked her head. "My malady has all but vanished
since I went up there."

Chloris did not know what Maura's malady was, but the
girl's positive comment made Chloris cling to the hope that
she, too, would be affected by the magic rituals she had undergone. "That is very promising."

They stared at one another, both curious about each other's malady, but divided by class and privilege. They did not
ask nor share. It had only been a moment's madness that had
inspired Chloris to interrupt Maura's whispered discussion
with another servant about the goings-on up at the house in
the woods. She'd happened upon the two in the library and

found herself compelled to listen to the discussion about magic and possibility.

"Would you do something for me, Maura?"

"Of course, mistress, if I am able." There was a slightly wary look in her eyes.

"I need someone to take this letter to the master at Somerled. Can you do it for me?"

Maura looked at the folded page and nodded, apparently relieved that it was something she was able to do. She accepted the letter and tucked it into the pocket of her apron.

"Thank you, you're a good girl." Reaching across the desk Chloris picked up the leather pouch she kept her coins in and opened it. Retrieving several coins she pressed them into Maura's hand. "Here, take this."

"No, mistress, I cannot. If the master finds me with money he will think I have stolen it." Maura glanced back over her shoulder at the doorway.

"Then tuck the coins in your undergarments and be quick about it. It is but a small thank-you for taking me into your confidence. I know you were afraid when I quizzed you about your discussion."

Maura lifted up her skirts and tucked the coins into a pocket stitched into her petticoat. Not a moment too soon. Her skirts dropped into place just as the door was flung open and Tamhas entered the room.

Both women tensed.

Chloris acted quickly. "Thank you, Maura, you may go about your chores."

Maura bobbed a curtsy and scurried off.

Tamhas stood in silence for a moment, observing his cousin.

Chloris shifted the items on her writing box, and then

smiled his way. "Your hearings have gone well this morning, cousin?"

"Well enough." He made his way over to her, glancing down at the page she was writing on as he passed behind her. For a moment he stared out of the window at the gardens, and then he turned to her. "Jean has expressed concern. She tells me that you went riding alone early in the morning yesterday." He assessed her as he spoke.

Chloris maintained her poise, but his questioning made her uneasy. "I found it most reviving. The spring air seems to improve my health."

And the Witch Master. Why, oh, why could she not stop the thoughts spilling within her mind, images of the magical, passionate encounters that were making her health more robust.

He considered her at length. "You do look well, quite rosy-cheeked, in fact."

The reason for the bloom in her was his lingering magic and passion, for she still felt Lennox's hands on her, molding her to him as they coupled in the bluebell glen.

"Thank you, Tamhas. I am grateful that you allowed me to visit at this time." Her voice faltered as she spoke. She hoped he would not notice her state of agitation.

Tamhas moved closer and perched on the desk where she was working. This had the unfortunate circumstance of bringing his torso far too close for comfort.

"I wondered if Jean's fortuitous news might be an upsetting matter for you."

Chloris was in the process of moving her chair back slightly when he made the comment, and jolted to a standstill, staring at him aghast. "Why, no, I am delighted for her. Despite the fact I have not been able to bear children myself, as yet, it does not mean that I resent others who have found it easier."

Tamhas nodded, vaguely, and then he studied her figure at length as if he might determine the cause for her lack of fertility. His mouth moved into a rather lascivious smile. "Perhaps I can be of assistance?"

Chloris swallowed. His meaning was quite obvious, and it shocked her to the core. Tamhas was forthright, and he had made lewd enough suggestions to her before, when she was a young girl and his ward. That was when they were both unmarried, however, and over time she had dismissed his flirtatious approach as the jest of a young man. A man who found himself with wealth and power before he had developed the maturity to manage it.

Chloris attempted an appropriate response. "You are being of assistance, allowing me this time of recuperation here at Torquil House."

"Come now, Chloris. Don't be coy. You know I have always found you an attractive woman, and a fine mistress you would have made for this house." A flicker of annoyance showed in his expression for a moment, forcing her to acknowledge his deeper motives. "I have sired three children with my wife now, and there are many more out there who could call me father."

"I'm not sure you should be sharing such information with me, especially when I am growing close to Jean."

Tamhas shrugged one shoulder. "Jean is content." Again he studied her, his gaze lingering around her bosom. "I could make you content, too. In fact," he added, "I'd put money on you accepting my seed well enough."

Instinctively Chloris turned her face away from him, but he only seemed to see it as an opportunity to reach out and grasp her hand, making a physical connection with her that she did not want. He squeezed her hand, forcing her to look back at him.

"I have made an offer, consider it well, cousin." The look in his eyes was cold. He was irritated because she had not immediately capitulated. "You might have better luck with a different lover. Most women in your situation would grasp any opportunity to fall pregnant. You are thirty years old and your husband will soon be seeking a more fruitful union elsewhere."

Chloris was well aware of the truth in what he was saying to her, but still she smarted. It was not only that he was saying it aloud, it was his coldness in delivering the information. It also suddenly seemed as if everyone in the world was privy to her secret failures. Not only that but they were all too willing to comment freely on it, and that was not easy for her. With Lennox she had been compelled to open herself to him, but she had not invited this discussion with Tamhas. It made her even more wary of Tamhas than she already was.

"It would be better that such a union be with a well-to-do, upstanding man," Tamhas continued, "someone who has your best interests at heart."

Upstanding? What upstanding man would make such a suggestion under the very roof he shared with his wife?

It was difficult not to point out she understood him better than he realized. Tamhas could not afford to have her turned out or wandering in mind or body. She had been Tamhas's ward until she turned marriageable age and she had been a canny investment for him. Her inheritance was substantial and what there was he split with her husband at the time of the marriage, and he still had an obligation to Gavin. No doubt he had been paid well by her husband to keep her away from

Edinburgh for a period of time, and to return her in good health and ready to bear him a son. If Tamhas was to secretly father her child it merely secured her position as Gavin's wife and therefore secured his dealings with Gavin.

Chloris had never felt more alone.

"Lennox, a letter has arrived for you." Ailsa stood in the arched entrance of the old barns. Sunset was close and Lennox was toiling hard with the other men in the fading light, building the framework for a covered carriage. Since Master MacDougal had praised their talents and he had been given access to the council, several requests for their craftsmanship had already been received. Despite Keavey's attempts to thwart him, and the delay for the guild, he had already begun to gain favor.

Lennox wiped his brow and set down his tools before striding over to take the letter from her. He examined the seal. He did not recognize it. "Who brought it?"

"Maura Dunbar carried it from the Keavey house."

When he did not respond, Ailsa gave a labored sigh. "It will be from that Mistress Chloris, seeking you and your magic I don't doubt."

Ailsa had a sour look about her and Lennox thought twice about opening it immediately. "The men are still hard at work and will be until darkness falls. Will you bring them some ale?"

Ailsa scowled at him, folded her arms across her chest, but nevertheless turned on her heel and headed toward the house.

Lennox broke the seal on the letter and read the contents quickly.

It was indeed from Mistress Chloris, and he frowned heavily when he read her words. Undue concern had haunted him all day long, after she had not arrived in the forest as planned. His goal was to irritate Tamhas Keavey. Why then did he find himself fretting over Chloris, wondering what had happened to her? Eventually he had to assume she was waylaid on her plans for a morning ride and had to abandon it. Nevertheless, Lennox found himself concerned for her safety, which shouldn't have been the case.

Now that he saw the real reason for her absence, Lennox found himself even more troubled by it. The more he thought on it, the more troubled he became. He wanted her again. The woman had got into his blood and he would not rest until he'd explored her at length. It was not the usual way of it, and he battled the urge to storm up to Torquil House and demand she reconsider.

What nonsense is this? he wondered. The woman had dismissed him. In all likelihood, that was the end of it.

Then he recalled the moment he saw the fear at the back of her eyes, and it had halted him in his tracks. Despite the fact she tried to hide it, she was vulnerable. Was she afraid now? Had someone made her send this note? Lennox could scarcely bear the thought of it. *It is because of my lost sisters,* he thought. If any man saw that fear in their eyes, he only hoped they would act on it, discover its cause and protect them.

Battling his confused motives, he shoved the note in his pocket.

When Ailsa returned with a flagon of ale for the men, he scarcely acknowledged her. His mood turned dark. It wasn't meant to end yet. In his blood, he knew that.

Such selfish motives could easily lead him into reckless behavior, and he could not shrug off the doubts he had about his own judgment. Nevertheless, after another hour's work, he gave in to his instincts. When the men went inside for supper, Lennox went to the stable instead, saddled his horse and took the moonlit path across the glen to Torquil House.

For whatever reason, he could not fight the need to see the woman again.

chapter Nine

The yearning that Chloris felt to see the Witch Master again was immense. It was a burden every bit as weighty as her guilt. Morbid thoughts crept up on her easily that evening, the realization that she might never see him again affecting her badly.

The dinner conversation did not help.

Tamhas rambled about council matters, occasionally making disparaging remarks about Lennox, which made her discomfort grow. Not only that, but his opinion of Lennox was so very low that she had to bite her tongue in order not to challenge her cousin. Lennox was by no means a perfect man, she was not foolish enough to believe that, but she felt her cousin did him a great disservice. Besides which, Tamhas was no saint, and each time he caught her attention there was an unwelcome intimacy there, a reminder of how untoward he'd been that very day.

It had been the same with Eithne, she recalled. Tamhas had an instant distrust of anyone who was attempting to heal others and provide comfort where there was none. He had listened to too many tales about those who practiced witchcraft and his mind was made up on the matter.

When she took her leave, Jean frowned.

"You look a little pale this evening," Jean commented.

"I am well, do not concern yourself."

Jean did not seem convinced. She rose to her feet and rested the back of her hand against Chloris's cheek. "No fever. That is a relief. If you feel unwell you must tell me, we can arrange for the physician to call."

"Please, don't fuss. I am just a little tired." She glanced at Tamhas.

Tamhas pressed his lips together and stared down at his goblet of Port. If she was not mistaken he looked a mite sheepish. He thought it was because of him that she was pale. Well, it wasn't, although Chloris was content to let him believe he was right.

She almost ran to her bedchamber, relieved to be away from the difficult situation. She could only hope that it would get easier now that she had ceased her involvement with Lennox.

Once inside her chamber, she reached for the candle that stood on a shelf inside the door and struck the flint next to it. Lifting the lit candle she carried it to the mantel where she set it down near a small looking glass to reflect the light. The fire burned low in the grate. She stared down at it. As she did the skin on the back of her neck prickled with anxiety. Turning on her heel she scoured the dark shadows of the room.

That's when she saw him standing there.

Shocked by his presence, she put her hand to her throat. "Lennox."

"I had to come. I had to be sure you were safe."

Chloris couldn't see his face clearly, but she could hear the concern in his voice.

He'd come to her, that indicated he cared enough to fear

for her safety. Her heart swelled, emotions brimming. She'd longed to see him, and he was here. "You received my letter?"

"I did." He stepped out of the shadows.

"You shouldn't have come here, it is too dangerous." She was about to dart over to him, to chastise him for taking the risk, when she heard the floorboards in the corridor outside her chamber creaking. "Oh, no, it is the serving girl. She will come in to stoke the fire and turn down the bed."

"Fear not. Act as you normally would."

His voice was calm, but Chloris felt only distress. Then she blinked and stared, but could barely see him at all. He had retreated into the dark shadows. A moment later there was a tap at the door and it opened. If she distracted the girl, perhaps she would not notice him. Chloris turned and smiled.

"Mistress Chloris." The upstairs serving girl curtsied, then darted over to the fire and stoked it from the nearby basket.

Chloris could scarcely believe it was happening. Lennox was in her chamber and the threat of discovery was immense. She took another glance at the spot where he'd stood. Mercifully, she could not discern his outline.

"Do you require any assistance with your disrobing, mistress?" the girl said as she straightened up. She always asked. It was her duty to do so.

"No, thank you." She realized her voice was barely audible because she was so tense. She forced another smile.

The girl wiped her hands on her apron. "I will just turn down the covers, in that case."

"No, that will not be necessary." Usually the girl undertook the task, but Chloris could not risk her moving closer to the place where Lennox stood.

The girl needed no further encouragement to be on her way. She bobbed another curtsy. "Good night, mistress."

As soon as the door closed and the sound of creaking boards faded away down the corridor outside, Chloris turned and ran to him.

He captured her in his arms.

"You should not have risked coming here," she chastised.

"I had to. I do not believe that you want to put an end to our endeavor."

She stared up at him, taking in the intensity of his expression. "It has gone far beyond an endeavor, even you cannot pretend otherwise."

He gave a gentle chuckle. "You are a brave and honest woman, and it is one of the things that draws me to you."

"Brave, because I have faced the truth of it, that we have become lovers when that was not my original intention?"

"Aye." Reaching for her hand, he drew it to his lips and rested a gentle kiss there. "We became lovers, and you cannot deny that you wanted it as much as I did."

His forthright remark only served to remind her how pleasurable it had been, and Chloris could not respond immediately because her body was wildly stimulated by his proximity. She could smell his aroma, hot and male and alive with the scent of the forest. "Lennox, please."

With his free hand pressing her close to him he ducked his head and kissed her mouth. Firm and persuasive, his lips covered hers. His hands were around her hips and he kissed her deeply, passionately, his mouth opening hers, forcing her to receive him. Locking her hands over his shoulders, she moaned into his mouth, unable to hold back for the touch of his mouth on hers made her clamor for him.

"This is too good to deny," he said as he drew back, his voice husky and determined, "and you will not send me away until we've coupled again."

"But we cannot. The serving girl might come back—"

He held her tumbling hair in one hand, drawing her head back so that he could look into her eyes. "You are as needy for it as I."

She was, and the hot tide of shame she felt was momentary in the face of her desire for him. She nodded.

He smiled. "You will not regret it."

"I will not, if you are fast and then make your escape," she blurted, "before my cousin finds you under his precious roof."

Lennox laughed beneath his breath as if delighted by that. "He could not stop me, for right now all I can think of is being inside you. The taste I had of you yesterday only whetted my appetite for more."

The appetite he referred to was there in his face, and she could not refuse him because she wanted it, too. Chloris could scarcely control her breathing. Her corset felt painfully tight, her pulse racing.

"Make haste," she whispered, clutching at his hips.

Backing her into the shadows beside the curtained bed, he pressed her to the wall. He cupped her head in one hand, stroking her hair as he did.

In the hidden shadows her desire intensified. Chloris ached for him at her center. Her head dropped back, her lips ready to accept his fierce, hungry kisses. In the gloomy niche they were shielded from the fall of the candlelight and she could not see him clearly, but she felt his passion enveloping her.

Hitching up her skirts, she lifted one foot from the floor,

riding her knee up the side of his leg. "You have made me wild with your spells and your wicked ways."

"If you wish to give me credit that is your prerogative, but I fancy it was there in you all along, Mistress Chloris, begging to be unleashed."

He undid the lace that held his breeches closed and freed his manhood. Chloris went to touch it, but before she had the chance he lifted her with his hands around her buttocks and encouraged her to wrap her legs around his hips. It made her feel so wanton, so womanly, cleaving to him that way that she had to gasp for air.

He pressed hard against her and she leaned into the wall at her back, one hand clutching at the velvet bed curtains at her side. Between her spread legs she felt his hard length pressed against her splayed flesh. She caught her lower lip between her teeth to anchor her emotions. They were about to couple, here, where her cousin would have Lennox strung up if he found him. She squeezed her eyes shut. Even though she knew it was wrong and dangerous, there was nothing she could do but submit to him because her body craved him so.

Lennox was calm and focused. That made her doubt the wisdom in this all the more. How could she have fallen into this so quick and so deep that all her reason was gone, that she took such great risks to be with him?

Because I've never had a taste of anything like this before.

Tears dampened her cheek. She brushed them away, annoyed.

Then his hard length was against her most sensitive places. Her breathing altered, speeding, for it was as if he freed life itself in her swollen bud, the pressure of his erection massaging it so intimately.

"Hold tight to me, for I must be inside you, now."

It was so true, need had them both. Not magic or her quest for fertility, but pure mutual need. She moaned and clutched at him, resting her weight back against the wall where she pivoted. He held her steady with his palms beneath her bottom. Then he eased the crown of his cock inside her, stretching her open. She breathed even quicker, her mouth opening in response to his penetration.

"You are so damp, mistress, my cock is doused in your precious juices."

Her entire body flamed. "Lennox..."

"Oh, aye, you're lush tonight, my beauty, tears or no tears."

The husky way he spoke and his warm breath on her face were maddening. She clutched at him. "Please, Lennox, please."

Shifting his weight, he pressed the blunt head of his cock deeper.

"Fill me," she whispered.

As he drove his full length into her, she cried out with pleasure.

Lennox covered her mouth with his, silencing her, then slid deep to her core in one fast move. He was inside her, his blood pounding inside hers. Her hips were angled to take him in, her flesh melting onto the hard, hot shaft. Sensation burst at her center and rolled through her. It felt too good. Her hands went to his head, holding him as she arched her hips to accommodate him.

Chloris moaned in ecstasy, her head falling back against the wall. He moved his face into the curve of her neck. Her sheath clutched at him, and Lennox cursed. He drew back, and then reached farther inside. She rose up, her hands on his shoulders, matching him. He was riding her hard and Chloris struggled for breath. Her hands fisted on the fabric of his coat. She contracted, tightening on his throbbing length.

He pushed one hand between them. She cried out in ecstasy, another rush of pleasure taking her.

"Chloris, oh, yes." His thrusts grew urgent.

She responded, wanting more, wanting it all. Pressing down hard onto his length she relished that it brought about both pleasure and pain in her. She wanted to feel it all, for it made her feel vital and alive. Her hands roved over his back, and as she did he whispered her name on a sigh and pulled free.

Chloris found herself lowered to the floor, swaying unsteadily as her feet met the floor. Staring down she watched as he rode his erection with his fist until he spilled.

The ache that loosed in her inflamed body was almost too much.

He put his hand to the wall behind her head, his head bent close to hers while he gasped for breath in his release.

Silence surrounded them, but for the sounds of their mutual labored breathing.

Then he sought her mouth with his.

The tender kiss they shared was interrupted a moment later.

A noise sounded in the corridor outside the door. It was the boards creaking again, signaling someone's approach. Chloris reacted, drawing him deeper into the shadows next to the head of the bed. Chloris had almost forgotten their surroundings, and the discussion had been heated earlier, their lovemaking fierce, perhaps too loud. Had they drawn attention to themselves?

Footsteps approached her door. She held her breath, one hand on Lennox's chest, protectively, her eyes trained on the door. Then Lennox whispered something. The strange words made her look his way. His eyes went bright, then faded. He smiled softly and put one finger to her lips. "Stay quiet."

There was a tap at the door. A moment later Jean entered the room. Her shoulders were shrouded in a heavy shawl and it hung down and covered most of her nightgown. She glanced over at the bed.

Chloris's heart hammered in her chest. She recalled the way Jean had fussed over her at dinner. She was obviously still concerned. Chloris rued the fact she had not sent Lennox on his way as soon as they'd talked. They were going to be found. In a moment she would be discovered harboring the Witch Master in her room at night. Jean would call out for help, and Cousin Tamhas would find Lennox here.

Jean lifted the candlestick from the mantel and held it aloft as she looked toward the bed. Chloris dared not breathe. Jean replaced the candle, then turned and left the room, closing the door quietly behind her.

"She did not see us?"

"I made it so."

Chloris realized the curtains around the bed had obscured Jean's view. Jean must have assumed she was asleep and decided not to disturb her. But the curtains had been open before, she remembered it distinctly. "You obscured the bed by magic?"

"Aye, and cast us deeper in shadows. Although it is the first time I have used magic since I entered this room tonight."

Chloris stared up at him. At first she thought he was clarifying about the earlier interruption, when he'd hidden in the shadows and she'd distracted the serving girl. Slowly, it dawned on her what he was saying. Magic had not played a part in their frantic lovemaking, only mutual desire. There was no ritual, no chanting, and yet it had been every bit as powerful an exchange as it had the day before in the bluebell glen. More so, in fact, because they came together with open, mutual longing, and because she could see his expression while they coupled.

He ran his fingers through her hair and smiled. "You seem surprised."

"I am. When you made love to me I assumed it was...magical." Her face flushed. She felt a little silly.

"It *was* magical, but only by virtue of the fact that we are well matched in both desire and appetite for each other." After he said that, he stroked his fingers along her upturned face, looking at her for a long moment, as if he, too, was considering the import of that connection.

Chloris tried to take it in. They had come together for ritual magic, a task, and yet what had happened between them that night was driven by something entirely different, a mutual need that had to be fulfilled. Could it be true, or was this part of his seductive repertoire, a performance he delivered to any woman he wanted to bed awhile? She wanted to believe, but it was a difficult task, given all that she had been told.

For her own part she wanted him, she couldn't deny that—couldn't deny him when he'd come to her. Before Lennox she'd known no other lover aside from Gavin. Their couplings were cold and perfunctory, at best. She assumed a man such as Lennox experienced pleasure this way with any woman he chose to couple with, and that she was one of many he was well matched with. Yet the way he looked at her made her wonder as to his meaning.

Then he bent to kiss her. It was gentle this time, a confirmation, not a demand.

Chloris returned the kiss, wrapping her arms around his head when he held her to him, savoring his embrace. Never before had she experienced such bliss, and she wanted to claim every part of it.

"You must go, all is quiet now," she insisted as they drew apart, her growing need to protect him taking over. "Promise me that you will not come here to the house again, it is too dangerous."

"I will promise you that, if you promise to meet me at the old oak in the mornings instead." He searched her expression as he awaited her response, and she felt the strength of his will. He wanted her to agree to the request.

Could she even begin to think about denying him? She would be denying her own desires, too, for her instinctive response was to agree. She wanted to meet with him again. She'd already broken her vows—just as her husband had done, long ago, when he took a mistress—and this was a source of happiness she had never imagined could be hers. She was also afraid, though, because the dislike Tamhas had for Lennox was so fierce, and Jean had made it clear that her husband was looking for a good reason to oust the witches who lived around Saint Andrews. Chloris did not want to put any of them in danger of that. If she met him in the forest, though, the risk would be much smaller. Would she be brave enough to claim a few more moments of happiness with Lennox while she was in Saint Andrews?

"Please, Chloris," he murmured, "say you will."

"Yes, I will."

The tension in his expression vanished, and the smile he gave was broad and infectious. Chloris laughed softly then stood on her tiptoes and cupped his face in her hands in order to kiss his mouth. The swelling emotion in her chest should have made her fret, but it didn't. Not then, not when he was holding her and it felt so right and true. The doubts would come later, she knew they would, but for now, she denied them.

chapter Ten

Tamhas Keavey supped his ale and scowled at the doorway to the inn. It was well past the agreed meeting time and there was no sign of Master MacDougal. It was important that he wait, though. As head of the town council MacDougal was often called upon to adjudicate in urgent matters.

When MacDougal eventually arrived, Tamhas signaled for another jug of ale and rose to his feet.

"My apologies, friend." MacDougal took his seat. "Affairs of the council take precedence over social time, I'm afraid."

Tamhas forced a smile. "It is a matter of the council I wish to speak to you about this evening."

MacDougal frowned. "If that is the case it should be discussed in council."

"It is imperative that I warn you about a suspicion I have, one that I cannot speak about openly as yet."

They fell silent when the serving wench arrived with a jug and a second mug. While she poured the ale, Tamhas was pleased to note that MacDougal looked curious, despite his reservations.

Once the girl had gone, MacDougal nodded for him to continue.

"It is Lennox Fingal."

MacDougal's frown returned. "You have already raised concerns about Master Fingal and we made a compromise in recognition of that."

"The concerns I have are weighty and therefore need to be broached. Believe me, it is the council and our town and families I fear for."

"Fear? You fear Master Fingal?"

Tamhas twitched. "I fear for the innocents because I believe Lennox Fingal is a wrongdoer. I am more than ready to step forward and defend our town."

"Master Fingal hasn't given me any cause to doubt the decision we arrived at regarding his presence on the council. And his men are good workers, skilled."

"It's a sham!" Tamhas paused to rein in his anger. It wouldn't do to lose control. "A respectable cloak behind which he hides. His allegiance is to the dark path of the Devil, and he engages in witchcraft up there at his house in the forest."

MacDougal pursed his lips and considered Tamhas at length.

"I believed you to be more of a forward thinker than this, Keavey."

Tamhas tightened his grip on his mug of ale. He wanted to crush it. "I *am* a forward thinker. I am thinking of our country, our families and their future."

"That is not what I meant." MacDougal pushed his ale away. His expression was disapproving. "There is no evidence of witchcraft in Saint Andrews, only hearsay. I understand you are suspicious of anyone who does not have a long history in the town, that is natural caution, but we are responsible men. As members of the council we must set a good example to all. We are leaders, and we must think and act carefully. An accusation of witchcraft against one of our townsmen would bring disrepute on the whole town."

Tamhas's frustration grew. "But witchcraft has been rife all over Scotland for centuries, why not here?"

"We are the religious capital of Scotland. That is no small thing."

Enraged, Tamhas gesticulated with his hands. "And therefore a temptation of the highest order, to such as them."

"Our good name cannot be tarnished by hearsay."

"Are you saying you would ignore a person you thought was capable of such heinous acts, for the sake of the reputation of the town?"

"No, I'm not saying that." MacDougal leaned forward and kept his voice low. "But we would require sound evidence and it would need to be handled discreetly."

The tension that had built between them diminished a modicum.

"Nowadays caution is key...humanity," MacDougal continued. "There are many in government who doubt the existence of witchcraft, and who question the death sentences that have been so readily doled out over the course of our history."

"They are fools," Tamhas blurted. "I've seen three of them hanged and they were evil to the core."

MacDougal observed him in silence, and Tamhas regretted speaking out again after they were drawing closer to an understanding.

"If Master Fingal has evil intensions it will be revealed in the course of time and we will make a decision on how to act upon it." MacDougal prepared to leave without having touched his ale. "For the time being, we will watch his performance on the council. By the close of summer, we will either revoke his invitation or his wainwrights will be recognized as a town guild."

Tamhas gritted his teeth. MacDougal was clearly humoring him, but he had raised his concerns and there was nothing more he could do without evidence.

Evidence I intend to get.

The next time the coven came together in ritual it was to summon a good harvest for the sake of a local farmer. Griffin had come to Somerled when his family had fallen on hard times after the death of the eldest son, and they needed a good crop to trade or they would lose their tenancy.

Lennox made his way to the clearing where the group met for ritual. Dusk was closing in. The sun was low on the horizon and the sky was streaked with radiant shades of russet and pink. It sent long shadows through the forest and across the place where they gathered. When Lennox took his place and glanced around the assembled group he saw restlessness in their eyes, questions. Something was amiss.

"We are only twelve," he commented.

"Nathan is still scouting about," Glenna informed him, "to make sure we are not being observed." There was an unhappy set to her mouth.

"I would know if there were strangers nearby." He had already circled the forest on his horse while the others built and kindled a fire on the clearing.

Glenna nodded, but she looked uneasy.

"What troubles you?"

Glenna glanced over at Ailsa and then at Nathan as he made his way through the trees to join them. It was Ailsa who spoke up and when she did Lennox saw distress in her eyes.

"It is Keavey's men, the ones who visit the tenants at the far reaches of his land. These last two days they made their way through the forest instead of skirting it when they returned to Torquil House."

"Through the forest?"

"The first time I saw them I thought it was by chance. Then I was out there late this afternoon and they came through again. I was hidden in a thicket between the trees and when I glanced back I saw they were watching Nathan from a distance. I heard them talk amongst themselves."

There was a hunted look in her eyes, and Lennox knew why. Bad memories of what she'd seen haunted her. It was how she'd looked when he first found her, and it returned when her liberty and her innate craft were under threat of discovery by those who would lead them to the gallows.

"They were trying to observe what Nathan was harvesting. Once I knew, I caused a distraction in the trees and they moved on. But I fear they will return, and often. They are watching us, Lennox." Unhappiness poured from her.

"Do not fear, for this ground is protected by my magic."

"Is your magic strong enough to protect us all?" It was Glenna who asked.

"I will strengthen the bond this very night. They will observe nothing in the forest. In our domain we will be safe." He locked eyes with each and every one of them in turn, giving them his promise. "Be on your guard if you're elsewhere or in the town, however."

He reached out his hands and the circle followed, each joining hands. "Let us move quickly and call on nature's bounty for the sake of Farmer Griffin."

Lennox felt their concerns diminish as they pooled their craft.

He threw his head back and breathed deeply, allowing the tides of time and nature to flow through him. Beneath his feet, he felt the richness of the earth and channeled his thoughts to it. When he began to chant the ancient words aloud, the coven followed. Some of them stood still, some swayed gently. The essence of each and every person gathered there rippled around the circle, into him, and connected with the ground they stood upon. When it grew strong and vital he raised his arms, then knelt and thrust his hands into the earth. Behind him the circle closed and a charge like lightning ran up his back. Heat and light flooded from his fingertips into the ground. He lowered his head, humbly offering himself, requesting nature's good fortune to benefit the kindly farmer who had asked for their help. Again their pooled essence shot from his fingertips into the ground.

Only when he was satisfied did he break with the ritual and rise to his feet.

He noticed that the ritual had restored unity to the coven. Grateful that it had brought some peace, he thanked them. Glenna smiled and the men embraced the women.

Nathan spoke up. "Do you want me to stay?"

"See to the others, take them back to Somerled."

Nathan encouraged them and the crowd dispersed, meandering back toward the house in the woods. Only one remained. Ailsa.

When Lennox went to her side he quickly saw that the distress in her eyes was now tempered by a plea. A plea for understanding. "You are hurting, Ailsa?"

"Aye. I'm afraid."

"Do you wish to leave Somerled?"

She shook her head. For a long moment she was silent, and when she spoke her voice faltered. "Lennox, you came for me. When my sister was charged and taken to the gallows and my life was over, *you* came. You took my hand and led me to safety."

Before him, Lennox saw a woman humbled. He rarely saw her that way these days, for she had grown strong and boisterous within the safety of the coven. "I know what it's like to lose kin," he answered.

She nodded, a tear dropping from her eyelashes to her cheek as she did so. "It was only a matter of time until all of Berwick turned on me as they had my sister. Had you not come, I would have been unprotected. You saved me, Lennox."

Lennox saw it then. Far beyond the responsibility, her loyalty was deeply bedded, but she was opening her heart in ways he had never seen her do before. A prickly lass she'd been and it moved him to see her so humbled.

He cupped her face in his hands, gently wiping away her tears with his thumbs. "It is what I do. When I hear tales of brethren I seek them out. If I cannot help them, I will try to help the ones they've left behind."

She reached her hand to cover his and her lower lip trembled.

"As a lad I ran," he confessed, "in fear of my persecutors. If someone had come to rest their hand upon my shoulder I might have tracked down my sisters, but I did not. I do not want anyone to feel what I have felt, but so many of you have and will."

Her eyelids dropped. Still, she wanted to know that she was

more to him than the rest, he sensed it in her. "Ailsa, I will always try to protect you, but you must be strong."

When she lifted her eyelids, her eyes shone. "Lennox, you are everything to me, you are my laird."

"Hush now." He rested a kiss on her forehead, treasuring her as he had treasured all those he'd brought together. He did not deserve their loyalty, and yet it was freely given, for they trusted in the one who guided them, the one who nurtured them and their craft.

"The fear, it runs amongst us," Ailsa whispered, "and when one of us is directly threatened we all feel it. But you grow distant, you only want to win over the town council."

She spoke the truth. His attentions were divided, just as they always had been. And life had yet again played a cruel trick on him, for his intentions toward Mistress Chloris were shifting of their own accord, and that, too, played its own part in what he wanted and the actions he took. "I see it, I know it." He sighed. "It's hard for me because part of me yearns to stand amongst them, to be recognized for what we are, not feared."

Her eyes flashed in the moonlight. "That part of you will lead us to ruin."

"I will not let it happen, rest easy. All around us people have questioned the fear of witchcraft. Some simply do not believe it, they say the law was written by a madman who feared everything. I long to find my way to a middle ground where we are accepted for what we are. If it does not happen, we will go north to the Highlands."

Solemnly, she regarded him. "You are a strong man, but you are ruled by your emotions."

"Would you want me to change that?"

She shook her head.

"Right then. Away back to the house, I have work to do."

Still she hesitated. "Shall I warm your bed for your return?"

There was tension in her voice. They had not lain together for some time. Was she testing him?

Lennox shook his head. "It will be late when I return."

chapter Eleven

As spring came into full bloom and the foliage in the glens became more colorful and plentiful, their illicit meetings became a daily occurrence. Despite the danger, Lennox was completely bound up in Chloris, more absorbed with her than he had ever been with any woman. He woke every day before dawn broke, his body eager and ready for her. Images of her writhing beneath him, moaning like a wanton as he gave her his length, made him instantly hard, fueling his blood with fire as he made his way to the meeting spot and awaited her arrival.

Under the continued guise of an early morning ride Chloris would meet him in the forest. Sometimes it would scarcely be enough for him, and he was often tempted to go to her at night again, risking discovery for a taste of her—just to feel her relinquish herself to him, her body becoming supple in his embrace. It was hard, but he restricted himself to their morning meetings. Sometimes she would ask him to reinforce his ritual magic for the sake of her fertility. More often than not she would just run into his arms and they would be entwined as one.

As time went by Lennox found he grew increasingly concerned in the moments before her arrival in the forest. It was not that he was afraid she would not come. He knew with full certainty that she would. However, he did not want their illicit rendezvous to be discovered. Upsetting Keavey had been his primary aim. At first he had relished the image of Keavey discovering that his precious cousin had offered herself to the local Witch Master. Not once, but repeatedly.

As time went by Lennox wasn't ready for that to occur. There was too much pleasure to be had—to be shared. It wasn't how it started, but Lennox soon found that he wanted all of her. To touch her, taste and hold her forever locked in his embrace. So while he waited for her to arrive each morning he sought her out, glad when he saw her riding his way, always eager to lose himself between her soft, silken thighs. She'd made him come alive when he was weary of life, weary of fighting for a doomed cause and forever hunting for lost brethren. Chloris had given him something else. At first he thought it a momentary, sensory distraction. He simply could not get enough of her and fully intended to slake his lust for her repeatedly before this thing ended. Then he realized that she affected him in a deeper, more resonant way.

Somehow his involvement with Chloris was making him think more deeply about the driving forces in his life, and how much he owed those around him. It had been a long slow battle, and his search for respectability for the people he was responsible for was taking too long. Too many innocents had been put to death in the Lowlands. Glenna and Lachie were right. They should have taken to the North, to the Highlands and safety there, years before. He was torn, though, because he might never find his sisters if he moved his people north. He had thrust roots down here in Fife in order to find his sisters, and he had become part of the fabric of the place. It wasn't his birthplace. He'd been born in the Highlands, taken Fingal as his name after the place that was his true home.

The burden carried by the Taskills was not easily shrugged off. His mother had led them south to find their father. An ill-destined journey it had been. Their kin in the Highlands warned them against it, but his mother was a stubborn sort. To her detriment. In the Lowlands their craft was feared and shunned. Witches and healers were put to death, stoned and burned for their craft. Their mother became one of them.

He'd been split from his sisters, bound and gagged and thrown in an old stone quarry where he'd been left to die. But anger kept him alive. He used his craft and his wits to survive and fight his way out. The need to spite those who damned him was great, but it was also foolhardy, for he knew it might bring punishment or death to his sisters. Hollow and defeated he let his feet lead him, seeking work and food along the way, until he was back in the safe haven of the Highlands.

His mother's sister and his cousins had nursed him back to health, gentle people who lived with their hearts tied to the land and seasons. They sighed and fretted over what had returned to them, for Lennox Taskill had been a broken youth.

When he grew well he watched and waited for Jessie and Maisie, but his twin sisters were too young. Their feet would not know the way home as his had done. Within the year he was back in the Lowlands, his mission to find his sisters. First he returned to the place where his mother had been put to death, faced it, allowing the sorry memories to stoke his will to survive—and to help others of their kind to survive. He discovered that Jessie had been kept there in the village in the charge of the schoolmaster, until she'd broken free of her owners and run. Of Maisie there was no word at all. Vanished. Both of them. All these years later and he was still try-ing to find them.

Establishing himself in Saint Andrews, he'd forged a bond with others of his kind, people who became his new family, people who watched out for him as he did them. Most of them had been born in Fife and they had helped him settle there. However, there was a part of him that would always belong to the Highlands, for he had been born there and all his child-hood spent there, learning the old ways under his mother's guidance. Moving south had brought nothing but trouble, but it was hard to break with the hunt for Jessica and Margaret.

Scotland was on the cusp of immense change. He felt it, but he could not clearly discern its direction. There was some re-sistance building to the persecution of witches. That gave him hope. But how long until the change came, and would people like Tamhas Keavey ever accept it? His coven was eager to find the safe haven, and they trusted him. What of his sisters? If they were alive would they have headed north, too, home-ward bound? No word had come from Fingal, so Lennox had to assume they were still lost to him and the Taskill family.

They would be nineteen now, young women. How he longed to know what had become of them. Every few weeks he traveled the land, whenever he heard mention of strange goings-on, whispers about witchcraft and women who were gifted. He sensed that his sisters may not have had the oppor-tunity to hide themselves in the community and live a life where they could conceal their craft, or to use it to help others.

He thought on it while he guided his horse through the woodlands toward the bluebell glen. Looking across the land-scape he ached for stability, for kin. A woman like Chloris in his bed every night? Yes, that, too.

She was waiting for him, which chased away the darkest of the memories, if only for a while. He climbed down from his saddle and let Shadow roam free.

As Lennox approached, he gazed at her. Even though her eyes were wide and she was nervous, her inner strength drew him—everything about her called on him, and it was an intoxicating and unique experience.

The way her hair was pinned close to her head immediately made him want to pull it free of the lace cap that held it there, in order to watch as it fell over her shoulders. Her pale blue gown was simple, and yet everything about it emphasized her softness, her vulnerability. The stiff bodice was hard and unyielding, which only drew his gaze to the swell of her bosom at its edge. Her skirts were not overly full, unlike some of the wealthy women in Saint Andrews, but the folds gathered below the waist served to emphasize her elegance, her womanly poise. The lace at her cuffs drew his attention to her wrists, and then he noticed how she clasped and unclasped her fingers as he grew close. She was eager for him.

She smiled his way as he approached.

"You grow more beautiful with each passing day."

"And you grow ever more charming, but I am wise to your wily ways." Her smile was teasing.

"It is the truth."

"You have made me happy," she added.

"I am pleased to know that."

"I believe your rituals have brought it about."

"As they are meant to."

"I do not refer only to the changes in my…womanly state," she said, blushing endearingly, "but in other ways, too." Her eyes took on a distant look, as if she were thinking.

"How so?"

"My memories of my family…they used to be dark and unhappy, tied as they were to the end days when the illness came. More recently I think of the happy times, before then." She lifted one shoulder. "I do not understand why, but it is a good thing and I thank you for that."

He found her comments pleased him, unaccountably so. He did not like to think of her having only dark memories about her loved ones. He knew that state far too well. Craving her, he took her into his arms and kissed her.

Her hands roving his chest beneath his jacket instantly roused him. When her fingers brushed his bare skin where his shirt was open at the neck, he put his finger under her chin and looked down into her eyes. "Come, let me undress you. It is warm today and I have longed to hold you in my arms naked, skin to skin."

"No." Her expression altered. "Someone might pass."

"No one ever passes by."

"I do not wish to undress."

He cocked his head to one side. "That does not bode well."

"Why ever not?" Chloris shifted one foot, nudging a rock with her booted toe.

He was teasing her, they both knew that, but still he wondered about her hesitance. "Because my magic and our encounters have emboldened you as a woman, as a lover, and yet you will not be brave enough to undress before me."

"But I *am* emboldened."

Lennox responded by folding his arms across his chest and offering her an expectant smile.

"I can engage with you," she insisted, "and I enjoy everything we have shared."

"I would hope so, but how emboldened are you?"

Her pretty mouth lifted. "You challenge me, sire?"

He nodded. "What is it that you want from me today?"

His demanding question appeared to let something loose in her, for she cast down her eyelids but not before he caught the mischief in her eyes. "It is too hard to speak it aloud."

"Show me." With his fingertips he encouraged her, stroking over her skin from throat to the edge of her gown.

She responded visibly, her bosom swelling as her breathing quickened. "Have you put a suggestion in my mind by magic?"

"No." He laughed softly. "But now I am even more eager to learn your thoughts, since you think I should take the blame for them."

"I want you." With one hand on his shoulder she nodded at the ground.

He arched an eyebrow at her, then dropped to his knees.

She hitched up her skirts, revealing her legs, blushing delightfully as she did so.

"You truly have become wanton."

"Under your spell, yes."

It made him proud to hear her say that, but was that accusation he saw in her eyes? It was, but there was humor there, too. She had entranced him, too. Unruly passion built in him, his cock painfully hard for her.

Pausing barely a moment, she pushed him over onto his back and then stood over him with one booted foot on either side of his hips. She lifted her skirts and petticoats in order to straddle him.

"Ah, I see." He ran his hands around her stockings where they were tied with ribbons above her knees. She truly was attempting to show him how bold she could be.

She put one hand on her hip. "Are you outraged?"

"Intrigued, perhaps."

Her cheeks were flushed. Then she lowered herself over him, knees on either side of his thighs. Her skirt billowed out around them, her warm inner thighs a tantalizing weight against him, and so close to the straining erection inside his breeches.

"As I am intrigued by you." She tugged his shirt free of his breeches and pushed it up, baring his chest.

He rose to assist, amused by her actions. Casting the shirt aside, he arched one eyebrow expectantly. She stared at him for a long moment, and then began to stroke his chest, her touch inquisitive.

Lennox rested back on the ground. The pungent aroma of bluebells and moss and pollen rose all around them. She ran her fingertips over his skin, and Lennox felt more than just the stimulation, he felt the bond between them needling beneath his skin as she explored. A rich swell of fertile magic bedded in him, and he marveled at how potent their connection was. It strengthened his magic. That was irrevocable. Carnal congress always did, but not like this. With Chloris everything about the experience was enhanced and magnified.

She bent and kissed his chest, her tongue tasting his skin.

Lennox grumbled. "You're making me impatient for you."

She chuckled, her eyes flashing as she looked up at him from the place where she currently tended to him, kissing the hard line of his muscled rib cage as she moved lower to where his cock strained to be inside her.

"It is good to see you so emboldened, Mistress Chloris."

"Do not call me mistress or you will disarm me, and I know what I want."

He glanced down at her hand, where she fumbled with his belt. "That you do."

When his cock bowed out, free from the restraint of his clothing, she clasped it in her soft hand. For a brief moment Lennox had to close his eyes and think of something else in order not to come undone too quickly.

He could not resist watching her for long, however.

A possessive look shone in her eyes as she stroked his length. How good it would be to see her riding him, and he felt sure that was her intention. Her fingertips touched him tentatively at first, then she grasped him firmly and stroked him up and down while she bent to kiss his swollen crown.

"Chloris," he warned when her tongue made contact with his skin.

Again she chuckled. "You taste so good," she whispered.

Her breath on his inflamed member made him reach for her, but his hand on her shoulder did not stop her. She took the swollen head of his cock into her mouth and ran her tongue across its seam.

"Chloris," he warned again, speaking through gritted teeth this time, "I must be inside you."

"When you are inside me, I can't adore you like this."

"You adore me in other ways, and I feel every one."

Mercifully, she lifted her head and looked at him, her eyes shining and her lips parted. "You do?"

"The clasp of your body, it is the best thing I have ever known."

She seemed awestruck by that. Adjusting her position, she crawled over him and kissed his mouth. Meanwhile, her hand guided his erection between her legs. When he felt the clasp of her body as she eased down, he moaned into her mouth.

"Oh, yes," she murmured, holding tight to his length with her hand and sitting upright, so that she could bear down on him some more, "it is too good."

His cock was already slick with her juices. Then her sheath enclosed him entirely. He reached one hand around her neck and drew her down. When their mouths met, they locked together.

"I feel brazen, mounting you this way," she whispered.

He noticed the blush on her cheeks. "Being brazen suits you."

She rocked back and forth, as if discovering him.

"Ah, but that feels good," he murmured.

She lifted up and then eased back down, and as she did her lips parted, her expression revealing the pleasure she felt.

When she ground down, firmer still, the head of his cock was squeezed tight in her embrace, deep within her. Lennox withheld a curse and arched up, holding tight to her hips through her skirts.

Then she began to move with more speed, to buck and ride him rhythmically.

Lennox watched, reveling in her triumphant actions, her freedom.

Clutching at him with her hands she growled and writhed, her inner flesh clasping him over and over. She splayed her hands on his chest for balance, and it drew fire from him. Moaning loudly, she shivered, her eyes rounding as she looked down at him, querying him.

"Aye, you feel that, that is the magic our connection brings about." He put his hands beneath her skirts and thumbed her damp folds, making her cry out.

She threw her head back, her hips working faster still on him.

With his cock buried deep inside her, he savored the way her body tightened on his cock as she found her release. Lennox groaned deeply, for she was milking him and he wouldn't be able to hold back. He wanted it to last and last, but his ballocks were primed. "I am fast coming undone," he warned, urging her to break free.

As his climax approached she held tight to him, forcing him to stay inside. "I want to feel you," she insisted.

Lennox was powerless to do otherwise than grant her request. His sac lifted, his seed pumping into her tight sheath.

Her entire body rippled and shuddered, a startled gasp escaping her, but still she held tight.

Lennox moved his hands to her waist, holding her steady while she caught her breath. "You look so very beautiful."

She stared down at him, her eyes sparkling.

"Shall I tell you what I see?" he asked.

"If you must." She chuckled.

He glanced over her. "Your womanly power fully realized."

She flashed her eyes at him. "You set me afire, Lennox, and all of this only makes me wilder."

He nodded, stroked her hair back from her face, and then he rolled her over onto her back and pulled free, so that he could kiss her properly.

On her back on the mossy ground, her hair spilled free and it looked like a shaft of sunshine across the forest greenery, just as she brought sunshine to him.

The bower they sheltered in was redolent with fecundity.

Under him, his woman was passion personified.

Lennox groaned against her throat, kissing her there.

He felt magic surging within him, the most powerful ritual of all, because they were so intimately connected. The life force that surrounded them was palpable in the air. Drawing on it, he whispered in the Pictish tongue, requesting that she would be as richly fertile with nature's magic as was this precious haven.

chapter Twelve

Tamhas Keavey watched his cousin heading toward the stables from his window. Dawn had scarcely broken and yet there Chloris was, fully dressed and hastening along the path to the stables as if she had an urgent appointment to attend.

Tamhas frowned. She would rather be out riding than anything else, it seemed.

It occurred to him that he should perhaps accompany her on one of these early rides of hers. If the morning air benefited her as much as she said it did, she might be in a more pliable state when he next invited her to share a carnal tryst.

The foolish woman ought to look kindly on his offer. Her husband had begun to refer to her as if she was an embarrassment. It would be her good fortune if she fell pregnant by another lover, giving Gavin Meldrum the heir he wished for.

Tamhas stepped closer to the windowpanes, his breath clouding the glass.

As a younger man he had been quite smitten with Chloris. She had acted like a nun, though, rejecting his advances. He remembered it well. So many evenings spent together while she would read and sew, and he would sit and lust after her, imagining her undressed with her legs spread. How pale she was back then, and how he would have enjoyed putting a flush on her cheeks. It would have been so easy to slip into bed with her, but she denied him.

When he'd suggested marriage to expedite the matter, she'd refused him. He had pursued necessary fornication elsewhere, but even after all these years Tamhas found he still had a hankering need to possess the thing that he had lusted after as a youth, even if only for a short while.

The best he could do for her when she refused him was to marry her off and get a good arrangement out of it, but now she was back and in his house and he wanted her again. How enjoyable it would be to see her on her back for him, at last.

He pictured it, and found it most pleasing.

When her fleeting figure disappeared into the stable, Tamhas returned to his bed, vowing to rise earlier one morning and join her.

The sky was streaked with pink and amber light when Lennox left Somerled to meet Chloris that morning. He urged his horse to a gallop. Shadow had fast learned the routine and huffed on the morning air, relishing the journey as much as his master relished the woman who waited at the end.

Lennox dismounted and let Shadow roam free to graze while he strode to the edge of the forest and stared out across the land for sight of her. When her figure appeared on the ridge and she waved his way, relief poured through him. He steadied himself with one hand against a nearby tree trunk, biding his time, but he could not resist stepping out to meet her when she closed on him.

She looked tousled, as if she had rushed to dress. That made him want to undress her all the more. He wanted to see her completely naked in his arms, so that he might picture her that way when they were apart. He captured her in his embrace, teasing her with hungry kisses on her neck and bosom.

"Lennox, you are wilder than ever."

"That is what you have done to me."

The sound of her laughter made him so happy. He took her hand and led her to their favorite spot.

"It is so beautiful here," she said.

"It is, but especially so when you are in it."

She looked at him as if she thought he were teasing her, but he meant it. "You have become the forest queen."

"I am not one of your witches, Lennox."

"That does not matter."

She strode alongside him, smiling. "I will humor you because you are so charming."

Her resistance to flattery only made him want to flatter her more. She was not used to it, he assumed. That was a crime.

When they reached the bluebell glen she paused and sighed. "I will dream of this place, forever." She met his gaze. "Of being here with you."

That tugged at something deep inside him.

He did not want her dreaming of him. He wanted her by his side. The notion surprised him, and he pushed away the urge to state it aloud. Instead he drew her down onto the forest floor. Tugging at her gown, he edged it down at her bosom. Her creamy flesh swelled from the lace edge of her shift. Ducking his head, he kissed her, sighing against the soft, responsive flesh as he moved to crouch over her. With quick, nimble fingers, he prized the edge of her gown back, and one nipple rose up, stiff and eager for his tongue as he closed his lips over it.

"Oh, Lennox." Her hands closed about his head.

Kissing her heavily he worked his tongue over the stiff peak, his free hand worked her other breast free, until she was gloriously exposed, both breasts on display for him. Drawing back to observe, his cock grew rigid, for she looked so gloriously undone, so ready to be plundered. When he leaned closer to kiss her in the shadowy dip between her breasts, his rod pressed against her hip, and she cried out.

"Lennox."

"Something you need, my sweet?"

"You are outrageous, you know what it is." Her head rolled against the mossy ground, and several strands of her tresses came free to curl against the side of her neck.

"You want me to give you more air?" He backed away.

She grabbed his shirt, holding him to her. "No, I…I want you."

Lennox laughed softly. How adorable she looked with her cheeks flushed. "And you shall have me."

She viewed him with suspicion. "You tease me so. You make me say it aloud and make a show of myself for your fun."

"Of course, but I cannot help myself because you are so desirable when you are this way. There is no malice intended, only joy in hearing you whisper your need. A man cannot help enjoying that when it is so genuinely meant."

She stared up at him as if thinking on what he said, and her candid innocence was so beguiling that he vowed he would not take his eyes off her face, he would watch while he pleasured them both, eager to see every moment reflected in her eyes.

He shifted, placing one knee between her legs. With haste, he pulled her skirts higher. When she wriggled to assist, as eager as a wanton, her knees parting and rising up, Lennox once again had the overwhelming urge to see her naked, to adore every measure of her, to know it intimately.

She moaned with pleasure, and it drove him on. He closed his mouth over her shoulder. She rose up into his embrace. As he glanced down, the sight of her loosed hair tangling over the top of her pale shoulder blades made him reach for her laces, to see more of her. Chloris rippled in his arms and pressed her face into his neck. Speedily he pulled the laces free, then eased the flaps of her dress open.

A gasp escaped her. Her fingers tightened on him.

He took it as encouragement. Pushing her gown down from her shoulders, he unraveled the ribbons on the back of her gown, eager to have her completely naked. He'd only been able to imagine it, due to the hurried nature of their encounters, and it was not enough. He pushed his hand beneath her loosened gown. "Yes, I shall have you naked today."

"Lennox, no!" Her body stiffened. "Please don't."

Too late were her pleas. In that moment he felt the very thing she was attempting to hide.

"No!" She pulled away from him, turning her face away from his as she twisted her arms behind her back and attempted to pull her gown into place, her fingers trembling as she struggled to find the laces.

Alas, her desperate actions only exposed what she attempted to hide.

Lennox stared in disbelief, then drew back, horrified by what he saw. Beneath her gown her beautiful skin was marred by deep scars, scars that spoke of a harsh beating, so harsh that her skin had been torn and healed poorly, leaving welts that would remain with her for life.

Grabbing her by the shoulders he halted her attempts to cover herself.

She shook her head and there was a crazed look in her eyes, the nature of which he had not seen there before. "Let me go, I beg you."

"No." Possessively, he held her.

"Please, Lennox, don't look at me." Wriggling her shoulders she attempted to break free.

Lennox gritted his teeth and forced her flat to the ground, rolling her onto her side so that he could properly examine her back.

Chloris whimpered and covered her face with her hands, but he had to know.

With one hand he held her in place, with the other he pulled her laces completely undone. The fabric eased apart and he tugged down her shift to expose her skin fully as far as the top of her corset, disclosing a tracery of raised welts.

Lennox swallowed down the shock he felt. She'd hidden herself very cleverly all through their time together. He realized that now. Hiding her shame, keeping the secret. Tracing the scars with his fingers he attempted to hold back his anger when he felt pain there. It was as if he'd been thrashed, not her. It pumped into his fingertips, and it was not just this beating, but more. The anger he felt in response to the images that flared in his mind would not be kept in check—images of Chloris, and images from his childhood, pictures of his mother being stoned.

Chloris flinched at his touch on the raised skin.

That made his anger worsen. Forcing back the images of his own mother, lying on the ground stoned and bloody, frustration bit into him, his ire rising all the while. He voiced his opinion. "You wish to fall pregnant to a man who does this you?"

Her head lifted and she stared over her shoulder at him, dismayed.

"Answer me!" His indignation was making him unreasonable. He could see that fact reflected in her eyes, but he couldn't help being angry.

"It will not happen again," she snapped, "if I fall pregnant."

Lennox cursed aloud. "If you believe that then you are a fool."

Chloris recoiled in astonishment. It was she who looked angry now, the shame that had marked her expression quickly changing as she pulled her clothing into place, covering the scars she had so cleverly concealed during their relationship. "What do you know of me and my situation?"

Lennox felt that old anger and frustration, that which was born of powerlessness, the mood that turned into white heat in his veins. He saw the men who stoned his mother almost to her last breath, then hauled her bloodied body upright so that she could take the final steps to the gallows where she would be hanged and burned. He'd cursed them all, until they bound and gagged him, but he had never forgotten the looks on their faces. Their fear twisted into glee, that ugly thing that turned them to animals. It disgusted him. "A man who does that to a woman will never change. There will be another cause for him to beat you, another day."

Fear flitted through her eyes as she considered his words, but she shook her head. "No, it is his anger at my barren state that is at the root of his black moods."

He resisted the urge to growl. She was too trusting, and he knew that too well for he had preyed on it, too. Annoyed at himself for forcing her to consider what was likely the truth of the situation, he reached out for her, moving to comfort her. The urge to remove her from her current situation was growing larger by the minute and he could scarcely trust himself, so unruly was his desire for her. It was in that moment that he knew with certainty that she was his destined lover, and the realization that he was irrevocably bound to Chloris shocked him to the marrow.

But she was rising to her feet and backing away. "If you have done what I paid you to do, then it will end." Tears shone in her eyes, and she trembled. "Your ritual, it had better work."

Lennox's thoughts were in chaos as he realized just how desperate she was. This was why she had come to him. He'd thought it her own desire for a child, but it was fear of her own husband that had put her in this position—fear that had forced her to be brave and venture to Somerled—and that was not right. He could not allow her to go back there. Rising to his feet he went after her. "It will, but my magic will not protect you if you go back to Edinburgh."

Striding over, he attempted to hold her. More than ever, he wanted to claim this woman as his own. He could not bear to think of her sacrificing herself to a man who would do that to her.

Chloris tore her arm from his grip. "You have said enough. You have shamed me, and now you have put me in fear of my situation in Edinburgh. Yet you are no saint, for you are a seducer of many women." She glared at him. "I know that I'm not the only one, for I am not the fool that you apparently think I am. This has been a pretty diversion for you. I know that you wanted more than your fee in return for your magic, and you took it."

Lennox reeled. Her words hit him harder than he could have imagined. "Chloris—"

"No, you will not charm me with your magic or your clever ways now." She held his gaze. "I just pray that you are as good a witch as you are a seducer." With that final remark, she lifted her skirts and ran through the trees, back to her mount.

Turning away, Lennox gripped a low hanging bough, forcing himself to stay there, not to go after her in anger. He was no longer in control of himself in thought or deed. Closing his eyes, he drew strength from the old oak, from the rising sap and the fertile ground beneath his feet—the things he was sure of, the tenets of nature that he clung to in faith when he felt madness beginning to descend on him.

A single shard of clarity shot through the chaos that reigned in him. He would not, could not, let her go back to Edinburgh. Even if she refused his protection, Lennox knew he had to make her see and understand that.

And as much as Lennox hated Tamhas Keavey, he suspected she was safer there under her cousin's roof.

Somehow, that only made his bitterness grow.

chapter Thirteen

Chloris's mood was so inflamed that she ran through the forest to her horse as fast as her feet would carry her, not caring if her gown ripped when it caught on the brambles or whether her boots and stockings became stained with mud. When she mounted she urged her horse to a gallop, her blood pumping, regret filling her.

Why had she allowed herself to drift into this situation with him? It was a risk in every respect and yet she had ignored the voice in her mind that had warned her. The answer was of course a simple one. Lennox had seduced her, thoroughly, and because her passion for him had grown beyond bounds she could not resist. *Foolish woman,* she chastised herself, and rode without concern for safety, covering the ground fast.

When she saw Torquil House on the horizon, however, she drew up and turned her mount away. Instead she rode in the direction of Saint Andrews.

It was not a conscious decision, but as she battled with her inner turmoil she soon found herself on the familiar streets where she had spent her childhood years. It was the need to address her substance, to feel that she belonged somewhere— even if that time had come and gone—that guided her from the depth of her emotional chaos.

Chloris had never wanted to see the place again, before now. However, she'd begun to exist only in respect of Lennox and that bond had shattered so suddenly that she sought some other anchor. That was how she found herself in front of the tall town house where she had been born, and where her parents had lived and died.

Chloris dropped down from her saddle and stared at the familiar building. She had not been on this street since she went to Edinburgh to marry Gavin, and she had not stepped inside the house since Tamhas had taken her to his home as his ward. She took a deep breath and told herself she was strong enough to do this, to face the past, in order to ready herself for the future.

Calling out to two passing lads, Chloris offered them the reward of a coin each if they stood with her mount for a few minutes. They gladly obliged, taking off their hats and petting the animal while she went to the door.

"The master and mistress are not at home," the serving girl said when she opened the door and saw Chloris standing there.

"It is not your employers I wish to see. I used to live in this house many years ago," she explained, wishing that her voice did not waver so. "Is anyone at home other than yourself?"

The girl shook her head. She was a timid girl.

"I will only ask for a small amount of your time. If you will allow me to visit the old nursery I would be most grateful."

She chewed at her lower lip for several moments before she replied. "I should not, mistress."

Chloris opened her hand, revealing the coins she offered in return for the favor.

The girl's eyes lit.

"I promise it will not take long. It is just to preserve my memories, you see."

After a prolonged ponder the girl's decision was made and she ushered Chloris inside. "Just the old nursery, you say?" She closed the front door quickly and gestured to the stairs. "That would be the long room at the back of the house over-looking the garden?"

"You understand me well, that is the very one." Chloris pressed the coins into the servant's hand. The girl curtsied and then led the way quickly up the stairs.

Chloris glanced about as she followed, noting the changes that had been made, and the things that were the same as she remembered. As they closed on the door to the old nursery, she steeled herself. There would be sad memories, but happy ones, too.

The serving girl opened the door, then stood by.

"Thank you." Chloris took a deep breath. It was time for her to accept her lot in life and not chase fancy dreams, nor allow herself to grow fond of a man who she should not have allowed into her life in the first place.

The room was more sparsely furnished than it had been the last time she had been in it, the work bench and chairs she had known gone, and in their place a fancy armoire and several storage trunks. "The mistress of the house has no children?"

"Oh, yes, but they are long since grown and married. This room is not used at all now."

Chloris nodded and then stepped farther into the room, her feet tracing the familiar path to the fireplace where every morning she'd sat at her mother's side. Together they would read and study and Chloris had grown from a child to a young woman here. Eithne was her companion in the afternoons, and while they worked on their sewing—Eithne busy with the household repairs, Chloris on her embroidery—Eithne would talk about the clans in the north and how they lived very different lives to the Lowlanders. Eithne would sometimes tell her fairy tales as well, stories of the strange and magical creatures who lived in the sea and the mountains.

So it was that her mother had made her an educated young lady who felt safe and loved, and Eithne had made her believe that magic was all around. They had been golden days, until the illness came and took her parents, and Chloris had found her world broken apart.

She ran her fingers along the stone mantel, but there was no fire in the grate.

There had been no fire in the grate the last time she'd stood here. It had not been laid because it was the day of the funeral and she should have been walking alongside the cart that carried her parents' coffins to the Kirk.

Eithne had understood, even though she said it was wrong. "You must do this, child. I know you do not want to say goodbye to them, but you must."

Chloris had clung to her, weeping. "I cannot."

"You must hold your head up, whatever comes your way in this life."

Eithne was upset, and Chloris remembered her trembling even as the buxom woman embraced and comforted her. Looking back on it, it occurred to Chloris that Eithne had probably been warned that Tamhas Keavey would not welcome her amongst his servants, and Eithne was doing her best to encourage Chloris on a safe, respectable path.

"Come now," she had said, "they are waiting for you to go down, it is time."

"I cannot, I do not want to live. I should be with them."

Eithne kissed her forehead, and Chloris remembered the sense of calm she had bestowed upon her then. Like magic.

"There is happiness ahead for you, my girl, dark days, too, but you will always carry your loved ones inside you, and even when you cannot hold them they will be in here—" she put her hand to her heart "—and that will help you through. Look to the future, to those days when the sun will shine in your heart."

Chloris blinked. That's how it had felt, when she was with Lennox. Like the sun was shining in her heart. From the moment he had unlatched the pearl choker from around her neck, he'd begun to free her of the deepest grief she carried and replace those emotions with something fonder, something happier. Memories to be cherished instead of grieved over.

Unfettered, is what he'd called it. And now she'd been brave enough to come back here and face her history. Had Eithne the gift of future sight? Would the brief happiness she'd known with Lennox over these past weeks stay with her always, even though it was over now?

Yes, it would. Just as the love she had for her family was locked in her heart and her memory. For a moment she felt Eithne's warm embrace—like a promise.

Then it was gone.

chapter Fourteen

Somehow Chloris made it through the rest of the day. The memory of Eithne stayed with her, warming her. She even managed to be convivial during dinner. Once she was alone in her chamber—and after the servant turned down her bed covers and retired for the night—her emotions grew tangled again. It was because she had lain here with Lennox. His presence still lingered, it always did. She looked about the room, the one she'd always had at Torquil House. The familiar damask curtains and the solid wooden furniture were anchors in her turmoil, but it was him she ached for.

Then, as she undressed and reached for her nightgown, she was reminded of Lennox's horror when he thought that she was a weak woman, despised by her husband. It was to be expected, she concluded. The women of Saint Andrews that Lennox consorted with were no doubt much stronger than she. They would keep their husbands happy and seek a secret affair bravely. Or they were witches, strong women who upheld their beliefs when all around people feared and condemned them. Nevertheless, she'd had a true taste of passion, happiness and forbidden love. There was no love in her marriage, and to partake of it outside of her marriage was a sin.

Yet these had been the happiest moments of her life.

It was over now. She sat on the edge of her bed in her night-gown and considered the fact that she might never see Lennox again. The ache in her chest was so great that when she lay down she thought she would die of it.

She buried her face in her pillow, her thoughts running back and forth over what had been said and why it had troubled her so.

"Chloris?"

It was a whisper so quiet, so gently inquiring, that she thought she'd imagined it at first. Rolling onto her side she peered into the gloom. The door clicked shut.

Lennox stood there in the shadows by the door, just as he had that first night.

It wasn't the same as before, though. Strangely enough, this time it felt almost natural that he had come to her, and when he stepped past the fireplace and the light from the embers caught his expression, it was a very different man that she saw before her. Troubled, just as she was, if not more so. The knot in her chest unraveled, threatening to unleash a barrage of tears.

"Lennox." As she rose to face him she battled the urge to run into his arms.

Before she could leave the bedside he closed the gap between them in fast strides and dropped to his knees before her. Grasping one of her hands, he drew it to his lips and kissed her palm. "Forgive me, I had to see you."

Chloris stared down at his now familiar head and stroked his hair distractedly. The way he approached—the yearning she felt—all of it threatened her unsteady emotions. "You shouldn't have risked coming here again. You should *never* have risked it."

He looked up at her, eyes glittering in the candlelight. "The only thing I shouldn't have done was be angry. I am in no position to judge. Can you forgive me?"

Chloris inhaled slowly. "There is nothing to forgive, your reaction was understandable."

"Understandable?" He looked dismayed. Rising to his feet, he held her gently by the shoulders. She noticed that his hair was tousled, his shirt neck open. "That is why you hid yourself from me, isn't it, because you expect people to be upset by the sight of it?"

She nodded.

"No, Chloris. I was upset because I felt it, just as you had, when I touched you."

"No." Could it be true?

He nodded, then leaned into her, kissing her forehead gently. His voice grew quieter still. "Our connection is deep."

Why did that make her ache so? Words were so easy for him. Seduction was his way of life. To hear such a thing and wonder if it was true tortured her.

"I could not bear to witness the images of him doing that to you," he added.

She closed her eyes. "I'm sorry. It was wrong of me to involve you in my...situation. I tried to keep it to myself. Our time together was so precious to me that I indulged. I let it last longer than it should have."

His mood changed instantly. Grasping her shoulders more tightly he looked into her eyes. "Don't say that. We both wanted it, every moment of it."

The knot in her chest tightened again.

"You have changed me, my precious lover." He cupped her

face in his hands. "The time we spent together has made me crave more. I want you, Chloris. I want all of you, forever."

Her lips parted and she went to respond, to deny him, but his mouth covered hers in a possessive kiss, claiming her completely. Her body pulsed with need. She acted on instinct, her hands moving up around his head, her fingers tangling in his thick hair. With her emotions so raw, she could only welcome him, running her tongue along the underside of his. There was no doubt their desire was mutual. She wanted him, too.

His words made her realize that everything she felt was too much, too dangerous. It was the tears that made it impossible to deny him though, the nature of what had passed between them in anger and regret only making her want him all the more.

She pulled back, swallowing hard as she looked up at him. Could she trust him? Could she trust her instincts?

Not where he was concerned. Lennox was a forbidden pleasure for her, and he was dangerous. He could easily weave a tall tale and make promises that his magic would make the stars fall at her feet. She feared her desire for him would blind her to the reality of her existence. But today she had gone home, and she'd opened her eyes to everything—to the truth of the past, the reality of her future. "It cannot be."

"It can. I do not want you to hide anything from me ever again." He gestured at her nightgown. "Let me see you."

It was a command.

The look in his eyes made her wonder if he was working magic on her. But no, he needed to see, and she was shocked to discover that she was compelled to show him, to reveal her shame to someone who cared for her in some way.

Her fingers trembled as she went to the silk bow that held

her thin nightgown in place around her shoulders. As she undid it and let it fall away, he surprised her once more by capturing the fabric before it fell from her breasts. Holding it in place there, he stepped behind her to examine her exposed back.

Chloris expected her shame to deepen. Instead she found herself distracted by sensations—the sheer lawn cotton gathered around the curve of her hips, embracing her. The heat of his body so close to hers. His scent, so familiar, so redolent with his power. With his hand covering her chest as it was, her breasts ached for more contact. Was this his doing? Was it simply his presence, or was he seducing her by magic?

Chloris did not care. She leaned into his touch.

With his fingertips he touched the uppermost of her scars. She arched her back in response.

He traced the lines, and warmth traveled into the places he touched. Not just the heat of his fingers—more than that—and it seeped as deep as her bones.

Was he using magic on her? Trembling, she clutched her nightdress over her chest where it was sliding away because he had loosed it. "Lennox, what are you doing?"

"Hush." His warm breath stirred over her bare shoulder. "Trust me, I am healing you."

She tried to respond but couldn't, for the sensation was too intense. Her body arched under his touch, for it was as if he had opened the wounds. "Lennox!"

"Forgive me." He withdrew his fingers. "I can feel it, every ounce of pain, and yet I am compelled to seek it out and quell it because I cannot abide the fact it was done to you."

The room crackled with his vitality just as it had when he had first performed his rituals on her. The fire leaped in the hearth. A warm draft of air raced around them—a draft carrying with it the scent of a laden orchard and ripe berries. Heat like a candle flame licked her back.

The state of her skin altered, the tightness that she always felt there easing. More than that, something deeper occurred, for it felt as if he drew the very experience of being beaten to the surface, before taking it away from her.

Chloris felt the tears come when memories of the beating flashed within her mind, shocking her. She had foolishly questioned Gavin on some minor matter. His mood had not been good and he'd fast become enraged. He'd hit her before that night, but on this occasion he'd taken a strap to her, a sturdy length of stable leather.

The first crack had floored her, but he did not stop there. Before he was done, she had fainted away from the pain. She saw herself lying there, where he left her, and then that image, too, was pulled from her memory. She'd crawled to her bed. Or at least, she thought she had. When she tried to remember what had happened it was suddenly vague, as if it had happened to someone else, someone she cared about.

Lennox kissed the back of her shoulder. Then lower, across her back, as if he needed to be certain of his own magic. His kisses entranced her, making her back feel warm and supple, shooing the badness and shame that she had carried there for so long.

She swayed, for she felt as if she might faint away entirely.

"Chloris," he whispered, his voice hoarse. "Come, sit down."

He guided her to the edge of the bed, where she sank down gratefully.

Her body shivered, not with cold, pain or fear, but with sensual pleasure and relief. He truly had unburdened her.

It was only after she had recuperated somewhat that she realized he was no longer close by. Chloris lifted her head, seeking him out. He was facing away, pacing back and forth, close to the fireplace. As she looked at him her chest swelled, for his actions meant so much to her. Not because of what he had done, but why. He had wanted to ease her suffering. She had not even asked him to do so. However, as she looked at him she also saw the turmoil in his expression.

Had he truly taken it into himself?

Eventually he stopped pacing and faced her way. His head was lowered, his hair shrouding his face in shadows. Tension emanated from the place where he stood. "You cannot go back to him."

Yes, he really had taken her burden into himself.

Chloris knew from the way he was that he had felt and seen it all. "I have to," she whispered. "I made marriage vows."

"Vows that you have already forsaken."

Shame engulfed her, but it was the truth and she could not chastise him for his words. "That may well be, but it was with honorable motives to begin with." *Then I fell in love with you, and that has torn me asunder.*

"What is there to lose by leaving?"

"Honor. Redemption."

"Redemption? You do not believe in it, otherwise you wouldn't have come to me and my kind, desperate for our help."

Even though he spoke the truth, his words wounded her to the core. She lowered her head. "Please, Lennox. Take pity."

He closed on her. Forcing her chin up with his fingers

under her jaw, he looked down into her eyes. "Pity? I do not want to pity you. It is not something you deserve and you should never ask for it."

His eyes narrowed, his expression determined. "Leave him."

"And where would I go? I cannot stay here. Tamhas will have nothing to do with me if I leave my husband." Discomfort assailed her, but there was no way to make her situation clear to Lennox without telling him its true nature. "They have an agreement. I was the seal. If I break it Tamhas would cast me out. Trade, money and power depend on it, for them both." She wanted him to see there was no way out, but her words only seemed to make him more possessive and angry.

His eyes were wild. "Damn their agreement! Neither one of them are worthy of you."

"Lennox, please. There is no one else, all my kin have gone. Tamhas currently harbors me under certain conditions, and being a loyal wife to Gavin is one of them. That is why you should not be here. I was foolish in allowing you to come here in the first place."

Was that guilt she saw flit through his expression? Had he woven magic over her that day in the market? Before she could quiz him on it, he shook his head.

"You will come to *me* for safe harbor, not Tamhas Keavey." His tone was low and commanding.

She shook her head. "It cannot be. We are too different. Your people would treat me with suspicion. I would not be welcome amongst them."

"They will grow to understand. They will grow to care for you, just as I have."

He cared for her. Hours earlier he had spilled scorn on her for being beaten at her husband's hands, turning away from her as if she sickened him. Now he turned her in his hands as if she were a mere rag doll he tended to. Although it gave her sweet succor, she could not risk letting him toy with her again.

"Do not make promises that cannot be kept." She showed him she was serious. She was the stronger one now, the one who had faced the reality of this. It could only bring trouble to them both. Nevertheless, it was hard to stop him making these wild statements, because deep down she wanted him more than life itself.

His mouth set in a tense line. He was a passionate man, and she felt that he meant it—in this strange moment of honesty he did believe he could make it happen, but it could not be. She expected him to argue, but he did not.

Once again he surprised her.

He drew her to her feet, then moved her hand from the place where she held her nightdress in place over her breasts, allowing the garment to drop completely.

The pale fabric pooled around her feet like a garland of May lilies.

It was the first time she had stood completely bared before him, but she did not feel shame. She felt desire. The man before her exuded power, and she wanted to feel it again. *One last time.*

He gazed at her naked form in the bedside candlelight, and the look in his eyes was both passionate and possessive. Chloris swayed under his scrutiny, her body pulsing. Yet he stood tall and unwavering, studying her as if she were the most important thing he would ever see. The man was a consummate seducer, for he had ways in which to make a woman feel his desire that were too powerful to resist. His gaze made her tremble. She wanted him so badly. Wanted him to take her and fill her and join them together completely. Was it so wrong? Her mind said it was, but her heart and body craved him like no other.

Beyond him she caught sight of the door and what it represented—a futile barrier between them and discovery. "Lennox, there is not even a key here to lock the door."

His gaze lifted and held hers, silencing her. "No one will enter."

Had he made sure of that by magic because of what had happened the last time he came here?

"Let me make love to you."

It was so hard to deny him. She stepped closer until she was right against him and cupped his face in her hands. "I want that, too, but I am afraid you will be discovered here. I have heard Tamhas ranting about you. I dread his mood if he found us this way."

His mouth tightened for a moment, but he ignored her comment.

Instead he ran his fingers over her up-tilted breasts, and his eyes glimmered with firelight that was of his own making. "I sense your need. Let me slake it, let me bring you sweeter dreams than you might have had tonight."

Oh, how his words stoked her fires. The ache at her center grew.

When her body shivered and her head dropped back, he covered her neck with fevered kisses. "I was ready to be inside you this morning, and that need has only grown."

She could not fight it.

He bent, lifted her easily into his arms and laid her out on the bed. Looming over her, he sighed deeply. Slowly, he began to caress her body, trailing his fingertips over the surface of her skin. As he touched her, from shin to thigh, from hip-bone to breast, he seemed to draw the breath from her body, quickening her blood, sending wild her senses.

"Lennox." She ached for him desperately. Desire the likes of which she had never experienced before washed over her and it made her eyes smart, for her emotions could come undone far too easily.

"Let me love you," he replied.

Chloris shut her eyes, savoring the words. *Let me love you.*

She felt him shift and he breathed over her nipples, then kissed them, one after the other, his tongue swirling over the peaked surfaces. Chloris melted into the bed, yet his intimate attentions were almost too gentle. Every moment they had seemed stolen, and she wanted to clasp him to her, frenzied, to bond with him hard and fast for as long as she could before their paths were forced to diverge.

Instead, Lennox shifted down the bed and lifted one of her feet, clasping her gently around the ankle with one strong hand. When she realized his intentions, she moaned softly. He parted her legs, his hands moving along the inside of her legs as he climbed onto the bed between her knees.

Glancing down, she stroked his thick black hair with trembling hands while he kissed the inside of her thighs. Each kiss was like sunlight dancing on her skin, teasing her. Worse still was the pounding she felt deep at her center and at the crest of her folds, where her swollen nub was tingling wildly, anticipating his touch.

"You are adorable." His breath was warm on her sensitive skin.

"Oh, please, Lennox," she murmured, her body shifting, her hands clutching at the bedcovers.

Splaying his hands around the top of her thighs, he sank his mouth onto the mound of her sex and kissed her deeply, his tongue moving between her folds.

Arching, her head fell back against the pillows. She moaned and twisted on the bed when his tongue moved faster. Pleasure blossomed fast, her heightened emotions bringing her closer still to him. He buried his face between her legs and tongued her faster. Her back arched, her bud growing tight and sensitive under his ministrations. A sudden tremor ran through her and she bloomed into climax. Still he kissed her there, making her spend again. In the distance she heard her own voice crying out. She all but fainted away.

His voice drew her back to him. "I want to hold you in my arms forever."

"Hush," she whispered. "Please, let us only think of this night, for the rest is an intrusion."

A shadowy smile passed over his face. "It is, but we will have more than this one night, mark my words."

He pulled his shirt over his head and off, casting it aside.

Chloris savored the sight of his muscular shoulders. Then, when he stood up to undo his breeches, the bulge of his cock made her mouth go dry.

He eyed her possessively as he kicked his boots off and undid his breeches, shoving them off. His cock sprang out, long and thick, its head beautifully defined and dark with blood. Her thighs instinctively rolled together as she took in the sight of him and damp heat trickled onto her thighs. This is what he had done to her, and it was so intense that she could only wish it could be the way he suggested, that they might lie together every night.

Then he was over her, his cock resting against the tingling

folds of her sex. His closeness overwhelmed her with a re-
newed fever of desire. She was intoxicated by him, wanting
him above and beyond anything. When he entered her she
clutched him in welcome and let out a loud moan of relief.

His eyes flashed, his mouth in a passionate curl. He nudged
then drove the full length of his shaft inside her slick channel,
until the blunt head was pressed to her center.

Chloris arched up from the bed in response. She reached
up to wrap her hands around his head. "Lennox, when you…
when we are like this, it is the most beautiful thing I have
ever known."

"I know." He looked down at her, studying her face, his
body supported on his arms, his hips hard against hers. "It is
the same for me."

They stayed that way, locked together by the intensity of
the moment, until a sob escaped her. "You have made me
know what it is like to be a woman—" she paused, because
she had to swallow back her emotion "—a woman fulfilled."

"We were meant to be this way," Lennox replied, and then
he lay over her, stroking her hair as he kissed her mouth,
soothing her.

His cock throbbed inside her. It made her desperate.

Shifting her legs to wrap them around his hips, she invited
him deeper still.

He began to thrust. Slowly at first, tenderly.

Oh, how she wanted it to last forever. Desire, fate and circumstance would not allow it. That made each point of contact
between them more poignant. She reached around to caress
his broad back, her body rocking to meet his, each and every
time he thrust into her. In the candlelight she saw how he held
back, how he made every moment last. Each thrust was so

exquisitely full of sensation that she felt as if she was about to spill again, every time his swollen crown crushed against her center. All the while, he locked her gaze to his, not allowing her to look away as they shared the intensity of their joining.

When their movements became more fevered she clung to him. She felt another sob building at the back of her throat. When it escaped her, he slammed home and she tipped over the precipice.

"Oh, yes," he whispered, and she felt his cock jerk.

Release flooded her, her entire groin filled with heat, her body alight as far as her peaked nipples and her throat. Then Lennox spilled his seed, and in the moment of their mutual release, his mouth covered hers, owning her inside and out, and Chloris thought she would die of the pleasure.

Lennox lay on his side and drew her tightly against him, arranging her body inside the curve of his. That warmth and closeness made her feel cherished.

At first Chloris dozed in his arms, supine with pleasure, comforted and loved. But before long her mind pushed forward objections. She fought sleep, concerned for his safety. "Please, go before you are discovered here."

He did not seem surprised, but he had an answer ready. "I will go if you promise to meet me at dawn in the usual place."

"But—"

He hushed her with his finger on her lips. "We will talk then. Now promise me you will come."

Uneasily, she considered the suggestion. He would not rest if she said no, he would keep coming back here, and that had to end. "I will come, Lennox. However, it is only talking we will do."

The closer she allowed him to get, the harder it was.

He narrowed his eyes, his lips curving.

"That was not meant to be a challenge," she added.

"I agree, we need to talk, because I need to convince you that we will lie together, every night."

She attempted to give him a chastising look. "And I need to convince you of the many reasons it cannot be."

The brooding look in his eyes was only belied by his lingering smile.

She clasped his arm. "Lennox, I promise to meet you, if you promise me you will not seduce me by magic or otherwise."

He lifted her fingers in his and kissed her palm. "I promise." Then he rose and began to dress. "However, should you change your mind about doing anything other than talking, I will not argue."

Chloris couldn't help herself, she laughed. "You are a dangerous man."

"Only if I am wronged." He shrugged. "Tenacity is my strongest characteristic, keep that in mind."

Chloris caught the serious note in his tone, and it made her long for a different life, a life where they *could* be together.

She rose and pulled on her nightgown in order to say goodbye. As they stood by the door, and she strained to hear any movement in the corridor outside, she noticed he looked only at her. "Please, take care when you go through the house, I fear for your discovery."

He stroked her jaw with his warm palm, the look in his eyes thoughtful. "It is not me you need to fret over."

Then he bent and kissed her, quickly, and took his leave.

chapter Fifteen

Lennox dreamed of her that night as he had so many before, in those few hours before he rose at dawn to meet her in the forest. The dreams were pleasurable at first, purely carnal. Then an overwhelming feeling of despair filled him as her face swam before him at the moment when he shunned her. Her sense of pride had been raw and wounded after he revealed the scars on her back, her beautiful eyes full of betrayal and sadness.

Interleaved with that were more pleasant images, moments from their lovemaking. The memory that haunted his dreams the most was the way she looked up into his eyes as she offered herself again, her hands fisting against his chest. That precious moment when all her doubts had been cast aside, when nothing would hold her. Her voice whispered around his mind. *You have made me know what it is like to be a woman— a woman fulfilled.*

Lust surged in him. Tossing in his bed he fought the urge to wake fully, unwilling to break with the dream because he felt her hair brushing against his face and chest, and it was so soft, so real. Lennox wanted it to be so. He wanted to lie with her every night.

Her body pressed to his, and her soft lips on his mouth let loose his desire.

He reached out and clutched her to him, grabbing fistfuls of her hair and holding her close as the kiss took hold of him. *Chloris.* The urge to possess her wholly, to make her his and his alone, was taking root in him.

But her hair was long and silky under his fingers, and it did not tangle or bounce.

Something was amiss.

Jerking free he opened his eyes and stared up at Ailsa.

His heart thudded violently against the wall of his chest. "What are you doing?"

Ailsa ran her hand over his bare chest and flashed her eyes at him. "Waking you in the manner you enjoy most of all."

It seemed like some strange jest because his mind and body were filled with Chloris and her essence. Then Ailsa's hair spread over his chest in a silken curtain as she ducked her head and kissed him on his breastbone. Her hands moved lower to his breeches, where she began to undo the buttons.

Lennox grabbed her wrist, halting her. Pushing her aside, he sat up on the edge of the bed and rested his head in his hands.

"Lennox?"

"A moment, please." The error disturbed him immensely.

Ailsa laid her hand against his back, sending her warmth into his bones, offering herself to him for pleasure and purpose—to give strength to his day in deed and magic.

Lennox rose to his feet, drawing away.

He did not want to hurt her, but he did not want her.

Turning to face her, he saw a woman thwarted.

She half sat in the place where he had left her, resting her hands on his empty mattress as she looked up at him. A beautiful lass she was, with her black hair trailing to the bed and eyes that flashed with mysticism and magic—eyes that reflected her heritage. She was a powerful young witch, and she needed a strong master to guide her lest she strayed from the natural path. Ailsa wanted that master to be him, always, but it could not be. Lennox was sure of that.

Swallowing hard, he reached for his shirt and pulled it over his head.

"It is her," Ailsa accused. "Chloris Keavey, it is her you want."

Straightening his breeches, he secured the buttons. "Be careful of what you are saying."

"No. I know you, Lennox." Her tone was bitter and she stared pointedly at his fingers lacing up his breeches. "You are blinded by your desire for her."

When he met her stare, her eyes flashed with rage.

It occurred to him that she'd suspected it even before she woke him with her kiss. He'd wondered on it that night on the clearing. Had she set out to test him? He shrugged his waistcoat on. "I have never bound myself to one woman, you are well aware of that fact."

"Until now," she said accusingly, drawing away and rising to her feet on the other side of his bed. "You would bind yourself to her. I see it there in your eyes. That is why you do not want me anymore, because she is the only one for you now."

Lennox cursed beneath his breath as he attempted to do up the buttons on his waistcoat. Ailsa spoke the truth. He could not deny her words nor would he have been able to indulge in carnal congress with her, because it was Chloris he wanted. That was no surprise. He loved her and would always protect her. Being confronted about it by a member of his coven did not help his state of mind, especially when his foremost concern was convincing Chloris to leave her husband and be with him instead.

"She's not even one of our kind," Ailsa continued, seemingly determined to drive her dagger deep, "which is the greatest risk of all. Even if she loves you now, there is no saying what she will do to you in the future."

Irritated, Lennox shouted at her. "Enough!"

"Why? Am I not allowed my say?"

Lennox glared across the bed at her. She was as slippery and determined as a salmon leaping upstream. "You are allowed your say," he retorted, "but I am currently troubled on many accounts. I fear for Mistress Chloris, who has suffered greatly and took a great risk the night she came here for our help." The leaden weight in his gut made him shake his head. "It is the way of my life, and it has always been so, to fret over women." He paused, but it had to be said. "Until I find my sisters I will not rest. I do my best for you and the other members of the coven, but for my own part I cannot commit more than that to you and you have always known that."

"I have always known that, but that is not the problem now." She folded her arms across her chest and stared at him. "I have sympathy for your burden, believe me, for I, too, have lost people who were close to me because of the craft, but you use your sisters as an excuse far too often, Lennox."

Irritation was fast turning to rage. "Hold your tongue!"

She shook her head. "You will hear me out." Relentlessly, she held his gaze. "You say that you wish to gain respectability for us. Yet, at the very same time you try to impress them, how...? By seducing their women?"

Anger roiled in him. He wanted her to stop.

"Do you know what they call you in the burgh? The Libertine. And they do not say it in hushed tones of admiration, no. It is said by those who doubt your claim to respectability, and I do not blame them. Passion might be the source of our greatest power, but not the way you have sought it out... seducing women to hurt thine enemies. Well, now you are mired in a situation you would do well to pull away from, but you won't."

At one time he might have been able to ignore the words, but her description made his bones so tight that his teeth ground and he had to grasp the bedpost to stop himself marching around there and silencing her with his hand over her mouth. "I told you to hold your tongue."

She shook her head, fire in her eyes. "Not until you tell me why you do that. Why you take risks with their women when you have loyal witches who can satisfy you in ways they cannot even begin to understand?"

This was the second time in the turn of a day that a woman had faced up to him, exposing the deep flaws in his character, the ones he knew he had, but denied.

"Because it is easy," he admitted. "There are days when I am sick to my belly with fear for our kind and I hate them for their superior ways and their ability to call us on our beliefs. The witch hunters scour the land on the promise of an ousting and the tally of lives ended cruelly grows ever longer. I cannot bear it, and when I look at those men who smugly turn us away..."

He sighed, for the confession shifted the weight he carried.

"I am not proud of it, Ailsa, but my actions are often driven by the need for retribution. I have given them every chance to accept us, but when a reasonable offering is rejected, I see them stoning my mother to death and forcing my young sisters to watch, and I want them to feel the pain that I felt when *my* family was crushed and torn apart."

They stared at each other in silence, then Ailsa's lower lip trembled and she skirted the bed and threw herself into his arms, clutching at him.

He held her to him with one hand against her back. The sound of her soft weeping against his chest only confirmed that he was making them all unhappy.

"Everything you have said is true. You are a sensitive young witch." He stroked her hair. "You must ally yourself to a better master, for you will be immensely powerful one day and you need someone to guard you well."

Ailsa lifted her head to look at him. Her strange gray eyes glittered with tears. "You have guarded us well. I want to stay by your side."

Lennox gave a wry smile. She was attempting to mend the rift, but her accusations made him want to make amends in a different way. He set her from him. "We will find your destined lover, just bide your time."

He glanced at the window. Dawn was breaking. He was due to meet Chloris. He snatched up his belt.

"You are going to her." It was not a question.

"It is the time for action, Ailsa. Today the council issues the list of the tradesmen who have been accepted into the guild. I want to see it just to know that my efforts were not in vain. I will speak to the coven this evening and if everyone is agreed, we head north to a new beginning. I must mend things with Mistress Chloris in case the coven votes to depart soon."

"You would have her leave with us?"

"It will take some convincing on my part, but it would be my wish for her to come with us, yes."

Ailsa took a deep breath, lifting her chin. "Then you had better hasten to her side."

Hurt still shone in her eyes and Lennox felt her withdrawing from him.

"If you have doubts about me, perhaps you no longer accept me as your coven master?"

She gave a sad smile. "Lennox, I cannot deny that I ache for you, and I will miss you as a lover if you choose her instead, but you are the Witch Master who gave me life when death took my sister. I remain loyal to you and will follow wherever you lead us."

There was honesty in her eyes, alongside the pain. "And I will do all I can to ensure you remain safe."

Ailsa nodded.

"We will talk more this afternoon, when I return from the council meeting." He wanted to reassure her, but things had been left incomplete with Chloris the night before and he needed to be sure she understood how much she meant to him before he went to the town.

Chloris watched him approach.

His tall figure moved through the trees easily, covering the ground between them. The day was already warm and the air hazy between the trees. Lennox seemed as one with this beautiful place, this hidden glen in the forest. It was how she'd always remember him, strolling through the trees as if he were king here. How was it that she had been allowed to love such a man, even for a short while? He was gifted and handsome, and younger than she. He was also wild and unpredictable.

When he closed on her, she smiled but she also put up her hand, indicating she wanted space between them while they spoke. She'd set her mind on how this would happen, and she meant to stick to it. But when she looked at him—adoring the very sight of him, intoxicated by it—she knew it would be hard. Nevertheless, it had to be done.

His smile faded somewhat when she raised her hand, but he halted in front of her and bowed his head. "How are you today?"

"I am well. But there are things we need to say and things I need to know."

"Ask me anything." The look in his eyes was brooding.

"There are things I've heard whispered, and I need to hear the truth about them from your lips." She put her back to the tree, resting against it. "Tell me, how many women have you seduced?"

He looked uncomfortable.

That only confirmed her suspicions that Jean had been right. He was a libertine, bent on satisfying his need and ruining women's reputations as he went. And she had fallen for his seductive ways. Even Jean had wanted to taste his magic, she was sure of it. The question had haunted her, and it was hard to state. She wanted to know his answer, though, and it pleased her somewhat that he did not shrug it off, that it mattered what she thought.

He opened his lips.

She reached over and pressed her finger to them, halting him. "Only the truth, I will respect you more for that."

The truth was she needed to know this, to make her stronger. She had to deny this scheme to have her run to him.

He looked somewhat rueful. "I do not keep count, but there have been many. But…until you, they were at best a source, the vital life force that I could harvest for my magic. At worst they were nameless, faceless lovers, a momentary escape."

Until me?

His eyes narrowed. He was silent a moment, as if he was gathering his thoughts. "Physical congress is the cornerstone of our beliefs. There is no greater power, and I am able to harvest it and use it to right wrongs, to heal and to influence. And yet, until you…I did not perceive the true value of what passes between a woman and a man, the simple act of sharing one another when there is deep affection as well as desire."

Chloris inhaled. This man who had so much understanding of the possibilities between a man and a woman, more than any person she had ever known, and his confession about not understanding it was almost unthinkable.

"I love you, Chloris." There was a look in his eyes that pleaded with her to understand. This was not easy for him. "You changed everything for me. I treasure our moments together. They bring me closer to the fundamental beliefs I subscribe to."

This was not helping her to make distance between them. They could not be together, she recognized that.

"I promise you I will love you always."

Chloris felt as if she would faint.

"Leave that other life behind you, be with me." He reached for her hand and held it in his.

She squeezed her eyes tightly shut to hold back the tears that threatened to spill. "I cannot, surely you know that Tamhas would despise me if I left my husband, and he would come after me to set me right."

"Aye, I know that." He squeezed her hand tighter still. "It

has long been my plan to take my people north, where we will be more readily accepted."

Startled, she stared at him in wonder. Her lips parted, but he continued to speak.

"But I also have to be honest with you about how things will be. Hard. Life in the Highlands is very different to what you have known here in the Lowlands. But I have kin there and we will be welcome. Those who believe in the laws of the natural world and draw on its vitality to heal and create magic are not hunted and persecuted in the Highlands. We will be safe there, but it will be a simple life that awaits us at the end." His eyes flickered. "An honest life."

An honest life. She knew he meant that to contradict the life she was living, where she pretended to be a happy wife when it was so very far from the truth.

"It will be a difficult journey, though, and danger comes in many guises. Once we leave Saint Andrews those who speak against us will see our departure as an admission of guilt. They will send out word and hunt us down to be brought to trial."

"It is safer not to run," she murmured, her belly turning at the thought of him being hunted down that way.

"I didn't say that." A wry smile passed over his expression. "Troubles lie ahead for the south, too. The Jacobites are growing restless. They are ready to rise up and fight once again, to restore a Stuart king to the throne. The English will be ready for it, but our country may once again witness many fierce battles."

Chloris inwardly recoiled at the idea of more violence for Scotland. As a child she had grown up listening to her father relating stories of feud and resistance. The union with England was not accepted willingly by most she spoke with in Edinburgh, but she had not heard talk of a new uprising. "How do you know these things?"

"When I am away I travel from village to village, and I listen. With King James in exile and supported by the Jacobites, rebellion has been inevitable."

Uncertainty surrounded them, and it took many forms. As she looked at him she knew one thing with certainty. She did love him. If he wanted her, as he said he did, could she risk her heart and go with him? Hardships ahead, yes, but there would be hardships aplenty if she stayed with Gavin.

There was more to it than that, though. This could be a whim on his part. She reminded herself that there were others he had responsibility for, and they would not readily accept her. "I will bring trouble to you and yours if I go with you."

He shook his head, reached out and took her other hand in his. When she met his gaze, he continued. "It has always been a matter of time. Leave now and we will go together."

"If that was your plan, why have you not left before?"

"I stayed only to find my two sisters who have been missing here in the Lowlands for many years."

Chloris was dismayed. Not only for his lost siblings and the obvious pain that caused him, but also because he had not shared this information with her before. That saddened her. She did not know him well enough. She knew him as a lover, but there was so much more. Would they ever have the chance to learn everything there was to know about one another? "I am so sorry. Tell me more. Why are they lost to you?"

Lennox released her hands. He inhaled deeply and ran his fingers through his hair, then turned away. It was not easy for him to discuss the matter with her, Chloris could see that. Was it because she was not of his kind? Did he discuss it with his people, his coven? That only made her feel further away from him.

A moment later he turned back, but he had a distant look in his eye. "Our mother was put to death when we were bairns, on a charge of witchcraft."

Chloris covered her mouth with her hand, shocked to the core by his statement. Shaking her head, she tried to take it in. "Oh, Lennox, I am so sorry."

The nature of his family history held so many implications. In particular it made her even more afraid for him. He had come to Torquil House to be with her, time and again, the very place where he was in deep danger. Tamhas would happily see a similar ending served on Lennox and his people. She knew that without a doubt. Yet so much of what she was learning about him made sense of the man she did know, his rebellious nature, his strong will and his tenacity.

"We have always been ready to take our leave, but I had hoped to find my kin before such time. It has not happened, but I have found you." He sighed, then gave her a gentle smile. "There seems a certain destiny in our meeting at this point in time. Locating my sisters is the only barrier to perfect contentment."

"That's where you had been, wasn't it, looking for your sisters, when I first visited Somerled?"

"It was." He stared at her in silence a moment and she could feel it, his affection for her. He truly did believe in it. "Chloris, we are meant to be together. You cannot stay with a man who treated you so badly."

"It is the way for many women, as well you know."

Anger shot through his eyes. "It is not the way for the women under my protection."

Chloris saw and felt his dream, but she knew it for what it was, a dream, at least where they were concerned. "You want to make me one of your women," she whispered.

"Yes."

Her eyelids lowered. A heavy weight pressed upon her chest, emotion swelling in her. When he went to say more she put her finger to his lips. "Lennox, say no more."

One of his women…

As if she could ever be like those women, gifted and magical. Chloris thought about Ailsa, who had opened the door to her that first night, so wild and sure with her misty eyes and knowing ways, even though the threat of discovery stalked them.

No, he grew bored of the women who weren't of his kind. The affairs that he had with the women of Saint Andrews were pastimes to him. That is what Jean had indicated in her warnings. That was the way of it, and that's what would happen between them. If she went to him he would soon tire of her, and she would be cast aside. Too long she had avoided the truth about her situation in life, and now that she had faced it so thoroughly she would not shy away ever again. How it hurt, though, because she craved him badly. Knowing that he wanted her, too—and it could never be, that it was doomed to failure—only served to make her feel as if her life was forever ill-fated.

"It is too much, all of it." She turned away, covering her face with her hands. Tears threatened to spill from her eyes and she didn't want to cry in front of him again.

His arms were around her inside a heartbeat and he kissed the top of her head. "Why? We will be happy together, I promise you."

"Stop," she whispered. Covering his hands with hers, she rested her head back against his shoulder, allowing herself to absorb the feeling of being comforted in his arms safely while he made promises that neither of them could guarantee.

He turned her to face him. "There is council business to take care of later today. We will meet again tomorrow morn, and you will give me your answer then."

There was hope in his eyes, perhaps even a touch of desperation.

She wanted to say she would, badly. An aching maw in her chest forced her to the brink of agreeing to his demands. "You would not use magic on me now, would you?"

"Never. Not for something as important as this. You must come to me of your own free will, otherwise it is worth nowt."

He wanted to do the right thing, trusted her to do the same. She would, but it would not make him happy. Eventually he would understand. He would mate with a woman of his own kind, and he would know that it was for the best.

But she wanted him so. Frustration drove her, and she pulled him by his shirt, drawing him to her.

"Make love to me," she demanded, one hand lifting her skirts as high as her thighs.

His eyes lit from within.

The ache in her chest grew. He thought she was agreeing to his demands.

Before she could deny it he had her in his arms, guiding her to a spot where they could lie together. "I knew you would see the sense of it."

No, she had only seen the truth of it.

But she could not deny herself this one last pleasure.

chapter Sixteen

During the council meeting Lennox could barely stop himself glowering at Tamhas Keavey. Keavey kept glancing his way, smiling smugly as if he was head of the council. Had he ensured Lennox's short membership? It mattered not. Lennox was no longer concerned about that. They would be gone soon. His relationship with Chloris had tipped the scales.

It was, however, tempting to inform Keavey he had not the slightest clue what was going on around him. That would be fatal, and Lennox vowed to remain silent even if provoked. He was scarcely able to allow Chloris to return to Tamhas Keavey's home that morning. Now he had to sit and watch Keavey gloat over some perceived one-upmanship on his part.

The last thing in the world he wanted was for Keavey to find out about his involvement with Chloris. The very reason for the affair in the first place now appeared so blatantly wrong. It unsettled Lennox greatly. If Keavey were to find out about the relationship that had grown between them, there was no telling how he might treat Chloris. She had doubts enough about the wisdom of leaving her kin to be with him. If Keavey had even the slightest clue and quizzed her, those doubts would inevitably increase.

The very thought of it made Lennox feel powerless and

frustrated. He loved the woman and he wanted to be with her forever. The only way to make that happen was to begin a new life together, far away from the Lowlands and all those who would try to keep them apart. It would happen, he would make it so.

He scarcely listened when the list was read out and the Somerled wainwrights were added for a tenure of one year.

How things changed, he mused.

It mattered not a jot.

Lennox returned to Somerled with plans to gather the coven.

As he approached he heard his name being called from a distance. Alerted by the sound, he saw Lachlan waving at him, as if encouraging him to make haste. Glenna was a few feet behind. Both of them looked anxious. Glenna hurried along the path, one hand reaching out to steady herself against a tree trunk and she realized he had seen them. His blood ran cold, the sight of them worrying him deeply. Was there trouble at the house? Or worse still, an ousting of one of their own?

He twitched the reins and urged his horse to gallop, quickly closing the distance between them. "What is it?"

Lachie eased Lennox's mount when he drew to a halt, stroking the horse's neck as he spoke. His face was flushed and his eyes bright. "Word has reached us that a woman is being held in the tolbooth in Dundee. She is on a charge of witchcraft."

A fist formed in Lennox's gut. It always did when he heard of innocents being persecuted. Then Glenna shook her head, her eyes widening, and Lennox knew there was more to it. He climbed down from his horse.

Lachie continued. "They say her name is Jessica Taskill."

Lennox gripped the pommel on his saddle, astonished. So long it was that he had hunted for Jessie and Maisie, and with no word. They had vanished—much as he had—into the fabric of the land, but he had always hoped that one day he would find them. Not this way. Not knowing Jessie was on trial for her craft.

Quelling his fear as best he could, he pushed his hands through his hair and leveled his mind. "How long ago?"

Glenna shook her head. "I'm sorry, Lennox. That was all the news there was. We can only assume it was not long since, or…or more details would have been passed on."

She spoke with obvious discomfort, as if unwilling to make him think about the immense possibility of his sister's end.

"That's true enough," Lachie added. "People are all too ready to gloat over the details. The news is fresh. Heed Glenna's words and hurry to her side."

Lennox nodded. Looking out across the land he reached his arms out with the deepest reserves of his divination—the most precious instincts carried by those gifted with the craft—and he felt sure she was still alive. He summoned a wish for a protective force to surround her until he got there.

He met Lachie's watchful, concerned stare. "Give Shadow a quick rubdown and a feed."

Lachie lifted the reins. "If you ride to Newport on the Tay you can stable Shadow there and secure a ferry to cross the water into Dundee."

Lachie urged the horse on to the stable while Glenna hurried alongside Lennox as they headed into the house. "I have readied a saddlebag with supplies. Is there anything else that you need?"

His thoughts turned back to Chloris, his mind racing. "A quill, ink and paper."

Glenna glanced at him with curiosity.

"I will explain." He had been intending to inform them that Chloris would be joining them soon and why. The time was nigh for him to lead them all north to safe haven in the Highlands. In his heart and mind he determined that would be with Jessie and Maisie in tow. He took strength from that ideal. Wits, magic and brute force may be needed to loose Jessie before she was put up for trial, but he would make it happen and soon. He would be across the Tay and in Dundee before the day was out.

First he had to alert Chloris of his unavoidable departure. A note had to get to her before the day was out. He could not risk her arriving at the meeting point with her answer or worse still, prepared to leave with him, while he was away.

Dark thoughts rose at the back of his mind—doubts borne of his concern about leaving her under Keavey's roof a moment longer than necessary—but he had no other choice than to ask her to wait until she heard from him again, and to not doubt his promises to her.

Tamhas Keavey spied the young woman approaching his estate from an upstairs window. At the time he was being measured for a new frock coat and he had stationed himself by the window so that he could admire his land in the morning sunshine during the tedious task. That's when he caught sight of her passing through the gates.

His sight was sharp and, although he could not recall her name, he recognized her. She was one of the pitiful women that allied herself with that heathen, Lennox Fingal. A lusty sort she was, with long raven hair and eyes that left him in no doubt that she was capable of evil—eyes that were not of this world. A witch, he had little doubt.

What was she doing on his land? Curiosity and suspicion built steadily as he saw her darting toward the house. She did not walk on the gravel track as most visitors did. Instead she sought the shelter of the trees and moved from one to the next with apparent caution. It was clear to him that she did not want to be seen.

"Enough," he said, and gestured the tailor away.

Both the tailor and his assistant froze midmaneuver. "Begging your pardon, sire, but I have only half the measurements I need for a good fit."

"My measurements are still the same as they were last time you measured me. I am well aware that you come up here and repeat this ridiculous performance just so that you can add another charge to my account."

The tailor flushed and stammered. "I assure you, sire—"

"I have urgent matters to attend to. Use the measurements you have on record."

Without waiting for the tailor's response, Tamhas Keavey turned away and strode out of the room. Quickly, he went along the corridor and down the stairs to the ground floor. The young woman had been headed for the servants' entrance. Was she in league with one of his workers? If that was the case it might be useful to know. Even the slightest bit of evidence of their craft would give him an excuse to go up to that lair they had in the forest with the bailiff and his men. Together they would uncover their evildoings for the purpose of bringing them to their just end. If one of his manservants was tupping the wench, all the better. A few well-placed coins would get him some snippet of information to warrant the bailiff's investigation of Lennox Fingal's property.

Marching through the kitchens, he pushed the cook out of

his way as he headed past her along another corridor to the rear entrance, where servants came and went and deliveries were made. He arrived in time to see one of the servants, a girl called Maura Dunbar, accept a letter from the hands of the strange-eyed wench.

"I'll take that," he stated, snatching it from Maura's hand as he stepped between them. The strange-eyed woman acted fast. She snatched the letter back from his hand and made an attempt to run. Entertained by her game, Tamhas grasped her wrist and held her tightly. "The letter or your life. It is your choice."

Relishing his power and eager for a sign he could use, he watched her carefully.

She turned to face him and stared at him. Those eyes of hers darkened, anger shining from them. She glared at his hand on her wrist. "Let me go. I will not give it to you, the letter is not yours."

"Ah, but it is, for you have delivered it to *my* house."

"It is not for you." She tugged this way and that, attempting to break free of his grasp. As she did her eyes glowed brighter, as oddly luminous as the garden pond shot through with sunlight at dawn.

Tamhas found himself unnerved by the strangeness of her appearance. Those eyes that had made her memorable now seemed to roil and surge with dark forces, and he knew for certain that she was evil to the core. He almost lost his grip on her, but then his deeper cause made him hold fast. "You will obey me," he bellowed.

He reeled her in against him, then clasped her around the throat with his free hand. She lashed out with one hand—the other keeping the letter locked tight to her chest—scratching at him with clawed fingers. When she drew blood on his face, he pushed her to arm's length. Fighting him tooth and nail, she kicked him in the shins, but he was a bulky man in comparison to her slight form and she could not get the better of him by brute resistance alone.

That's when she gasped for breath and then muttered words in a strange tongue.

Witchcraft. His hand tightened on her throat.

"Maura, you are witness to this." He glanced back and saw that Maura was huddled against the door frame, clutching at it, her eyes rounded and afraid as she observed the scene. "Look at her, remember it well, for you will be called upon to describe this demonic woman's change in appearance to the bailiff."

The witch clamped shut her eyes.

Maura whimpered, but when he sent a warning glance her way she nodded.

"Witchcraft it is," he stated, perversely delighted to see some evidence that his long held suspicions were well-founded, "and I will oust the lot of you. I'll march each and every one of you to the gallows myself."

The girl's eyes flashed open, and for one moment he thought looking into her eyes alone would be enough to ensorcel a man. Yet he found he was compelled to stare into those eyes, eyes dark with fury and yet so sure, so knowing as she looked upon him. "Dear lord," he muttered, "you are the Devil's own handmaid."

He'd intended to toy with her awhile, but something about those eyes made him think that the quicker he got rid of her, the better. For a moment he was tempted to put an end to her there and then, but that was not the way. "Think on this, witch. I could take you into the bailiff now, for Maura and

I have both seen your eyes turn and we've heard your despi-
cable satanic words as you call on your dark lord, but sending
you to your death is not enough for me. I will bring down
the lot of you."

The girl swayed and her hair flew up around her head, her
trapped voice hissing curses as she struggled against the hand
around her throat. As she did, he saw her grip on the letter
loosening.

Snatching it from her hand, he thrust her aside. "Count
your blessings I did not break your neck. Now get off my
land, away back to your lair. Enjoy it while you can because
you will soon breathe your last, the lot of you."

Once she was let free her appearance returned to normal.
Tamhas despised that most of all, for it was pure trickery.

The woman did not, however, run.

Instead she stood still and proud. She stared down at the
letter as if she were thinking of working her magic on it, but
then her hand went to her throat where the imprint of his
fingers was visible on her pale skin—just as the mark of the
hangman's rope would also be, and soon.

"I pity you," she whispered. "Filled with hatred as you are,
you will never be a happy man." Then she turned her back
on him and walked away.

Tamhas stared at her back as she retreated. He had expected
an attempt to slap him or spit in his face. Yet her final words
had been unnerving due to their calmness.

Gathering himself, he glanced down at the crumpled letter in his hand, and he quickly forgot the messenger when he
saw that it was addressed to his cousin Chloris.

Frowning, he turned the letter over, broke the seal and
opened it.

chapter Seventeen

Chloris had been attempting to read a book in order to rest her mind. She sat in the drawing room and her book lay open in her hand, but her thoughts were far away. Tomorrow she must give Lennox her answer. As she pictured him, her heart fluttered in her chest like a bird taking flight. *Is that what I am, a bird taking flight?*

Her thoughts were confused and contradictory. It was only the occasional mite of good sense that pulled her back from the wild notion of running away to join him, of following him wherever he led. Or so she told herself. Was it honestly good sense to stay in the life that she knew because of vows that had been meaningless to her husband the day he spoke them? *But they weren't meaningless to me.*

One thing she knew with absolute certainty was that if she didn't go to Lennox she would always wonder about what might have been. It was no easy place to sit, betwixt doubt and the sure knowledge of eternal regret. These dark thoughts were shot through with instinctive hope, and with the yearning she felt to be with him. Would it not be better to know happiness with him for a short while, than never at all?

Chloris did not believe he could be faithful to one woman— even though he had begged her to believe it—not after the life he had led. All of it filled her with uncertainty. She barely knew the man. *And yet I know I love him.*

The door sprang open.

Chloris's book fell to her lap. Seeing Tamhas at the door, she rose to her feet, closing her book and laying it aside.

Tamhas walked into the room slowly and then paused and scrutinized her.

Heat rushed to her face. It was as if he knew the matter she had been contemplating. She urged the thought away, blaming the odd notion on her state of indecision. "Cousin?"

"I have a letter for you." He gestured with a sheet of folded parchment, flicking it in his hand. Then he sauntered over, slowly, never once taking his eyes off her.

"Oh. Thank you for bringing it to me. That was not necessary." She frowned. Was it from Gavin? He had not written to her at all, but then she didn't expect him to. Moreover, something in Tamhas's stance and the way he regarded her so closely made her uneasy.

"Ah, but it is necessary, for I am eager to share it with you." He held out the folded page.

Chloris took it.

The handwriting was not familiar. She turned it over to break the wax seal. Her mouth went dry when she realized that had already been done. Tamhas had read it. Discomfort filled her, but why? Urging herself not to pause nor meet his gaze, she opened it and read.

Mistress Chloris.

I long to hear your answer, but I will not be able to meet you as planned. Forgive me. Word has reached me of my kin. I will contact you again when I return. The hope that you will agree

to our arrangement will sustain me. Until then, I remain de-voted to you,
Lennox.

The handwriting was not familiar because he had not written to her before.

Now Tamhas had read it. Tamhas knew that there was something between her and Lennox. The consequences let loose in her mind, filling her with horror.

Chloris folded the page with trembling fingers. "You read my letter."

Latching onto that injustice, she clung to it. Nausea made her feel quite unsteady, but she knew she must be brave.

The room was deadly silent, the tension between her and her cousin sapping it of air. When she lifted her chin and looked at Tamhas, he folded his arms across his chest expectantly. "I did. Would you care to explain its contents to me?"

Sarcasm dripped heavily from his words.

"I went to Somerled in the hope of a cure." It was the truth.

"A cure?"

"I am barren. I wish to bear my husband a child."

Tamhas inhaled loudly then snorted a laugh. "You wanted a child, so you went to Lennox Fingal."

Chloris bristled. "That was not the way of it."

"And yet the letter suggests a fair degree of intimacy, would you not agree?"

"I know you do not approve of their kind, but I went because I was desperate for help. Master Lennox offered to undertake the rituals himself, that is why he has written to me about a meeting."

"Rituals?"

"Magic." Her face was aflame, but she met his gaze. "A spell to make me fertile."

Tamhas regarded her with a scathing glance. "Please do not insult my intelligence, dear cousin."

His tone had turned threatening.

Chloris swallowed, for she realized that no amount of explanation for her original intentions was going to make it any easier. She wasn't afraid for herself, however. It was Lennox and his people that she was afraid for. She'd heard Tamhas rant about them often enough to know her connection to them must stay secret, for it would only fuel a fire he had well stoked in his soul—the funeral pyre he wanted for Lennox and his people. Chloris had often dwelled upon the danger of Lennox visiting her here in Torquil House. Never once did she imagine the truth would come out this way.

Tamhas unfolded his arms, then paced from side to side, occasionally running his finger over items of furniture as he passed as if examining them. It was almost as though he was enjoying her discomfort.

Chloris considered the doorway. That would only serve to anger him all the more. She had to make use of this moment to do all she could to deflect his attention from those at Somerled.

"Tamhas, I only went to them hoping that it might help… and they did not harm me. You should not shun them so."

"Why so concerned for them, cousin of mine?" His eyes narrowed and he studied her intently. "I'm beginning to wonder if there wasn't more to it." His expression grew angrier still. "You let that heathen beguile you, didn't you?"

There was nothing she could say in response to that.

In *his* eyes she was disgraced.

In *her* heart, she knew with certainty that she loved Lennox.

No one could taint him in her eyes. She also saw with more certainty than ever that it could never be because people would not allow it, because they were so different.

Tamhas lunged at her.

She turned away but he arrested her from behind before she ran, holding her with his hands around her shoulders, his face close against her ear as he pulled her back against him. "You could have been mistress here," he said low against her ear, his voice seething with rage, "I offered you that."

He moved one hand to her throat, where he stroked her.

The way he acted chilled her. "You're my cousin and my guardian, it did not seem right." She tried to remain calm and not inflame him further.

His palm was clammy against her skin, his fingers shaking with withheld emotions, dark emotions. "Yet you let him touch you, didn't you?"

She closed her eyes, reaching for the right thing to say. "I am grateful for your protection, and for the good marriage you arranged for me."

When she mentioned her marriage he shoved her away from him.

Chloris gripped the back of a chair to save herself from toppling over.

"If you are so grateful," he spat, "you would not have risked bringing shame on our family. If this is made public my good reputation will be ruined."

Turning to him, she shook her head. "I had already brought shame on my husband because I am barren. I was trying to right that wrong."

He looked at her in disgust. "Go back to Edinburgh, Chloris. You're a fool and I will not let you ruin my good standing in Saint Andrews."

It would harm him if it came out, she saw that. Would it work in her favor? "I will go, but on one condition, that you leave them alone, the people at Somerled."

Tamhas stared at her, his expression filled with disbelief. "You attempt to bargain with me, you ignorant woman?"

Every part of her wanted to run away from him, for there was madness in his eyes, but Chloris strived to contain her doubts, drawing strength from her convictions. She met his gaze levelly, determined to face him. "If you do not agree, I will stay here and I will tell Jean that it was me you wanted. See how long she stays loyal to you when she knows you tried to bed your own cousin on the very day she announced she was pregnant with your third child."

It was something she could never do, but it was her only bargaining tool.

It was also a great risk. He could laugh in her face, she wouldn't be surprised.

He did not. Instead he looked at her warily and with mistrust.

Chloris tried to get the measure of him. He was angry, and she had seen too much of anger in men's eyes.

"Make ready to leave at dawn," he muttered. "The carriage will be waiting to take you back where you belong. Do not attempt to leave your room until then, your food will be sent up."

Chloris nodded, turned away and walked as fast as her legs would carry her. She would return to Edinburgh because she had to. It was not where she belonged, not anymore. But she would do it to protect Lennox.

As she rounded the door she saw that Maura, the serving girl, waited outside in the shadows, observing the doorway.

When Maura saw that it was Chloris and not Master Tamhas, Maura emerged and ran to her. "I'm sorry, mistress," she whispered. "I tried, but he took the letter."

Chloris took the girl's arm, comforting her while encouraging her to move on. "Hush, it is not your fault. Come, help me prepare to leave."

Maura looked woebegone.

"It is for the best," Chloris added, "for everyone."

That was the truth.

It was only her misguided heart that made her feel so wretched about it.

Jean appeared fretful.

Tamhas knew why, but he did not want to discuss the matter.

Then she gestured to the serving girl, who stood by awaiting Jean's instruction to serve dinner. "Please could you go upstairs and rouse Mistress Chloris, I fear she must be unwell because she has not come to dinner."

"That will not be necessary," Tamhas replied. He'd assumed that Jean would have found out from one of the servants, but apparently no one wanted to share the gossip with the mistress of the house.

Jean frowned. "What do you mean?"

Tamhas signaled at the serving girl, indicating she should leave. "Chloris will not be joining us because she is returning to Edinburgh in the morning."

Jean sat back in her chair. "I had no idea. Why has she made the decision so suddenly?"

His wife appeared to have grown fond of his cousin. Well, it was too late now, their friendship would not flourish. "I ordered her to be gone."

Jean looked aghast.

"I'm afraid Cousin Chloris has abused my trust."

Jean stared at him, her brow furrowed.

"Don't breathe a word of it to anybody, but I intercepted a letter from that scoundrel, the Witch Master. It was quite obvious from the contents of the letter and Chloris's reaction that they had been meeting."

Jean turned quite pale.

"It is almost as if she has done this to provoke me. She knows what I think of them."

"I warned her," she said. "I told her that no woman was safe in his company."

Tamhas studied his wife carefully. Had she known anything about the affair? "The morning rides she took, did she ever speak to you of them?"

"Only that they invigorated her." Jean's cheeks flushed when she realized what she had said.

Tamhas gave her a warning glance. "You had no suspicion?"

Jean shook her head. "No. I was very careful to warn her because I myself found him a most intimidating personage." She paused and her eyes flickered, as if she regretted what she'd said. "So it is unlikely that she would have confided in me."

She looked away.

Tamhas sensed her discomfort. What had she let slip? "Whatever do you mean you found him an intimidating personage?"

"I misspoke, husband." She could not look his way, which only confirmed her guilt.

Tamhas rose to his feet, his blood boiling. "Tell me, or I'll beat it out of you, bairn or no bairn."

Jean lifted her gaze to meet his, terrified, as well she should be. "When I first came here, I encountered him. I spoke with him awhile, that is all."

The door opened, and the serving girl carried in a platter of food.

"Get out," he shouted.

The girl scurried off.

Tamhas returned his attention to his wife, who was now cowering in her chair. "I meet with the bailiff tomorrow to discuss ousting them. Before I do so you will tell me exactly what happened, and when."

Jean hung her head. "I invited him here, many years ago, to see to the ghost that lingers in the west wing."

"Did you let him touch you?"

"No, I promise you, I did not."

"Continue, tell me everything."

Tamhas pressed his lips together and forced himself to listen to every detail of her silly tale, even though he wanted to silence her, for it only reinforced his determination to see Lennox Fingal destroyed.

When she finished he let her sit in silence for a while, as punishment.

"We will never speak of this again, and there will be no need to." When she lifted her head to meet his gaze, he continued. "I intend to burn the vermin out of Fife myself."

chapter Eighteen

The long boat creaked as it crossed the gray, shifting waters of the Tay.

Restless and uneasy, Lennox peered across the expanse of water at Dundee. It was not a place he was familiar with, but he knew of its dark history. A busy port, the walled city had been the site of many battles. He'd heard tell of how it was thoroughly bombarded by the English navy from the sea, and then crippled again during Cromwell's civil war on the land. There hadn't been a witch trial there for many a year now, though, and Lennox could scarcely bear to contemplate the fact that it could be his own sister who would suffer the same fate as those who went before.

If she hadn't already been put to death.

He clenched his hands together and bowed his head, willing it not to be so.

"'Tis a good day to be doing trade in Dundee, sire." The ferryman stood alongside the narrow wooden seat where Lennox sat while they crossed the water, leaving his two scrawny young oarsmen to do the hard work.

The day did not look promising at all, neither was Lennox in the mood for a genial chat. As he was the only passenger, he didn't have a choice. The ferryman had stationed himself beside Lennox. His feet were widely placed, his stance easily managing the currents as they crossed the estuary.

Lennox mustered an appropriate response. "That it is."

Lennox scarcely listened as the man meandered on about the weather.

"Take care when you're in Dundee, sire," the ferryman said, eventually nudging Lennox's shoulder in order to get his attention.

Lennox lifted his head just enough to look at the ferryman from beneath his hat. "Why so?"

"There are witches about." The man raised his woolly eyebrows dramatically.

Lennox attempted to look disturbed by the suggestion. "Witches you say?"

"Aye, they captured one of them last week. A woman it was."

The nature of the conversation did little to quell Lennox's impatience. Bracing himself, he forced himself to ask the most difficult question of all. "Have they tried her?"

The ferryman shook his head. "They didn't have the chance. The vixen escaped their clutches and disappeared." He fluttered his fingertips. "Away into the night she went."

Lennox stared up at the man. Escaped? Could it be true, that Jessie had slipped from their fingers and was free once again? He considered his response, measuring his words carefully before he spoke. "You mean she is free and walking amongst us, the witch?"

"Closer than you might think." The ferryman leaned down and lowered his voice to a whisper. "She passed this way. Innocent of that I was, but she sat upon this very boat four nights since." He jerked his head back, indicating that she had gone toward Fife, from whence Lennox had come.

Lennox grappled with the information, looking back across the stretch of water they had already covered, fighting the urge to order the man to turn his boat about. It would draw suspicion if he did. Besides, four days or more had passed. She would be long gone. "One woman?"

The man nodded.

What of Maisie? "You think she's loose in Fife now?"

The ferryman—who obviously assumed Lennox's interest was based in fear or wariness—gave him a lopsided smile. "She could be anywhere by now, spreading her evil ways."

Was Maisie still in Dundee? Lennox had to be sure.

The burden he carried began to feel a mite less crushing, however. Jessie had escaped and was traveling in Fife, on land that was more familiar to him than Dundee. He stood a chance of finding her. On his return he could send his people to the villages to seek out word of a stranger who had passed that way. Tomorrow. In the meantime, he would find out what he could of Maisie in Dundee.

Hope fired his blood. Jessie was free. Maisie was likely in hiding. He would not rest until he found them both, but he breathed a bit easier than he had in the hours since Lachie and Glenna told him that Jessie had been captured by the bailiff of Dundee.

"Shrouded in a heavy shawl she was," the ferryman continued, "so I could not see her face." The boat was nearing the shore. As the ferryman straightened up he marked himself with the sign of the cross. "Thank the Lord I was protected that night when I carried evil across the Tay into Fife."

Lennox stared at the man, trying to reconcile—as he always

did—the image of evil and what most of them honestly were, curers, healers. They would protect themselves by magic if they had to, of course, and the lure of greater power turned one or two bad. But in the main they were peaceful people. They did not deserve the brutal, vile treatment they received when they were called out.

It brought about a deep sense of bitterness in Lennox, a sense of injustice and anger that was rooted deeply in his character. Despite his will to be accepted and be allowed to uphold their beliefs, his thoughts did sometimes turn dark. If their persecutors were not careful, those who practiced the old craft would rise up as one and wreak havoc. He had the capability to become what they said he was, and sometimes it was so close to the surface that he knew it was a necessity to gather his brethren and head to the Highlands before he became everything they feared. Most of all it was the fact he had found Chloris—whom he loved—that now gave him the strength to endure and move on.

The boat thudded heavily against the narrow wooden jetty. The ferryman reached out for a sodden rope that was piled on the end of the landing point and used it to haul his vessel in alongside the jetty.

"Thank you for safe passage, good man." Lennox rose to his feet, fished the requisite fee out of his pocket and handed the coins over. "I will be availing myself of your services to return to Fife on the morrow."

Nodding his head, he climbed onto the jetty and set off at a pace.

"Aye, I was here when they brought her in." The jailer was a large, unkempt man who regarded Lennox with a wary stare.

"The witch whore they called her. The Harlot of Dundee, one and the same."

Lennox lifted a brow. Jessie had garnered herself quite a reputation. Before he'd even reached the tolbooth he'd heard about the lusty young witch who had escaped her jailer. They talked of it readily in the inns around the harbor.

The jailer frowned. "What of it?"

The man had obviously been admonished by the bailiff of the burgh. Together they were responsible for keeping the prisoners here until they could be tried, and this man had failed. Lennox fished for coins from the pocket of his greatcoat and offered them to the man. "Tell me all you can."

"Why are you so interested? What concern is it of yours?" The man was wary, despite the fact he stared at the coins Lennox held out with hungry eyes.

Lennox had prepared his excuse. "I have my suspicions that the woman who was brought here is someone who did me an injustice in the past." The lie passed his lips readily enough, for it was one he had used before when trying to discover the whereabouts of his sisters. He glanced down at the coins lest the truth be seen in his eyes.

The jailer nodded and took the coins.

"Her and her sister," Lennox added. He knew that only one had been brought here under a charge of witchcraft, but this man might know something of Maisie, as well.

"Sisters?" The man grumbled beneath his breath. "It does not surprise me that there is more than one of them, for I heard they gather together in a flock like animals." He frowned heavily. "I would not like to meet two of them. One was enough of a handful, a wild one she was."

Lennox wondered if the man was exaggerating in order to

cover up his failure to keep Jessie under lock and key. However, he also had to face the fact that he had no idea how his sisters had fared. Jessie had been the most fae of them, and when they were children they often had to search in the woodlands for her when she wandered off. It was hard for him to picture his sisters, who would be well over eighteen by now. The last time he'd seen them they were children. The two girls had been forced by the villagers to stand on the pillars by the gate to the Kirk and watch while their mother was stoned to death. This cruel act was done in order to teach them the error of their mother's ways, to redeem them. The church gate was open to them—they could make the choice to turn away from what was called evil and wrong.

Even remembering it made the old familiar pain gnaw at his guts. He'd tried to stop it, let loose chaos through his magic, cursing them. But there were too many of them and they made the strongest man take Lennox before he could do any more damage.

"She wasn't here long," the jailer said, drawing Lennox back to the moment, "but I will tell you what I remember." He pointed at the bruise on his forehead, indicating that he'd had a knock to the head.

Lennox nodded, encouraging him.

"She swore she'd done no magic, she did."

The thought of her fear, enough to bring about the denial of her magic, made Lennox sick. It was little wonder, though, after all she had witnessed, their own mother being put to death. While there was comfort in the fact that she had escaped, he regretted that he had not got here earlier. What he wanted most of all was to have been the one to liberate her. He wanted to take her home to his people. When he'd quizzed the innkeeper that morning, he was told that she was known in Dundee and had lived there for a year or more. It was little wonder that he felt at least one of his sisters was still in the Lowlands. One of the final things their mother had said to them, when she knew of her own impending witch trial, was that they never should have left the Highlands. There, they were safe.

"Will you show me where she was kept?"

The jailer looked at him oddly but lumbered along the corridor.

Lennox was closer than he had ever been, since they were torn apart as children, and yet he hoped that she had gone far away. North, to the Highlands. Torn between the fear for her safety and grateful that she had been loosed, he felt increasingly tormented. He glanced at the huddled figures in the cells as they passed. None were witches.

The jailer gestured into a cell and raised his candle outside the bars so that it shed a little light, enough that Lennox could see. When Lennox looked at the sorry circumstances his sister had been kept in, like an animal, the dark cloud in his soul grew larger.

Angered, he could scarcely contain his feelings. "They say she outwitted you?"

The jailer scowled.

"Come now. All along my route people are talking about her escape."

"She was helped."

Lennox cocked his head, waiting to hear more. Had Jessie gathered a coven around her the way he had? He could only hope that was the case. "Not by her sister?"

The jailer shook his head. "It was a man, strong brute he

was. Dressed as a minister he did and I left him with her in good faith, to share the Lord's words with her sorry soul."

A man had broken her free? A protector?

Lennox was about to turn away when he felt it—her residual vitality permeating the dank tolbooth. He wrapped his hands around the bars and imagined her there.

Where are you now, sister of mine?

chapter Nineteen

It was late when the Keavey carriage shunted into Edinburgh. As the coachman guided the team of horses through the outer reaches of the burgh the sun lowered in the sky and the buildings cast long shadows.

Chloris felt the darkness descending on her—both inside and out. For the early part of the journey she'd felt only the hurt of being torn apart from Lennox. They had not even had the chance to say goodbye. That pained her immensely. The taste of happiness she'd had with him was something she thought might strengthen her, but it only made her dread her return to Edinburgh. Her life there seemed futile, hopeless. She couldn't even think about what would happen when she returned home to Gavin. When she tried to prepare for it, her mind seized.

Everything that was vital and alive in her was linked to her time with Lennox. As the journey progressed and Tamhas's words flitted through her mind over and over again, she rued her sorry actions. Would he do as she requested and let Lennox and his people be? She covered her face with her hands, scarcely daring to consider the likelihood. No, Tamhas would not be placated on the subject of those at Somerled. He'd glared at her when she pleaded with him again on her departure from

Torquil House that morning. It was to no avail. He scowled and slammed the carriage door shut, ordering the coachman to be on his way, before he turned on his heel and headed into the stables. Chloris's heart sank as she watched him, her suspicions roused. He would not let it pass. She should never have gone to seek help from Lennox. She'd brought a terrible thing about, Tamhas's anger and another reason to hate Lennox and his people.

She also wondered if Tamhas would inform her husband of her misdemeanors by letter. She did not care if Gavin cast her out now. She had done, before. Now it was as if her life was over. Yet she did not need another reason for Gavin to despise her. *Foolish, foolish woman.* All for a few hours of happiness, stolen moments of passion with Lennox.

The rituals he had undertaken meant so little to her now because it was him that she cared about. *I love him, I have lost him, and I have left him in danger.* She could only hope that returning to her real life would restore order for Lennox. It was her only real concern. She recalled walking into his parlor and rued that simple act. Thinking it would aid her, she had unwittingly started something that now threatened the safety of so many people. Chloris realized too late that a love affair between two not only involves those two, but everyone around them. Secret meetings and stolen kisses had repercussions.

As the journey progressed the emptiness and regret she felt only grew.

The carriage slowed as it advanced through the crowded streets within the city walls. She stared out at the city that she had become part of since her marriage, and she did not want to be there. Originally she'd considered herself lucky to have made a good match and moved to the capital, which had initially been exciting for her. It was most unusual for a woman to leave the place where she had grown up, but Tamhas had made the match on her behalf. He knew Gavin through a mutual acquaintance, Tamhas's agent for selling wool hides. They had struck up a friendship and Gavin had introduced Tamhas to many notable people in Edinburgh. At the time Gavin was an established landlord in the city, and he had recently buried his first wife. As Gavin's true nature revealed itself, Chloris often wondered about that first wife, but when she asked him about it Gavin grew angry and would not speak of it. In time her female acquaintances enlightened her. The woman had died in childbirth within five months of their marriage. Both she and the baby had perished. Her informers hinted the child had been conceived out of wedlock. It was because of the tragic circumstances and Gavin's ongoing desire for a son that Chloris did not speak again of the matter. The fact that she subsequently failed to conceive when his first wife had been with child only made things more difficult.

As the coachman guided the carriage toward the older part of the city, where the well-to-do merchants had their homes, they passed through the more cluttered and ramshackle parts of the town. Here the street vendors and traders sold their goods along the narrow track left for the carriage, and noxious smells rose from the gully at either side of the street.

The coachman yelled from his perch, warning people out of his path. The man was weary, having been told to deliver Chloris and fast about it.

As she glanced out of the carriage Lennox's description of the Highlands whispered through her mind. Previously she had assumed it a lonely, barren place, only fit for sheep and wild Gaelic speakers, but Lennox's words had reformed her

Lowlands view of the heathen north. What he had described to her was a romantic place, a place where people could live and love without censure, a place where kin, clan and coven were cherished. On that last fateful meeting he'd also told her that it would be hard, that they would have to build a new life together. It was a dream that would never be realized, an impossible dream. And now that she was forced back to the life she had known before, the yearning she had for Lennox and a life with him twisted like a knife in her chest.

The bitter irony of her situation made her eyes smart with unshed tears. She'd almost been ready to abandon her fears and leave with Lennox, and instead she had to return to the pitiful existence she'd had before in order to protect him and his people.

As for her lot, she could not go on living the way she had been. Gavin did not want her, had not done so for several years. She had failed him in every way. Barren, and now an adulteress, she knew what she had to do. She would be brave and talk to him, be honest and offer to leave, in order to relieve him of his burden. She would seek employment. He could marry again, have children with another woman. It was the best she could hope for.

The carriage drew to a halt in the yard at the rear of the house.

Mary, the downstairs servant, gasped aloud when she opened the door and saw her mistress standing there.

"Mary," Chloris said in greeting as she stepped past her and into the hallway, removing her gloves as she did so. The hallway—so familiar, but somehow strange after her time away—was gracious and well-appointed. The walls were decorated with painted trellises and the stone slabs on the floor were highly polished. It was a fine home. Why did she feel like a stranger there now? The coachman followed, carrying her trunk. Chloris spoke again to Mary, who stood by looking amazed at her mistress's return. "Would you please offer my cousin's coachman refreshment and a bed for the night?"

"Yes, Mistress Chloris." Mary curtsied. "We were not expecting you," she added.

"I know, but don't fret on it. Is Master Gavin at home?"

Mary seemed rooted to the spot. The girl was usually quick to speak out, but now she fidgeted with her apron and looked awkward.

Chloris awaited her answer.

Eventually Mary nodded.

Chloris looked down the hallway. At this time of the evening he would either be in the parlor, if they had company, or in his study if they did not. "Is he in his study?"

"Yes, mistress."

Chloris noticed that Mary was quite flushed in the face as if shocked by her mistress's return. "That will be all, thank you. See to the coachman, I will announce myself."

Chloris headed off down the hall toward the study.

"But, mistress…"

Chloris paused and looked back over her shoulder. "Yes?"

Mary's cheeks flamed as red as her hair. "There is someone with him," Mary said, and nodded her head down the hall, "in there."

It was the girl's discomfort and her sympathetic glance that made Chloris realize what she was trying to convey. Gavin was entertaining a visitor. Quickly, she assessed the potential situation. If it was a friend or associate Mary might have warned her, but not with such a fretful stance. It was something potentially more upsetting and fraught.

Chloris wondered on it. She had to inform him she was here. She steeled her nerves, strengthened her resolve. Chloris was home, but she was not the same Chloris as before. "Thank you for your concern, Mary. You're a good girl."

When she nodded and smiled, Mary scuttled away as if relieved to be gone.

Chloris continued on to the study. She was about to knock, but thought better of it. Turning the handle, she opened the door. The sight that greeted her should have shocked her. It would have done several weeks earlier, but now it did not.

Gavin was there, and he was not alone.

The woman was facedown over his desk, her skirts pushed up to her waist, her ample buttocks on display. Gavin stood behind her, breeches around his knees, one hand pressing the woman to the desk at the small of her back. With the other hand he guided his erection into her.

Gavin's face was contorted, his eyes all but closed, and he did not see or hear the door open. For the woman it was a different story. Her face was turned on one side and facing the door while she was pressed to the desk. Her abundant brown hair was loose, her breasts out and crushed against the papers there. She was an attractive woman, with dark and dramatic looks, and her eyes flickered with uncertainty when she saw Chloris standing there.

Chloris wondered if the woman knew who she was, and suspected she did.

The woman lifted her head as if she was about to say something, when Gavin grunted heavily at her rear. Before the woman had a chance to announce the intruder, Chloris stepped out and closed the door quietly behind her.

She felt strangely calm.

This was why Gavin had sent her away. Not for her health or to visit with her relatives, but so that he could bring his mistress into their home. She had known he had a mistress, but he had been reasonable about it and kept the woman in rented chambers in another part of the burgh.

Chloris had never seen him with another woman. But now she had, and it did not touch her. At one time it might have reinforced the futility of her existence—a sham of a wife with no children, a woman who had brought finance, but nothing else. Now it only served to show her that she had been right to grasp the few hours of happiness that she'd had with Lennox. That had kindled a flame in her. He'd made her different, for he had brought out the deep, essential part of her, and that would never be fully submerged again. Above all her sense of calmness on the matter solidified her plans to take action.

Gavin wanted his mistress installed in their home.

Chloris could give him the freedom to do that.

The following day Lennox crossed the Tay back into Fife. By the time he rode across the land toward Somerled, evening was closing in. He was weary, having not slept at his lodgings in Dundee the night before, but he did not want to rest. Dark clouds hovered over him, an immense sense of foreboding building all around.

And he longed for Chloris.

The need to continue the hunt for Jessie was also fierce. He had to assure Chloris that his plans for them to be together had not altered. At dawn he would begin again. Getting so close to Jessie had given him hope, knowing that she was still alive and had so narrowly escaped trial and persecution. The truth of it was that she could disappear completely again, afraid for her life. Wherever she'd gone, staying hidden was crucial. Despite the fact he wanted to find her, he hoped no one else would. Least of all those death-hungry witch hunters. *Please, let her be safe.*

Who was her cohort, the man who had set her free? Lennox could only pray it was one of their kind, someone who would continue to shelter and protect her. Tomorrow he would encourage his people to seek word of Jessie on this side of the Tay.

However, as he skirted Saint Andrews and drew close to the place where he'd made his home, the sense of foreboding he felt multiplied, and fast. Something was amiss. He felt it—he felt his coven reaching out for him, urging him to return quickly.

Troubled, he pressed on at a pace.

That's when he felt magic rise from the ground. Beneath the horse's hooves a spell had been set. Shadow huffed on the evening air and tension rose from the beast. Glancing across the landscape Lennox sensed it was one of many such warding spells, designed to keep enemies at bay. He passed through, however. For whom had these boundary spells been set? His already troubled thoughts were stirred afresh. Something was badly wrong.

"Nearly home, boy." Shadow's flesh shivered when Lennox stroked his neck. The horse did not falter on the familiar path, but there was a sense of fear and urgency building in the air around them and the beast sensed it, too.

When he got closer to the house, he saw candlelight flick-

ering in the windows. Glenna and Ailsa always set them out
to guide him home when he was away. However, this time it
was not only so that *he* could see his way. The candles were
many and they lit the area in front of the house, where he
could see figures moving. They were going in and out of the
house, carrying goods. Glenna, Lachlan, Ailsa and the rest.
The largest cart they owned was at the steps, the one they
only used to bring wood and goods for the carriage making.
Two of the younger men were busy covering the contents over
with blankets and tying them down with ropes.

Lennox leaped down from his mount even while he approached, and urged Shadow to the trough. Glenna saw him
and made her way over.

"What has occurred?"

"I am so glad to see you." She wiped her hands on her
apron. "I feared you would not return in time." Her breathing was labored from her exertions. "It is Keavey. When Ailsa
took your letter up there he caught her."

Lennox grasped her by the shoulder. "Did he hurt her?"

Glenna shook her head. "No, but he threatened her with
the gallows if she didn't give him your letter."

Lennox froze. If he had taken the letter, Keavey would
know that he and Chloris had been secretly meeting. Cursing silently, he gripped Glenna's shoulder tighter.

"Ailsa was afraid, Lennox. She had no choice."

Glancing beyond her while she spoke, Lennox noticed that
Ailsa continued to work with the others loading the cart.
When she looked his way she hung her head in shame.

"It is not Ailsa I am angry with. It is myself for giving the
letter to her and sending her into harm's way. I am a fool, and

I am unworthy of your loyalty. She should not have been put in that situation."

Glenna hushed him. "Don't fret. We are ready to leave. It is time. And your woman is safe. Keavey has sent her back to Edinburgh."

Back to Edinburgh.

To her vile, brutal husband.

Lennox cursed and stared up at the sky, wondering if the tangled web of his life could get any worse. Why was it that he was doomed to fail when it came to keeping his women safe? He had vowed that no man would ever hurt Chloris the way she had already been hurt, and yet he had not been given the chance to see that through.

Life had dealt him another cruel blow.

"Edinburgh is no salvation for Chloris, believe me." He looked into Glenna's eyes and shook his head.

Glenna was watchful and canny and she quickly saw that he was even more afraid for his lover. Lennox paced from side to side, tormented by the notion that Chloris had been forced back to that bastard who had treated her so cruelly. If only Keavey had not found out. It was a particularly bitter twist of fate because when he first set about seducing Chloris he had anticipated Tamhas Keavey's reaction, and had wished to see his face. Because of what had passed between them it was now the worst thing in the world for Chloris, who he cared about immensely.

And it was bad for the rest of them, by the looks of things.

"You are making ready to leave?"

"Aye. Keavey told Ailsa that he would find evidence against us if it was the last thing he did, and he would see us all burned. We gathered together to discuss it. Then Maura Dunbar came down from Torquil to warn us. She'd overheard Keavey shouting at his cousin. Poor Maura felt bad because she was the one who'd sent Mistress Chloris up here. Maura said that Mistress Chloris cried in her room. She told Maura she'd begged him to leave Somerled's people alone. Keavey said he would, but only if she returned to her husband."

Chloris. Pain knifed through him at the thought of her so distressed. Lennox could scarcely contain his anger at Tamhas Keavey.

"Then, when Maura left, Lachie and I talked. We knew Keavey would not let it rest, despite his supposed promise to his cousin. He was bound to use this against us. Lachie went into Saint Andrews and asked about. Keavey had already been in to the town and has requested the bailiff attend the town council first thing in the morning. He put the word about that there is evil in the forest and with the bailiff at his side he would be seeking the witches out and bringing them to justice. Keavey is readying his men for a morning raid."

Lennox felt his anger turn inward as he realized he had lost control, and people who relied on him were being let down. All of them. How could this have happened? With his sister's ousting so fresh in his mind, the news of Chloris and Keavey meant that pure, undiluted rage pumped through him. It was only his concern for Glenna and the others that stopped him bellowing aloud in his fury.

"When Lachlan returned," Glenna added, "we made the decision to be ready to leave by dawn. There was so little time, we had to make the decision without you."

"You made the right decision. If you are gone by dawn you will have a good start on them. Keavey will not be able to act alone. He'll need the agreement of the town council and the power of the bailiff's men. It'll be midmorn before they get here."

"What news of your sister?" Glenna was cautious in her question.

Lennox took a deep breath. "Gone. Escaped before her trial, thankfully."

Glenna grasped his forearm. "You see, there's no holding any of us."

Her eyes glistened.

He sensed her relief, and he knew that she was taking strength from his news. News of running, hiding. That should not be something to gain hope from, but for them it was. The history of torture and death for those who practiced the craft was too long and too sordid in the Lowlands. He looked over at Somerled, where his people loaded the cart with their most prized possessions.

"You are ready for this," he whispered, commenting more to himself than to her.

It would not be easy on them. The people he had gathered beneath his wing were a mix of witches born in and around Saint Andrews, and those from farther away, like himself. For a while it seemed as if they could be safe here. With an outward life of respectability and commerce, nurturing their practices until they became more widely accepted. Now they had to gather their chattels and leave, head north to the Highlands where the terrain was tough and unknown to them.

Glenna nodded. "You prepared us. We've been ready for this for a long while."

Lennox was grateful for that much. Now he had to choose between seeking the trail of his sister, protecting Chloris and urging his people on their way.

The situation rent him asunder, for it tore his loyalties in three different directions. He looked at the members of his coven and saw what they were. Kin. Not family, but people brought together to support each other and protect each other. They would make their journey north and they would be strong. He would find them again.

That meant he had to choose between Jessie and Chloris.

Pain drummed at the back of his eyes. He closed them.

When he did he saw the scars on Chloris and his gut turned over, bile rising in his throat as he thought about the fact that that bastard Tamhas Keavey had sent her back to the cruel man who treated her so badly.

Jessie was not alone, and she had magic on her side. He was determined to find them both but he had to go to Chloris first. It was a hard decision, one of the most difficult he'd ever made in his life, but logic determined it would be so. He lifted his face to the sky, watched the passage of the moonlight and knew that he had to follow Chloris. Time would allow him to pull all the other pieces together, to find his sisters and to reunite with his coven. "You have closed the gate to Keavey?"

"We have. Lachlan sent three of the women out and they made magic between here, Keavey's place and the roads into Saint Andrews. It will not hold them off for long, but they will find their path treacherous when they come."

Lennox was proud of them. They had come together and taken action, everything he would have done and perhaps more, given his present rash of ill luck and lack of good sense. "Make haste, take only what you can, your tools and anything that ties you to your craft."

"What are you going to do?" Glenna's eyes were filled with concern.

"I know what I should do, go up there and give Keavey what he deserves."

"No, Lennox, reel in your anger for you put yourself at risk. You will only give him what he is after, a reason to hunt us all down."

Lennox stared down at her and realized that she spoke wise words. The fact that Chloris had been returned to the man who beat her was making it hard for him to act with caution.

Glenna covered his hand with hers and fed her calm and nurturing spirit to him. "We will not leave until we are certain you are not going to put yourself in danger." Still she waited to be reassured. "What will you do?"

He grasped her hand, squeezing it. She was the closest thing to a mother he had ever known, since his own was so cruelly put to death. "I must try once again to find Jessie before I head north but first I'll go to Edinburgh to fetch Chloris."

"You truly love this woman, Chloris." Glenna's mouth lifted at the corners and her eyes glistened.

"Aye, that I do."

"Then you must find her and tell her."

Lennox nodded. He had not told her enough. He had spoken most of all about desire and destiny, of forging a new path for them both, but he had not told her exactly how much she had come to mean to him. "You're right, and I will be on my way to Edinburgh. Come now, I'll help you clear the house. We need to be gone from here by dawn."

As he covered the ground into the house in easy strides, Ailsa set down the goods she was carrying and came to his side. She rested her hand on his arm, drawing him to a halt. "I am so sorry, Lennox, I tried to hold tight to the letter when he descended, but he was strong. He taunted me and he threatened to bring us all to justice if I gave him the evidence he needed. It was as if he wanted me to show my true nature."

"That does not surprise me. He's long since wanted his proof." Lennox remembered the conversation they'd had, the day he'd presented to council. For Keavey it was a step too far, and he could not abide it.

Ailsa peered up at him. "Even if I had used my craft to hold or destroy the letter, there was no telling what he would have done to us, and to her."

She was afraid he would think badly of her.

"I could never hurt anyone that you loved," she added, "believe me."

Last time they had spoken, they had argued over Chloris. Ailsa had been jealous then. Lennox stared into her eyes, so mysterious, so capable of witchcraft, and yet deep down he knew she spoke the truth. "I do believe you."

Her lower lip trembled and a plump tear rolled down her cheek.

Lennox embraced her. "No tears, please. Soon you'll be safe in the Highlands."

Looking down at her upturned face, her misty eyes made him think of the mountains, of the glens. "I do believe that you most of all will be at home there."

Ailsa mustered a smile.

"Come, we must hurry. I'll help you clear the house and then I must be gone. We must not leave a shred of evidence that will give Keavey and the bailiff's men cause to come after us."

They worked through the midnight hours and by the time the sky began to lighten the carts were loaded and ready to go. Lennox peered at the horizon, watching the sky. It was time. The house was stripped of all evidence of their craft, and Lennox's precious papers that he had repeatedly presented to council in Saint Andrews were burning in the grate.

The mood amongst the coven members was stoic.

"It's time to go," Lennox called out. He gathered up Shadow's reins and the horse lifted his head. "Head inland to Perth and from there turn north to Inverness. Be sure that you carry plenty of supplies at all times. If I do not find you along the route, wait for me at Inverness."

He mounted his horse, then took one last glance at Somerled. "Protect one another, stay strong. I will find you again, never fear."

"We will be with you in spirit," Lachie answered, "until you come back to us."

"Inverness," he repeated.

Glenna nodded. "Take care, my dear boy."

Lennox forced his gaze away from the house and the people who had come together under his wing. They would be long gone from here before Keavey came. Thankfully.

Then he turned his mount and urged it to a gallop, as he had so many times before when he set out looking for his two sisters, and now Chloris. His mate, his lover, the ruler of his heart. It was with no small sense of irony that he realized Mother Nature had deemed him this role. Nature had seen fit to make him an eternal hunter for those he loved. Knowing that was how his fate was cast only steeled his resolve.

He would find them all. He had to.

chapter Twenty

Chloris sat at the dining table and observed her husband with cautious detachment. It occurred to her that she did not know him very well. That had worried her about Lennox, but now she felt as if she knew Lennox better than she did her own husband. It was the closeness, the intimacy they had shared. There had never been any intimacy with Gavin Meldrum.

Gavin was an austere-looking man who rarely smiled. He had a neatly trimmed beard and he wore a wig, as befitted his landlord status, but it was not too fanciful. As a habit he dressed in somber clothing, which he felt appropriate for the business of collecting rent from tenants. The properties he owned were now many, and although Gavin had workers who could take on the matter of collecting, he preferred to collect the rents himself. Chloris had often suspected he enjoyed seeing the poorest tenants beg for leniency if they had not enough coin, but she always dismissed the notion as cruel and unfounded. She did not know how he went about it. She only knew that many people would be homeless in the burgh were it not for his property.

"Tamhas sends you his regards," Chloris stated, trying to raise a conversation.

Gavin nodded and continued with his meal.

Chloris ate some of the roast pheasant and sipped her wine. They had to talk, and her intention was to launch on amiable matters then venture into the real subject that weighed upon her. "Jean fares well. She and I became good friends during my stay in Saint Andrews."

Gavin met her stare briefly but did not comment.

It was the first she'd seen of him since the night before. He seemed intent on ignoring her presence, and now she knew why. When she quizzed Mary that morning, her maid revealed that he had gone out early. Although uncomfortable about it, Mary also answered Chloris's other questions. Gavin's visitor of the night before had left at midnight but had stayed in the house overnight on previous occasions during Chloris's absence.

Now he had returned for his evening meal and it was quite obvious that Gavin had no intention of mentioning either her unexpected arrival home or the scene she had witnessed in his study. Chloris felt quite sure that the woman had been about to say something, and would have done so afterward. If Gavin had quizzed Mary, he would know that it was his wife who had entered the room.

He barely acknowledged her presence there when he entered the dining room. It was as if she had not been away. Chloris also noticed that he had not asked after the state of her health, which was supposed to be the reason for her trip to Saint Andrews. She smiled wryly at the idea of it. It was now blatantly obvious that he wanted her out of there in order to indulge himself further with his mistress. Traveling across Edinburgh to the district where her chambers were located was obviously a tedious task and he would rather have her here with him. Fair enough, she thought to herself, let it be that way.

The servants came and went with the dishes, and when they finally took their leave she steeled herself. "And you, have you fared well in my absence?"

Gavin stared across at her coldly, eyeing her body as if she were merely a vessel. Which of course she was. A vessel that would not hold his seed. Had he always looked at her that way?

He nodded. "Well enough."

"Your mistress's company made it easier, I'm sure."

The tension heightened in the room.

Gavin set down his cutlery with a clatter and dabbed his mouth with his serviette, peering across at her with a warning glance. "What of it?"

"I will make this easy for both of us. I will leave, in order to make room for her to replace me." She stated it simply enough, then clutched the stem of her wineglass to keep her hand steady.

Gavin's eyes flashed angrily. He threw his serviette down on the table. "You will not."

Chloris braced herself. "It is quite clear that you would do better to replace me with your mistress. I do not intend to question your motives or argue on the subject. I will move aside."

He shook his head. "Don't be absurd. I have a reputation to keep."

"You were not concerned about your reputation when bringing a mistress into our home?"

The cold, dismissive look he gave her was tempered only by a wry, almost smug smile. No, such infidelities only added to a man's reputation. A woman was damned if she dared to do the same. Even if the marital bed had turned cold, it was not the woman's place to find passion and comfort in the arms of another, but it was a man's *right* to do so. The tension she felt built. She had hoped he would find her suggestion agreeable at this point. She had no idea where she would go and what she would do, but she could no longer continue to live this sham of a marriage. "Under the circumstances, I cannot stay."

Gavin shifted in his carved wooden chair. Pushing it out from the table, he crossed one leg over the other. "I forbid you to leave."

That smug smile was back, and the way he had moved his position meant he was ready to pounce.

Her heart thundered in her chest. This was so wrong.

She stood up, pushing her chair back so quickly it crashed to the floor behind her. Even as she turned away he was on his feet and in pursuit. She almost reached the door and he snatched her from behind, grabbing her by the arms and hauling her away from the door.

"You will stay and you will bear me an heir," he barked into her ear. His hands tightened on her arms, straining her shoulders and forcing her to arch her back.

"I would prefer that your mistress took on the task."

It flashed through her mind in that moment, what Lennox had suggested to her. What if it were not her that was infertile, but her husband? There was no guarantee the child his first wife had carried was his. Could it be true, that his mistress had not borne him a child, either? If she had given birth he would already have announced it. Chloris felt the rage at her back intensify, and realized that she had stumbled upon the truth—that his mistress had not fallen pregnant by him, either. Was that his purpose on having the woman installed in their home, to fulfill his dream of an heir? If he had been successful, would she have been banished to Saint Andrews forever?

His grip on her arms was viselike, and then he shook her, violently, bending her arms back as he did so. Chloris bit back a scream, for the pain in her shoulders was immense. For a moment she thought he intended to break her arms, and then he pushed her harshly against the wall, where she slumped.

She turned to look up at him.

"If she falls pregnant before you, you are out on the streets for all I care. But I forbid you to bring humiliation upon me by leaving before there is good cause."

She gripped a nearby chair and her feet scrabbled beneath her. Pushing herself up against the wall she stood up straight, facing him. "I already have good cause to leave you."

The hard, brittle character she saw in his eyes intensified. "I have warned you before. I will have you weighted and drowned before dawn if you deny me my rights as your husband."

He had threatened her with it before, but Gavin had men that would take on the unsavory task, the brutal types who protected him when he went amongst his tenants demanding rents.

"Do so. I care not to live under these circumstances." It was the truth. In fact she'd rather drown herself than carry on in this manner.

"Ungrateful bitch. I have given you a home and comforts any woman would be happy with."

"Aye, and most of it bought with my dowry."

He ignored that. "If you fail to fall pregnant before this summer is over, you will be out in the gutter, worthless and abandoned. You would do better to open your legs and pray that you are not barren."

"I would rather be in the gutter than receive you in my bed again."

"You will receive me, even if I have to bind and gag you."

The threat did not surprise her. He was at best coldhearted and selfish, and now he was threatening to force her. However, in the old days it would have made her tremble in fear, now it only made her angry. "I take it your mistress has not provided you with a bairn as yet."

That enraged him. He slapped her across the face.

It was such a harshly delivered blow that her neck twisted, her head knocking up against the wall. The pain was extreme only for a moment, then it turned to a slow burn. Her eyes smarted but Chloris held her head high, using the pain to reinforce her determination. She saw it all clearly now, saw the way he had channeled his disturbed emotions into her, making her feel guilty and ashamed because she had not produced an heir. He was the desperate one here, not her.

His eyes turned blacker than she had ever seen.

He lifted his arm again.

Once she would have cowered and begged him for mercy. But Chloris suspected that only incited him. She straightened her spine and shook her head. "You will not hit me again, Gavin."

He looked at her with outrage, with hatred.

None of it moved her. She had become whole, a woman fulfilled, a person in her own right. She'd grown stronger, flourished in ways far more immense than she ever imagined when she went to Somerled that fateful night.

Continuing to fix him with her steady gaze, she leveled with him. "Only a coward beats a woman."

His raised hand trembled, but it trembled with rage. He spoke through gritted teeth. "Get to your chamber and prepare to receive me."

"I have already stated my feelings on that matter. Go to your mistress instead." Before he had a chance to reply Chloris turned and left the room.

She darted up the stairs and dismissed the upstairs maid quickly, eager to be alone. Once the girl was gone, she bolted the door to her chamber. Under normal circumstances it remained open at all times, except for when Gavin came to her bed.

It would only hold him back for so long, but it was all she could do.

The dark furnishings in the room made the place feel bleak, bleaker than it had been before. As she undressed and pulled on her nightgown she looked into the fire and wished herself far away. She blew out the candles in the wall sconces and took a lone candlestick to the bedside table. Then she sat on the edge of the bed and stared at the door. She knew he would come, and he did.

Within the hour he rattled the door handle.

It was only a matter of time before she would have to receive him. But not tonight, not with the fury he had on him.

When she did not answer he pounded the door with his fist.

Chloris wrapped her arms around herself, rocking slightly to and fro, afraid that he would batter down the door. Mercifully, he did not.

She heard him cursing and then his footsteps thundered down the stairs.

"To your mistress's bed," she whispered.

And please, please let her fall pregnant.

Despite her silent prayer, the cold hard truth of the matter reared in her mind. If Gavin could not father a child, and his mistress was his alone, this purgatory could go on indefinitely. She crawled into the bed and pulled the covers over herself. It was not cold. The fire in the grate was well stoked and burned low and steady. Nevertheless, she shivered because the images Gavin had forced into her mind brought no comfort.

In the morning she would begin her quest to find employment. She would query her friends. She was well educated and could perhaps find work as a governess. An acquaintance had recently taken on a teacher for her children. The teacher was a widow woman fallen on hard times. Could she find a similar position? There had to be a way to escape this marriage and build a humble, honest life for herself.

An honest life. That's what Lennox had called it. She had been living a lie, thinking wrongly that appearances, vows and loyalty mattered.

Watching the candle flicker and grow faint, she let her mind drift away from the hell that promised to lie ahead and instead let her memories dance into the flame, back to that first night in Torquil House, when Lennox's touch had brought fire into her body.

He'd encouraged her body to blossom, like the flowers opening to the sun. And he was her sun, the passion he had unleashed in her was nothing compared to what followed. As her eyes grew damp, she closed them. She said his name, over and over in her mind, led by instinct. For some reason, it calmed her. She pictured him taking off her glove that first night and wished that she not been married. Then, if he had asked to run away with him as he had, she could have done so without moral doubt or recourse.

One thing she knew with full certainty, there would never be any man in her heart, for she gravitated to him and him alone now.

Even if she never saw him again, her heart would always be his.

chapter Twenty-One

Tamhas Keavey's horse reared up, almost dislodging him from his saddle. He held tight to the reins, cursing as he was forced to counterbalance his weight against the rise of the horse. When its front hooves landed with a thump, the horse backed up, neighing loudly and tossing its head. Below the animal's hooves Tamhas caught sight of a glimmer of light in the mud. Tamhas glanced left and right, but could see nothing on the ground.

"They have laid traps," he shouted back over his shoulder. "It is their evil spells. We will find a way to get past."

He ground his teeth together, furious with the situation. It had taken him a long while to convince the bailiff and the prominent members of the council to agree to this plan. He'd had to bring in the minister to speak about the evil ways of those who practiced witchcraft. Resistance was higher than he expected, many claiming Lennox Fingal was a decent man, a man who had brought new custom to the burgh. Others said that the practice of hanging and burning was unchristian in itself. One man had even gone so far as to say that the law about witchcraft would be changed, stating that there would be shame about what had gone on during the time of the witch trials and it would cast a shadow on Scottish history. Another had openly admitted he had sought them out to treat his gout. He described the simple herbs that a young woman had offered him. They were ground up and made into a liquor for him to sip, and he said that helped purify his blood and cure his condition. Others were most impressed by his tale.

They were fools, the lot of them.

Three of Tamhas's men had already been dislodged from their horses along the route, and now it seemed he, too, struggled to get near the accursed place. Tamhas could see the house through the trees, though, candlelight glinting in the window even though it was daylight. Behind him he could hear whispers of concern, the men exchanging their thoughts on the matter, but Tamhas ignored them, determined not to let a little bit of the Devil's trickery stop him from delivering these heathens to justice. He yanked on the reins and forced his mount to move away from the troubled spot, skirting several tall trees as he attempted to lead the men to their destination.

When they finally forged a path close to the clearing in front of the house, Tamhas saw that the door stood open. The inhabitants were gone. The candles in the window burned low, as if they had been left there all night. His chance to bring them to justice had gone, too. "Damn them all to hell. That is where they belong."

The bailiff drew his horse alongside Tamhas, then turned back to shout instructions to the gathered men. "Secure your mounts at the forest edge. We may need to examine the tracks that have been left here."

Tamhas looked down at the clearing. The ground had been heavily churned, and recently, the tracks of several large carts heading out by the looks of it. Frustrated, he dropped from his horse. He ventured up the steps and pushed the door wide-open.

"Traps might have been set," a man called out.

Now they think so, now when it is too late. Tamhas clenched his jaw, then gestured briefly in acknowledgment and made his way into the building.

The place was stripped. Doors stood open, empty drawers hanging out of the dressers. The large items of furniture were still there, but few personal belongings. Fingal and his cohorts had left in a hurry. With the bailiff's men following behind, Tamhas went through every room in the house.

In the parlor he found ashes still smoldering in the grate. Evidence, no doubt. Turning the remains over with the poker he stared into the grate. It was Lennox Fingal's determination to establish himself in Saint Andrews that had convinced Tamhas they would stay, no matter what. There was some small sense of satisfaction that Lennox Fingal had been forced to accept defeat on that point, but it was not enough to pacify Tamhas's need to destroy the vermin. They had gone because they knew he was on their trail. Had his cousin Chloris sent word?

Tamhas cursed beneath his breath as he considered her foolish behavior, how it angered him. He'd had her watched, though, and he was sure she'd not had the opportunity to leave and pass the word before she left for Edinburgh. Yet somehow they had been one step ahead. He had not gone to all this trouble—engaging the support of the council, the bailiffs and his men—to end it now.

"They fled," he informed the men as they gathered outside, "but not long since. The fire is still warm." He turned to face them, glad to see several of them still had the bloodlust in their eyes. "I will ride after them and bring them to justice. Who is with me in my quest?"

"Are you sure of that, Master Keavey?" the bailiff said. "If they are gone from the burgh it is no longer our concern. We can spread the news, warn others who might encounter this unholy coven. But I say we celebrate the day they have left this place, for we will no longer be subject to any wrongdoing on their part."

Tamhas frowned. The bailiff's job was to secure the burgh for which he was responsible, so Tamhas could not fault him for his view on the matter. It did not tally with his own, however. Cousin Chloris and her weakness for the Witch Master still needled at him, and the fact that his wife had let slip she'd had dealings with the blaggard only angered him all the more. He was determined to sniff Lennox Fingal out, to oust him as a servant of Satan and see him strung up.

"I understand your position, Bailiff. However, it is in my nature to be sure that they will not return. My peace of mind and my family's safety demand that of me." He looked beyond the bailiff at the gathered men. "Who rides with me?"

Some of the men stayed silent, unsure about the value of the ongoing chase. However, there were enough who were still eager to give him support. He looked their way. A dozen or more of them said "aye."

Before they left he examined the tracks once more. "They are headed inland, away from the coast."

"Sire," one of the older men called out, and drew his attention away.

Peering down at the sight, Tamhas frowned. Then he saw what the man had seen, the hoofprints of a large mount traveling a different path. Glancing first at the sky and then at the landscape on the horizon, he gained his bearings. The carts had, as he first thought, headed inland—to who knew where. This lone rider had gone a different direction. To Cupar or beyond?

Beyond. It was a journey he knew well—for it crossed Fife to Edinburgh.

Words from that revealing letter he had intercepted crossed his mind. *The hope that you will agree to our arrangement will sustain me. Until then, I remain devoted to you.*

Could it be that Lennox Fingal was set on having Chloris? Had he ridden after her? Anger built steadily in Tamhas as he considered the possibility.

What arrangement did that letter refer to? Chloris had said it was a magic ritual, but there was more to it. "Damnable stupid bitch," he muttered beneath his breath, "I would have sired a child for you if you had been more amenable toward me."

The implications continued to unfold.

If Chloris's husband discovered what had gone on while his wife was under Tamhas's protection, a large share of Tamhas's wool trade in Edinburgh might be at risk, for it was Gavin who had established the majority of his commercial contacts.

That threat, and the real possibility of shame brought on his family because of Cousin Chloris's dalliance, meant that there was only one possible path for Tamhas to take—to follow the lone rider.

He had a dozen men, and Lennox Fingal was alone. Even with witchcraft on his side, he was well outnumbered. With a sense of satisfaction, Tamhas headed to his horse, assured that he was finally going to see justice done.

★ ★ ★

Lennox rode as if he could beat time by doing so, watching the sun's passage across the sky, trying to stay ahead of it and only slowing when the path became more treacherous. Even then he urged Shadow on, picking his path carefully, always taking the shortest route, no matter how hard.

By midday he had skirted the Burgh of Cupar. There was still a full day's ride ahead before he reached Edinburgh. Chloris was already there and subject to her husband's will. It turned his belly to think of her sacrificing herself, returning to the life she'd confessed she hated, in order to protect his people. It was her trust and her honest faith in people that meant she could not see her cousin had no intention of keeping his word. Of that Lennox was sure. Chloris's nature was kindly, even though her wish to discover the best in people had so often been unfulfilled. He would not allow her tentative trust in him to be shattered.

Then it occurred to him that Chloris might have realized he had come to her because of his feud with Keavey. Keavey might have pointed that out to her when he read the letter. The thought of it made Lennox wish he could change what had happened, that he had realized from the outset how much she would come to mean to him.

He was so deep in thought that he jolted in his saddle when his horse stumbled. Grasping tightly to the pommel on his saddle in order not to be thrown, he saw that the ground had become rocky. They were passing through a glen flanked by a rocky ravine on the left-hand side. A stream trickled through moss covered rocks to his right. Heavy gorse and heathers covered the spot, the only bare patches where it was too rocky even for the hardy gorse to thrive. "Easy, boy, easy."

When he soothed the beast, he realized Shadow needed to rest. Perhaps he did, too. Several nights had gone by with little sleep. With a long ride ahead he had to pace them both. Forced to dismount he reluctantly took a respite, leading Shadow to the stream. Alongside the horse he ducked down and scooped the icy water in his hands, splashing his face, sharpening his senses. Then he sat on a nearby rock.

Exhaustion was creeping in on him. He needed his full faculties when he arrived in Edinburgh. He could not afford another misstep. Three days earlier he'd been confident in his endeavors and fully expected to have Chloris by his side now. An error on his part. He would not let her return to that sad fate, to be unloved and unwanted, and worse still—beaten and berated. But he had to be able to think clearly.

Resting back against the mossy rock, he allowed his eyes to close.

It was images of Chloris that swam in his mind. Chloris breathless with need for him. Chloris on the verge of agreeing to forego her previous life, to be with him. For a woman like Chloris, who had battled her desire to stray so fiercely, that was no easy choice. It made him long to hold and shield her. The tightness in his chest knotted over again, and he forced himself to consider images of her in a better life, vowing to make it real. He could never offer her the privileges she'd had before, but he could give her much more in other ways, and he would cherish her.

Drifting on vows and promises, Lennox dozed.

The sound of voices did not reach him for some time.

When they did he inhaled sharply, but forced himself to keep his eyes closed as he sought awareness. Someone had approached. An urgent discussion was taking place nearby. Lennox kept still. He honed his senses then attempted to rise to his feet as he opened his eyes.

"Stay down." The man who stood over him had a pistol pointing at his chest.

Lennox eased back while he stared up at the weapon. Inwardly, he groaned and cursed. A quick side-glance alerted him to three other men several paces away, one with a musket and two others with swords. They were soldiers.

Was the hunt for the Somerled coven already under way? That was not good, although he could quickly distract this party from their cause by means of magic. Chastising himself for resting, he rued the extra time this intrusion would add to his journey. It was an irritation he could do without. Chloris was in danger. Every moment he wasted might be recorded in fresh scars, and he could not live with himself if that were the case. However, if he could draw these men away from the coven's trail, there was some purpose in it.

The man standing over him was smartly dressed in civilian clothes but appeared to be their leader. Lennox assumed him to be a bailiff. The man did not remove his tricorne hat, and he booted Lennox in the hip as he looked him over. "What have you done with the woman?"

Lennox frowned. "I travel alone."

He mustered an enchantment, readying to call upon the elements to deflect their attention from his coven, who would by now be well on their way and perhaps even past Kilmaron, north as the crow flew from his present whereabouts. Beneath his breath he whispered the Pictish words. The nearby stream bubbled and rose fast. Within moments it would breach its banks.

Shadow lingered by the stream's edge and he backed up and

neighed, but the strangers had their full attention on Lennox. One of the soldiers stepped forward and nodded at Lennox. "I think I was mistaken, sire, 'tis not the man I saw at The Drovers Inn, the one who helped her escape."

Lennox tried to make sense of what they said.

"And they were on foot," the second soldier added, "this man has a horse."

The leader of the group shot the two men a disapproving glance. "They could have stolen a horse by now," he barked. Looking back at Lennox he demanded more information. "What is your purpose and where are you headed?"

Lennox's mind worked furiously. They were looking for someone but it was not him, nor was it his coven. He kept his expression open and steady. "I travel to Edinburgh on a family matter. I am alone. Search my goods, you will find I only carry provisions for one."

The leader did not take his attention from Lennox and continued to train his weapon on him, but he gestured at Shadow and one of the men darted over and began to search the saddlebag.

Lennox didn't bother to watch. There was nothing there that would connect him to Somerled. It was not Somerled's coven they were after, though, of that he was now sure. Something nagged at him. Who was it that they sought? A leaden feeling in his gut grew, alongside the suspicion that it was people of his own kind. They sought a man and a woman, by the sounds of it. As the men's comments came together in his thoughts, Lennox's heart thumped wildly. A woman, a woman had escaped them. *Escaped*. He recalled what he'd been told in Dundee, that Jessie had been aided by a man. Could it be that these men hunted his own sister, and that she was hereabouts?

Sharpening his senses, he sought knowledge by reaching out for the presence of the person they hunted.

"Who is it you seek, sire?" Lennox asked the man who watched him, to hold his attention. "Perhaps I have seen them. Perhaps I can assist you in your quest." He opened his hands in an innocent gesture.

The man pursed his lips thoughtfully.

Before he had a chance to answer, Lennox felt the woman's presence.

A witch, there was no doubt about it, and she was hiding nearby. Without taking his attention from the man who stood over him, he honed his deepest, most innate senses, and attempted to discern the woman's whereabouts. A moment later he sourced her heat, and recognized therein her pagan heart, her burgeoning craft. She was hiding some forty strides beyond, at his back, sheltered in the deep gorse that grew at the place where the steeper slopes sprang from the more sheltered glen.

He also felt her fear.

The woman had faced this situation before. She'd been hunted and scorned. She'd seen dreadful things and she'd run many times. Worse than that, she feared her end was near, and the end of someone she loved who accompanied her.

That age-old pain rose inside him. With effort, he kept it in check. That was hard because he felt as if someone had put a fist in his chest and wrung his heart. Could it be Jessie? Could it truly be his sister crouched there fearing for her life? Through the pain, hope flared.

"There are witches about," the man with the pistol answered.

Aye, there are. And I will use every whit of the magic I know so that you never discover the one who is hiding at my back.

"Witches, you say!" He widened his eyes, but he could not do more than whisper the words, for they were all but trapped in his throat. Meanwhile, he assessed the danger. He had to protect her from discovery. The men had come into the glen the way he had, and if they passed on in the same direction they would skirt the woman's hiding place.

The soldier had completed his hunt through Shadow's saddlebag. "Nothing there, sire, and he spoke the truth. He carries only enough for himself."

The second soldier nodded over at the stream. "The water is rising, sire."

"A bit of water won't hurt you!" The man lowered his pistol, his expression angered. "Your brains are addled."

"So would yours be, sire," muttered the second soldier, "if you'd been charged by a possessed pig."

Their leader rolled his eyes.

Lennox observed intently. It would appear the woman they sought had given them a runaround. Despite his caution and his increasing need to know who she was, that pleased him. He had to usher these men on their way, fast. Summoning his deepest reserves he whispered under his breath, evoking the elements. Within moments the sky darkened, clouds moving in from behind him. Thunder cracked overhead.

"We have bigger worries," the man said, looking at the sky. Looking at Lennox he added, "Be on your way quickly and be wary of a couple on foot." With that he gestured at his men and they headed off back to the ridge beyond, where Lennox spied their mounts.

Lennox rose to his feet, dusting himself off and taking his

time about it. The soldiers mounted and the leader directed them back toward Cupar. As he'd hoped, the threat of poor weather had sent them back the way they'd come. When one of the soldiers looked back, Lennox raised a hand then headed toward Shadow. Mounting, he set off quickly. Once he arrived at the ridge he paused and watched them gallop into the distance. He wanted to go back, but not until he was sure he would not lead them to her. There was a tight knot in his chest. It was born of hope. When he attempted to quash it, to allay the potential disappointment, he could not.

Only when he was sure the men would not return, he looped back and returned to the spot by the brook. Dismounting, he stood and waited. Hoping all the while—willing it to be Jessie.

If the woman wanted to come out, she would surely know she was safe in his company. Perhaps not. Not all members of the coven he knew well had the same level of skills he did, in fact they each had different abilities. He stood his ground because he had to know her identity. Even if it were not Jessie, he wanted to warn the woman of the direction they took, but he did not want to frighten her by stomping over there and hauling her out. If she came out of her own accord, he could reassure her.

"Those who hunt you have gone," he called out, "you are safe now."

A figure emerged and peered across at him, a young woman. Lennox felt her scrutiny, and it was so intense the hairs on the back of his neck lifted. Her head and shoulders were swathed in a dark shawl that obscured her features. Nevertheless a connection, deep and undeniable, flared across the space between them. He opened his mouth to ask her name, but found he could not speak.

"You…" Her voice faltered. "You are Lennox Taskill, are you not?"

The sound of his family name spoken aloud made Lennox's heart stall. Outside of his coven, only his sisters would know that.

A tall man emerged behind the woman. He attempted to block her, his arm in front of her causing her to pause. "Jessie, be careful."

Jessie. Lennox felt as if he'd lost touch with the ground beneath his feet—that he might stumble and fall. It truly was Jessie.

The woman shook her head at her companion. "Do not fear. He is brethren, I sensed it."

She took a few tentative steps forward and then removed the dark shawl that she had wrapped around her head. She lifted her chin.

Lennox inhaled sharply. For several moments he thought he was looking at the ghost of his dead mother.

"Jessie?" He spoke his sister's name gruffly, for he was overwhelmed at the sight of her.

She nodded then broke into a run, hurling herself into his arms.

Lennox clutched her against him, his vision blurring as he felt her real and solid—alive and safe—in his embrace. Staring down at his young sibling, he could scarcely believe the woman she had become. "Is it truly you?"

"It is."

"You escaped them in Dundee. I went there."

"Aye, a week or more since. Gregor here freed me."

Lennox looked beyond her at her companion. The man had followed and stood close by, observing, one hand wrapped around the hilt of an ornate handled dagger.

Lennox returned his attention to Jessie. "Maisie, is she with you?"

Jessie shook her head. "I have not seen her, not since... that day."

She did not say more, but Lennox read it in her face.

Not since their mother had been hanged and burned before their very eyes.

It was not easy to recapture the intervening years for one another, but Jessie's companion left them alone while he went in search of provisions. In the shelter of the rocky enclave they became brother and sister again. When Lennox quizzed Jessie about her life during the intervening years he found himself both fraught with anxiety and lost in admiration for her tenacity and her ability to survive the harsh reality of her young life. For his part, he kept things simple, but Jessie seemed equally awed that he had escaped the attempt to silence him forever, returned to the Highlands, then made his way back, intent on finding them. When he told her about his current mission in Edinburgh, she smiled.

He reached into his pocket and drew out the two magical charms he had crafted from wood and kept for his sisters. "I have carried these many years, for I made them when we were first parted."

He held out his hand, gesturing. "Keep it with you always. Hold it to your heart if you need me and I will come to your side."

Jessie looked down at the objects in his hand, and then

took one, studying it. "I feel your magic. You're most gifted, brother."

"I have had years to learn, and knowledgeable people around me, a coven of my own."

For a moment she rested her fingers over the second charm and he felt her yearning for her twin. Then she tucked her own into her bodice and smiled at him.

"Was there never anyone for you?" From the information he had gleaned, it seemed that she had always been alone.

"Until Gregor. Sometimes I wondered about people, but I was too afraid to ask them, after what I saw."

It tortured Lennox to think of her so lonely, in a time and place that did not accept their beliefs. "That will never be the case again."

Jessie stared down at his open palm.

Lennox closed it, pocketing the second charm. "You and Maisie were so close," he commented. "Do you ever feel anything of her?"

Jessie nodded. "Not often, but there are times when I feel how far away she is, and she longs to find us as much as we crave to find her."

"The villagers who kept you said nothing?"

"No. No one would even answer me if I spoke of my family." She fell silent awhile, and Lennox saw how hard her life had been, and for a long while. "I did see the carriage that took her, when they finally let us down from the pillars outside the Kirk."

"A carriage?" Lennox's attention sharpened.

"Aye. It was a fancy affair, with a crest on the door."

"Would you recall the crest if you were shown it?"

Jessie's forehead creased. "Possibly."

"Several members of my coven are wainwrights. We had good trade in Saint Andrews these past two years. It might be possible to study a record of crests, once we are all safe and can give the subject some time."

"Oh, Lennox, that would be grand."

"Keep the image of the crest in your thoughts and we'll find a way." The priority was to get everyone to safety in the Highlands, but there was a slender chance there and he could see Jessie's yearning, the hope that they might find her twin. Lennox could scarcely imagine how hard it must have been for her. They were inseparable as children. He'd assumed them together all these years, with each other for comfort.

By the time the man she called Gregor Ramsay returned from a nearby village with provisions, they knew the important events of each other's lives and how they both came to be at this spot where their paths had crossed.

"Jessie tells me you are a seafaring man," Lennox said, as her companion shared out bannocks and cheese.

"I was." The man seemed not to want to say more on the subject.

Lennox eyed him with curiosity. There was a tightly packed bundle that he kept close at his side, and Lennox sensed it was of great value. The man had a scarred face, and yet he was not cowed by it, nor did he try to hide it. How had he come by the wound, Lennox wondered, wary of the man's sway over his sister.

Jessie ate heartily, which encouraged Lennox to eat, too.

"We will come to Edinburgh with you," Jessie stated. "We can help you find your Chloris." She smiled at Lennox.

"You cannot go to Edinburgh," the man called Gregor

Ramsay insisted. "We take the road north." He directed his next words at Lennox. "Where Jessie is safe and unknown."

Lennox did not argue with him because the man was correct in what he said.

He was not sure he liked the man, though. Neither was this Mister Ramsay one of their kind, although he seemed to have accepted it in Jessie, as Chloris had in him. It affected him oddly because the sight of these two together made him think even more about his relationship with Chloris, and how they might manage together, despite their differences. They would make it work.

Nevertheless it was not what he'd wanted for his sisters. They held beliefs that meant they would be safest with a Witch Master, someone who would not be afraid of them and would not turn on them. He thought of the young men in his coven, strong, loyal young men. This man, Gregor Ramsay, had knowledge and wisdom in his eyes, something he saw in those who traveled to faraway places, but Lennox was not sure of him yet.

"Nonsense," Jessie retorted. "My brother needs our help and I am not known in Edinburgh."

Lennox shook his head. "Your companion is right in what he says. You should be on your way north. I was in Dundee two days ago, I went to the tolbooth. I spoke to people there. The hunt goes on. They want your blood." *As much as they will all want mine in Saint Andrews by now,* he thought, realizing it was well after noon and Keavey's men had likely breached the warding spells set for them.

Mister Ramsay looked concerned. "They did not realize you were Jessie's brother when you asked after her?"

Lennox shook his head. "No. I invented a tale to cover my

queries. But they are still looking for you, not just those three who we sent off earlier, but many more."

A shadow passed briefly across Jessie's expression and her lips parted, but she did not speak for a moment. When she did it was only to insist that she help him. "Aye, we know they are not far behind us."

She wrapped her hands around her upper arms and her companion moved instinctively, drawing her in against him with his arm around her shoulder. She rested her head against his chest and Lennox watched, touched by this strange sight. After all these years, while he thought of his siblings as young girls who were in need of his protection, he saw that she'd grown and thrived, too. She was a strong, passionate woman, and she was determined to survive. And now she had a lover, a protector of her own.

Jessie lifted her head and in her eyes he saw the weary, age-old wisdom that her life had brought her. "I will not be parted from you again, brother. Besides, there is strength in numbers. We will go to Edinburgh together and aid you during your quest. It makes sense, for we will then be together and united in order to travel north to where we had our beginning." She held his gaze. "I cannot risk losing you again."

How was it that she was the one saying things that he should be saying, binding them together as kin once more? Lennox observed his sister's companion as he considered the dilemma. The man would not be easily swayed, and Lennox could not fault him for that. Perhaps he could warm to the man. He had rescued his sister from the tolbooth, after all, and the bond between the two was clear to see. Time would tell whether Jessie's affection toward him was truly warranted, and Lennox saw that keeping both of them close at hand would allow him to be sure that his sister's affection was warranted. "Are you in agreement, Mister Ramsay?"

Gregor Ramsay had a shrewd look in his eye. "I will agree, but only because they're searching for a woman with one man. If we travel as three, Jessie gains more protection and is better hidden."

"I respect your argument," Lennox replied.

Gregor Ramsay shot him a look. It was a subtle, guarded warning, perhaps.

Lennox gave a wry smile. "You are as wary of me as I of you."

"At least." Gregor inclined his head.

"Gregor!" Jessie looked affronted.

Ramsay did not respond to that, although he still kept her close, holding her tightly to him. "We will help you in your task, but as soon as I have the slightest suspicion that the town bailiff has word of Jessie's whereabouts she will be gone, with me."

Lennox respected that, too, but he wasn't about to say so. He nodded. "That is fair." He was warming to this Gregor Ramsay after all. "We'll need to purchase two more horses."

Ramsay shook his head. "No, we go by foot or by enclosed carriage."

Lennox frowned. "A carriage will be harder to find."

"I'm sorry, Lennox." Jessie looked sheepish. "'Tis my fault. I cannot abide to look down from a height, not since they stood me on that pillar and made me watch…"

Something inside him jolted and he was back there in his mind, kicking and cursing, and he could see them, his twin sisters forced up on the pillars at the Kirk gates, forced to watch their mother being stoned.

"I have coin enough for a carriage," Ramsay said, which pulled Lennox back to the present moment.

"I, too, have money. We will go by foot until a carriage can be hired or bought."

"Thank you, both." Jessie mustered a small smile, but Lennox sensed she was ashamed of her burden—a burden no woman should have to carry.

"Well, now that we are all agreed," Jessie said, mustering herself, "we must make a plan to loose your Mistress Chloris from her current whereabouts."

Lennox stared at his sister in amazement. *A plan.* He was so busy reacting to what went on he hadn't even considered what he would do once he got to Edinburgh. A plan would be good, he realized, suddenly resigned to the fact that he was not invincible and he needed the guidance of his people, just as much as they needed him to validate what they were doing.

"Tell us more," she encouraged. "Tell us all that you know of her circumstances, so that we might form our plan."

"I fear her situation is little better than what you experienced in the tolbooth in Dundee, sister. The difference is that she lives in a life of comfort, but she is unhappy for she is beaten and abused by a husband who does not care for her and seeks to be rid of her."

"Oh, Lennox," Jessie whispered, and took his hand in hers. He stared down at the ground in front of him, the tender gesture threatening to undo him. The need to know that Chloris was safe and not affected at her husband's hands once again was overwhelming. It also made him wonder if she would ever forgive him. Then came the shame and the regret, for he had dallied with her to undermine his enemy. His emotions were awry, and he could scarcely think straight. "She went back to him in order to protect my coven from discovery, but her sacrifice was useless."

Gregor's head lifted, the look in his eyes sharpening.

Lennox nodded his way. "Aye, the soldiers will be swarming after my people as well as the two of you, by now."

"In that case," Gregor said, rising to his feet, "we will form the plan as we go. We had better be on our way, and be quick about it."

chapter Twenty-Two

"Mary, I will be out making calls later this afternoon. Would you please lay out my cloak and walking boots?"

"Yes, mistress." Mary hurried off, leaving Chloris to her embroidery.

It would be her second day of seeking word of a position that she might be suitable for. The previous day had resulted in sympathy from the two good friends she had called upon. The details of her failing marriage were greeted with curiosity, but not with surprise. It seemed she was the only one who was blind to the inevitable turn of events.

It also resulted in one hopeful offer of assistance, a possible post as a companion to an elderly widow whose hearing was failing. Someone else had been recommended, but it was not clear whether the post had yet been filled. If it had, she would keep searching. She would call upon all the women she knew in order to find employment.

She had many skills. Her sewing was good. She could also teach, and she would find a way to forge her own path in this world. Above all it gave her hope and something to occupy her mind, when her aching heart threatened to fill her thoughts with despair. Chloris thought she'd known low spirits before, but she had not. The sense of loss she experienced was like none other.

Moreover, it was only a matter of time until Gavin forced himself upon her, or punished her for her contrary behavior. There was nowhere else for her to go, not immediately, but she feared she could not abide Gavin's ways now, not since she had tasted something of freedom and respect. She could not return to Saint Andrews for fear of endangering Lennox and those he protected. Previously, she thought her few weeks of happiness would carry her through difficult times ahead. Now she knew it would only make it more difficult to endure.

So she prepared herself for a new life, one that was as yet unknown to her.

A knock at the door interrupted her thoughts.

Mary entered the drawing room and drew her attention. "You have a visitor, mistress."

"I am not expecting anyone to call." Chloris frowned, then wondered if it was news of the post mentioned the day before. She rose to her feet. "Is it someone carrying a letter?"

"No. It is a woman."

Chloris immediately thought of the woman she had discovered with Gavin on her return. "My husband's night visitor?"

Mary shook her head. "It is a tradeswoman at the door, mistress. She wishes to show you her wares."

Chloris frowned. Gavin had a strict policy on such things and she was surprised that Mary had not followed his instructions without drawing it to her attention. "The master allows no tradespeople into the house."

"The woman is most insistent, and she…well, she somehow made me believe you would want to receive her." Mary frowned. "That is why I thought I ought to mention it." Mary looked every bit as confused as Chloris felt. "The woman said to tell you she has lace for you, the lace that you purchased from her in the market at Saint Andrews."

Chloris felt light-headed.

Lace, from the market in Saint Andrews? She cast her mind back. Yes, she had looked at lace with Jean, but her thoughts had been entirely elsewhere, for that was when she had seen Lennox. Then he had stood behind her and whispered to her. She could not even recall the face of the lace maker, and although she had feigned interest in Jean's purchases, she'd bought none of her own. As she tried to order her thoughts on the matter, one image stayed solid in her mind—the sight of Lennox across Market Street, watching them, smiling her way and making that secret connection with her.

Her heart beat hard and fast. She put her sewing aside and nodded at Mary. "In that case you'd best show her in."

When Mary disappeared, Chloris stood perfectly still and watched the doorway with great curiosity. A few moments later, Mary showed a young woman in. In her arms the woman carried a basket that was covered over by a lace cloth.

When she entered the room she stared at Chloris with great curiosity. "Thank you for admitting me." The woman dropped a quick curtsy. "I have brought your lace, and I have some other items that may be of interest to you."

Chloris felt irresistibly drawn to the young woman, as if a secret would be revealed within the woman's basket. The young woman's eyes burned bright blue, as if sunshine was captured there. Chloris pressed her hand to her breastbone in an attempt to remain steady. She felt quite light-headed but suffused with warmth, as she often had when Lennox per-formed his rituals with her. The significance of the encounter dawned on her. The young woman was one of his kind, a witch.

The visitor seemed to sense her growing awareness and she gave a slight nod.

Chloris could not look away from the young woman, for her vivid blue eyes held Chloris's attention. Gathering herself, Chloris spoke to the serving girl. "Thank you, Mary, that will be all."

She could hear the tremble in her own voice. While she waited for the curious girl to leave them alone, she struggled to maintain her composure.

The young woman with the basket observed the servant leave. Then she set her basket down on the floor and walked over to Chloris. Taking Chloris's hands in hers, she peered at her closely and then broke into a broad smile. "You are just as pretty as my brother told me you were."

Lennox had told her. Lennox had sent her. Chloris found herself awash with confusion, with hope and with disbelief. But there was such warmth, such welcome in the young woman's face, and the heat from her hands seemed to reach into Chloris and soothe her troubled soul. "You are Lennox's sister?"

The woman nodded. "One of them. I am Jessie."

Chloris struggled to make sense of it. The letter he'd sent confided that he'd had word of his kin. Was this the matter of great urgency that he was called away upon, on that fateful day that he had sent a letter? "He was searching for you."

"Lennox and I have recently been reunited. He was on his way here, to find you, when our paths crossed."

"Being reunited with you again will be a huge comfort to him, for he has searched for you all these years."

Jessie nodded. "Aye, but if he had not been on his way to

find you, our paths would not have crossed. There is great significance in that for a man such as Lennox."

Destiny, he had mentioned it often. Chloris longed to believe in it, too.

"But it is you that he needs now for his comfort," Jessie continued, "you most of all."

Chloris withdrew her hands from Jessie's, difficult though it was to turn away from the succor she offered. "It cannot be. My cousin will have his coven ousted if I dare to see Lennox again." She picked her words carefully, aware of the pain the young woman had suffered because of her mother's persecution.

"I do not know the full circumstances of the situation, but Lennox has already sent his people north."

Chloris was startled. "They have gone from Saint Andrews?"

"They had to leave, your cousin was determined to oust them all, every last one of them."

Horrified that her worst fears had almost been realized, Chloris struggled to put the pieces into place.

"We must speak quickly in case your servant returns." Jessie retrieved her basket and withdrew a folded page. "Lennox is here in Edinburgh and he has taken rooms for us just a few streets away. He has written the address for you, and he will remain there until you are able to meet him."

Chloris stared down at the page, saw that it was written by the same hand, and her heart beat wildly. Lennox was here, in Edinburgh. "He has come here?"

"He's in love with you, Mistress Chloris." Jessie laughed softly. "He is in a terrible, sorry state. I must say it is quite endearing to witness."

Chloris could scarcely breathe.

"Can I tell him you will come?" Jessie asked.

"Yes, I will be there within the hour."

Chloris was ready to leave the house immediately, but she forced herself to wait a little longer, lest someone spied her following in Jessie's footsteps. Her heart was all aflutter, her thoughts dashing this way and that. Lennox had come after her, he had hunted her down. Why hadn't he gone with his people? How had he found her? The questions spilled through her thoughts as she attempted to bide her time.

Mary entered the drawing room. "I've left out your cloak and boots, mistress."

"Thank you, I will be going out immediately."

"Shall I order the carriage to be brought round?"

"No. I want to take the air, so I will walk." She followed Mary out of the room, then hurried to her bedchamber where a cloak hung over the dressing screen next to the armoire. Changing into her boots, she grabbed the cloak and raced downstairs.

Once out in the street she glanced about to check that she wasn't being observed, and then hurried on her way. It was not far, but every step felt as if she had to make haste, lest she awaken from the dream and discover she had imagined this situation.

As she approached the building where Lennox had taken lodgings, she saw Jessie watching from a window, waiting for her. Before she even knocked at the door, Jessie opened it and directed her up the stairs.

"The first door at the top of the stairs, he's waiting for you. Hurry, before the landlady sees you."

"Thank you." Chloris squeezed Jessie's hand, then lifted her skirts and darted up the stairs. She almost tripped in her haste, but when she got to the landing and saw the door ajar, she felt suddenly nervous. It was as if it were a dream and if she stepped through the door she would awaken and find herself alone.

A moment later the door opened wide and Lennox was standing there, one hand against the door frame, looking out at her.

Chloris stared at him, almost too nervous to speak and break the spell, for it had to be a spell, this vision of her handsome lover standing here in Edinburgh. He was barely five paces away, and yet she could not believe it was really true. *Lennox*. His posture was poised and the atmosphere around him filled with his presence—with a sense of anticipation and tension that was palpable. He looked so handsome, so wild and passionate, and the light burning in his eyes was intense.

The frown he wore vanished when he saw it was her who had clattered up the stairs. Chloris could not hold back her joy. She fled across the landing and into his arms, her hands locking around his head as she welcomed his hungry, possessive kiss.

When they drew apart she stared up at him in wonder. "Lennox, oh, Lennox. Why did you risk your safety to follow me when you should be with your people?"

He smiled down at her. "Because I love you, and I promised you I would love you forever. That meant there was only one thing for me to do, to find you and keep you safe."

Her hand went to his chest, her emotions spinning. All the doubts she had harbored about his intentions—all the fears that it was fanciful nonsense and he felt no lasting affection for her and that she was nothing more than another conquest for a wild libertine—disappeared because she could see it in his eyes. Possessive, proud and filled with desire, he had come to her.

"Oh, Lennox," she whispered.

"Are you well and safe?" He smoothed back her hair from her forehead as he studied her intently.

She nodded, unable to do more. She knew the real meaning in his question. He wanted to know if Gavin had harmed her.

His finger beneath the chin forced her to look up and meet his gaze. "You look tired."

"I've been worried." She prayed that he would not press her to say more.

He took her hand and led her into the room beyond, a furnished parlor of some comfort. Closing the door, he shut the world out. Again she found herself held in his arms, held tight and thoroughly kissed.

"I missed you more than I thought possible," he whispered to her, and his voice was husky with emotion.

"As did I. The thought that I might never see you again made me wish to die."

"Don't say that." He shook his head, as if he could not bear her words.

How deeply he felt, as did she.

Desire shot between them.

She arched in his arms, her body kindling. Memories of their lovemaking flooded her with need to be coupled with him again, to prove this reunion was real.

His hands enclosed the curve of her bosom, cupping her breasts from beneath.

Breathlessly, she responded. Standing on her tiptoes, she pressed her hips to his. His hands roved quickly up and down her back and around her waist, as if he wanted to touch all of her at once.

"Come, sit." He led her to a long couch. She glanced about and saw a bedchamber through the doorway beyond.

Perching on the seat, she sighed with relief and undid her cloak where it was tied at her neck, letting it fall away. She could not take her gaze from her lover's face. Here in this furnished parlor he looked like a laird. The gentle ticktock of the clock that stood behind him seemed almost incongruous. It was so calm, when between them their passion for one another was as wild and powerful as it had been out in the bluebell glen.

But he was here, and that very real fact made her afraid for his safety.

Chloris felt the dangers closing in.

If Tamhas knew about Lennox's action, he might send word to the Edinburgh witch finders. They might already be armed with information that could quickly arrange for her lover to be put to death. Her belly turned over and she felt light-headed, her emotions tangling. "You shouldn't have taken the risk. Tamhas will be angered you got away, he might—"

Lennox silenced her with one finger on her lips. "My people are safely gone, headed for the Highlands."

A deep sense of guilt tugged at her innards. "I'm so sorry to have brought this dreadful situation upon you and yours."

Lennox shook his head. "You did not bring this upon us. The feud between Tamhas Keavey and my coven has gone on for a long while. He has done terrible things, and long before you and I met. One of my men…Keavey stole the use of his arm when he found him picking forage. Broke him by beating him and then trampled him with his horse."

Chloris shut her eyes, ashamed and horrified by Tamhas's actions.

"He was set on having us turned away from Saint Andrews, or better still put to death, if he could organize that."

Chloris whimpered and shuddered. She knew of the witch trials, of the gruesome manner in which they put to death those who were convicted, but she could not bear to hear it on his lips, not about him and his people.

"Hush. What happened between us is not to blame. This was always our destiny. It was only my stubbornness and the need to find my sisters that kept me there. I thought I could change people's opinions of the old ways, but there are long held grievances and suspicions, and human nature does so like to have someone to persecute."

Everything he said made her fret all the more. He was trying to comfort her, to reassure her, but guilt weighed heavily. She wrung her hands together, remembering those final words she had exchanged with Tamhas, how angered he had been when she tried to bargain with him. Lennox was too precious to her. She could not put him at risk any more than she already had. "Tamhas might have left you alone, though, if it were not for me."

"That is not the case." He cupped her face in his hand. "Chloris, until you came into my life it was as if I were trapped, unable to find anything I needed to find, unable to make a true sanctuary for the people I care about. But you have been a lucky charm, for you unleashed a level of madness in my life that has resulted in good things." There was affection and humor in his eyes and although she could not fully believe in his convictions, she felt compelled to listen to him.

"We needed to leave Lowlands, that has been the truth of

it for a long while. The persecution of witchcraft is embedded in the people's minds here, as it has been for over a hundred years. I had tried to bring about change, but with enemies such as Keavey, I cannot take any more risks. You have given me the strength and purpose I needed to move on. There is also the matter of Jessie." He smiled. "If it had not been for the fact that I was coming to Edinburgh to find you I would not have found my sister, who I have hunted for all these years."

There was luck in that, Chloris reflected. Could she truly believe this was meant to be?

"Most of all, you have given me what I needed, a woman to love, a woman to cherish. Every man needs those things, but I did not know how much loving you would alter the way I live, the way I see and feel. I am stronger, I am a better man."

She saw what he was trying to say, not only as a man, but in his magic.

Nevertheless, she still wondered if they were too different. She shook her head and turned her face away, breaking contact. "I fear it cannot be, or will not last."

"It can and it will."

She met his gaze. It was there in his eyes and she all but melted.

"I know that you could not wait for me," he said, "but this is our true beginning. I love you and I know that you love me."

"When we were together…when we were there that last day in the forest and you painted a picture for me of how it could be, it was too much like a dream, Lennox. I am older than you, a married woman, and a burden because I am so different to you. I do not share your nature." The shortcoming she felt on that score grew deeper still. She lowered her eyelids, afraid that he would see the grief and pain she carried.

Lennox shook his head. "All of that means nothing. You cannot turn away from a life with me. You were not happy when you came to me, you as much as admitted it, and I have seen you blossom while we've been together. You cannot deny that."

"No, I cannot deny that."

He drew her to him and looked into her eyes beseechingly. "I will not let you say no to what we could have together."

"You told me it would be hard, but that is the truth for you, too."

"Do I need to remind you how we are when we are as one?" He closed in on her, his mouth covering hers.

Chloris whimpered, then melted and relinquished herself to him.

His kiss was soft and persuasive at first, reminiscent of those first few kisses he'd given her, and then it came as she knew it would—the full-blown passion that flared between them. How she adored it, the sheer and absolute immensity of the reciprocated desire they shared.

Cradling the back of her head with one hand, he moved the other around the outline of her breasts and waist, where he gripped her tightly and drew her closer against him. The firm, hard line of his body against hers—together with the feeling of being held in his arms while he plundered her mouth—shooed everything else in the world away. She let it, savoring him.

He eased her down onto her back. Chloris sank gratefully onto the couch, not breaking from the embrace. To feel the closeness, the presence of his body over hers, made her heart soar. "Lennox, you make me…you make me feel, everything."

"It is the same for me, and you and only you make me feel this."

He meshed his fingers with hers, and she stared at their joined hands. She wanted this, wanted him—for always, just as he suggested.

He looked down at her with passion in his eyes. "Let me love you."

Chloris groaned. When he said that, she could not resist. Turning her face to one side, she was ashamed of her blatant reaction, here in this borrowed parlor where everything should be proper and moral.

Lennox swooped down upon her, kissing the soft, sensitive skin that she had exposed in turning her face, raining kisses down her throat and into her cleavage, his hands around her waist.

Desire sprang at her center, heating her groin, making her entire body throb with need. Between her thighs her core clenched, reaching for him, reaching for the certain pleasure of his hardness inside her.

With one hand on the couch above her head, he rested his knee by the side of her hip and caressed the curved underside of her bosom through her bodice and corset. It made her breath come ever quicker, the damp heat between her thighs growing. Moaning softly, she shook her head, but her hands moved and she ran her fingers into his hair, craving every part of him.

Sensation overwhelmed her, her need for him blinding her to their surroundings, to the danger inherent in their situation. She looked at him, her lips parting, and put her hands against his chest, her head pressing back as her body arched to his.

His hands roamed, squeezing her through her clothing. Even through her skirts she could feel his erection solid and real, promising her untold pleasures such as those she had experienced with him over the past few weeks.

"We should not," she whispered. Yet she did not resist when his mouth lifted at one corner and he lowered his hand and pulled up her skirts, his fingers quickly working between her thighs to delve into the heat he found there.

"Lennox," she breathed. The stroke of his fingers opening her up sent her spinning. She felt panic, and bliss. Pressing back against the cushions, she shook her head. "Please, don't."

Even as she said that she knew she was helpless. She could barely resist him, she was powerless under his hands, and now it seemed even worse than before because he had professed his affection for her, affection she reciprocated deeply.

Lennox laughed softly. "You pretend you can resist me, yet this—" he stroked his thumb over the seat of her pleasure, making her moan "—says something different."

She cried out, her hands fisting.

Again he chuckled. "Even when your words deny me, your body tells me what it is you want. It has been that way since the beginning."

He was so sure, just as he had always been.

"Of course I want you. I always have, for you have seduced me thoroughly. That is a task that you are very good at. It is the wisdom of our actions that I query, that and matters of the heart."

"You will be able to consider our matters of the heart more honestly, while I reacquaint myself with you." Again he stroked her sensitive folds.

Chloris writhed against the couch. "You are terrible! I need you there, inside me."

His smile was triumphant. "A moment longer. Let me study you while I touch you, and then I will have to be inside you."

"You are shameless." She gave him a rueful glance.

He ducked to press a kiss in the cleft between her breasts, then thrust one finger inside her. "I am merely demonstrating how well we are matched."

Chloris covered her mouth with her hand to stop herself from crying out. The hard intrusion felt too good, and her body clasped it, instinct taking over. Her hips bore down, and when they did his thumb rode over her swollen bud and released a tide of heat that bloomed within her.

He lifted his head and looked down at her, holding her gaze. His finger stroked in and out of her damp niche. Slowly, so slowly, he moved, coaxing her to enjoy. He circled his finger around her sensitive opening. "I want every ounce of you, Chloris."

Her body was trembling, so intense was the connection. She saw what he meant now, about considering matters of the heart. When he had her this way, she could think of nothing else but how much she loved him, and that she wanted to be with him for all time. She clutched at him. "Please," she whispered.

He pulled free the laces at his groin, freeing his manhood. It was hard against her and when she felt its size she shivered.

"I am needy for your most precious embrace," he murmured.

She wrapped her fingers around his girth, testing him. He was solid, long and thick, and the skin was hot to the touch. She stroked her fingers down around the shaft, then cupped his sac, squeezing it gently in her hand.

He shot her a warning glance. "Tread carefully, my love."

He spread her legs, arranging one over the side of the couch. The other he lifted along his flank, encouraging her to bend her knee. Slowly, he eased his length inside her, his hands cupping her bottom as he lifted her to arrange her and gain entry. Chloris moaned as he stretched her open, moving his cock deeper.

Then she was gloriously full and he held his position.

His breath was warm on her mouth and she breathed him in. His hair fell forward, enclosing them as he kissed her softly, the stubble on his jaw grazing her face. It was too good. Chloris wanted to stay locked that way forever.

But then he stroked the leg that pressed alongside his flank and shifted it, folding it high against his side as he ground his hips into hers, slow and deep, his teeth gritted, and she was soon close to spilling. They both were. She could see the muscles in his neck working, his eyelids lowered as he watched her reactions.

A trickle of her moisture slid free and ran down between them.

He smiled at her. "You are awash, my love."

Chloris didn't respond, but her cheeks flamed.

"And how you blush."

"I cannot help it, my emotions are tender."

"Good."

She felt the swollen head of his cock throbbing against her deepest point, and it made her whisper his name, over and over, her release imminent.

He pulled back when he felt the depth of her response. "Oh, Chloris."

Then he drove her on, riding her slow, hard and deep, until she began to pant aloud. He arched up his shoulders with effort. She bore down, meeting him, and the release came sudden and sweet and hot and wild, flooding her groin with pleasure. When she clenched on him, her core rippling, he groaned, jerked inside her and spurted hot and copious, equaling her release. Chloris held on to his shoulders with weak hands, shuddering.

When he drew away, it was only after he had kissed her for as long as he could stay inside, and then he stood up and laced himself up, before he lifted her in his arms and set her upon his lap. "There, now that we are reacquainted, did you think on our matters of the heart?"

"Long and hard." She laughed and rubbed her face against his.

"And you see it, don't you, this will always be the way between us. This is nature's way, the most powerful vitality there is, and when it grows this way between two lovers who are meant to be together, it is immense and undeniable."

She nodded her head, clinging to him. That first time in the bluebell glen, when she had wanted to turn him away but had begged him to fulfill her, was close in her mind. There was regret, but it was nothing in the face of her growing desire for him. She'd woken the next day longing for more, longing to be in his arms again.

For the first time she let herself believe this was right.

"When you first came to me we met as if strangers, both driven by different needs in our union. The draw between us was powerful even then, and because of that I fast grew to care about you and nothing else mattered, not your cousin nor what he thought, or how well I could fox him by seducing you."

Chloris drew back. Her breath caught.

Lennox, whose passion had clearly undone him, cursed when he realized what he had said.

"You...you are saying that you seduced me in order to upset Tamhas?"

Even as she said the words, her heart ached. More fiercely than all the pain and loss she had experienced over these past few days, a knife ran deep in her heart. She shifted, climbing off his lap.

Lennox hung his head. "For a while, I thought that was why you had gone from Saint Andrews, that you had thought on it and realized."

"I left because he threatened to punish your people."

"That is what he is like. You have seen it. He detests my people, you know he wanted to run us into the ground and have us burned at the stake. I cannot help that I reacted to that." He reached out for her.

Chloris pulled away. "But you...you made a fine show of your talents, in order to get to me, because of him."

"It is how it started, but soon discovery was the last thing I wanted, because most of all I wanted you."

She stared at him, remembering how it had been, her mind going back to that very first evening when she had asked his assistance. He had questioned her, and when he saw her with Jean his mind was made up. He had set out to ruin her in Tamhas's eyes. That is why he was so driven, why he pursued her even when she wasn't sure if she wanted to go ahead with the ancient ritual he described. "The ritual to increase my fertility, was that even real?"

"Of course it was real." Dismay filled his expression. His chest rose and fell rapidly, and he ran his fingers through his hair and cursed beneath his breath. "What we do cannot and should not be taken for granted. We can summon the gifts of nature to share with others but we must do it with respect."

"I thought you wanted to help me."

"I did." Wild-eyed, he rose to his feet, opened his arms out at his sides and faced his palms upward. He bowed his head, but still he held her gaze, and his eyes shone with unruly fire. He spoke beneath his breath, strange words.

The fire she saw in his eyes leaped from his palms, too.

It was so sudden and so powerful that Chloris backed away, astonished.

When she did, he put an end to it, closing his hands and extinguishing the fire. "I love you, Chloris. What I showed you there is as nothing, compared to what flares in me when I am with you."

And I love you.

Determinedly, he continued to plead with her. "Please understand, Chloris. There was some temptation in seducing you because of who you are, but that became insignificant for me very quickly, I assure you."

Chloris looked at him with fresh vision. She could not bring herself to think of being without him, but she saw that his cause had been far from the pure, nurturing thing that he had described when he spoke of the ways of his people, in tune with nature and the seasons rather than the Church and its rules. No, she was torn between what she felt, and what she saw before her—a man who she did not know well enough.

"Please do not look at me that way," he begged. "I was in error, badly so. I had been working for years to make my people accepted, to avoid the fate that has fallen upon so many of us this last century in the Lowlands. Your cousin was the worst contender, constantly trying to undo everything I did to guarantee our acceptance in Saint Andrews. I have told you what kind of man he is."

"I know what kind of man he is," she responded coolly. "What concerns me is that I do not always know or understand what kind of man you are." That hurt him, and it hurt her when she saw the pained look in his eyes. But it had to be said. "I had not realized you were driven by that. I thought you wished to help me."

"I did. I cannot deny that there was some pleasure in thinking how shocked he would be if he knew I was under his roof and in your bed."

Chloris reeled. Covering her eyes with her hands she shook her head. "Please do not say any more."

"But I must, for that is how it began. I beseech you, Chloris. It is very far from being that way now. When I asked you to meet me, to be with me forever, it was because that situation had changed. I love you. That is why I came here to Edinburgh, to plead for you to leave with me, to plead for your hand and your heart."

There was contrition in his expression, and she wanted to believe him, but it was all too much. "I cannot order my thoughts, please. There is too much to think on."

The chime of the clock marking the half hour brought her back to their surroundings. "I must leave now. I do love you, Lennox, but I need to let my thoughts settle."

"Promise me this, for all the precious moments we have shared, that you will try to forgive my poor judgment."

Chloris stood there, looking at the desperation in his expression, and her whole world was spinning. She nodded, then collected her cloak and forced herself to turn away and walk to the door.

He whispered her name.

When she paused at the door, he said, "I will be waiting for your response."

"I know, and I will return and give it to you soon."

Her legs trembled under her as she went down the stairs. When she reached the hallway, Jessie emerged.

"You will come with us, yes?"

The question, her smile and the fact that Chloris was quickly warming to Lennox's sister, made the tears well. Chloris wiped them away and looked back up the stairs. "I fear we do not understand each other well enough."

Jessie studied her silently for a moment before she responded. "That will come. It is not easy at first, because the things that draw us together also conspire to keep us apart. We have to sacrifice part of what we were to meet in the middle."

Chloris stared at Jessie. "You are a wise young woman."

"I know that he loves you."

Chloris nodded. "And I love him. But I am not like you, I do not understand your nature and your ways, and I think that puts distance between us."

Jessie grasped Chloris's hands in hers. "But you will. My lover, he is not one of us, and he is my defender still."

"I had not realized." Chloris felt her encouragement.

"It will be that way for you, too. Lennox is fierce in his affection for you."

"I need to be sure."

Jessie studied her and squeezed her hands. "You already are."

"Perhaps." Chloris mustered a smile.

Jessie reached into her pocket and drew out a small wooden object. She pressed it into Chloris's palm. "Here, take this. It is a charm that Lennox crafted for me and it will protect you. If you need him hold it to your heart. He will know."

Chloris stared down at the small wooden object. It was roughly hewn but pretty, and it resembled a wildflower. It made her think of the forest where they had lain together amongst the spring blossoms. She shook her head, offering it back. "I cannot take it if it is yours."

"Take it." Jessie lifted the flower from Chloris's hand and pushed it into the pocket on Chloris's skirt.

Behind them a door clicked open and a woman stepped into the hallway.

Jessie reached over and kissed Chloris on the cheek. "It is the landlady."

Chloris nodded, understanding.

Jessie saw her on her way.

As she turned the corner of the street, Chloris's footsteps slowed. Ahead of her lay her home. She knew too well what that meant. At her back, the home of her heart, and she knew so little of what might lie ahead if she took that path.

Her footsteps grew slower still, but each step she took made her want to turn back, and that's what she needed to feel. She needed to be sure. She would return home and collect the few small possessions she had that belonged to her mother. Then she would go to him and give him her answer.

No matter what had brought them together, he was everything to her.

I love him. I always will.

chapter Twenty-Three

"Witches?" Gavin Meldrum reacted with astonishment.

"Believe it, for it is true." Tamhas Keavey observed his friend closely. He stood in Gavin Meldrum's study, choosing his words carefully. He wanted to incite Gavin to action against Fingal, but it was also important that Tamhas himself came out of this well.

His determination to put an end to Lennox Fingal had only been strengthened during his journey. After all that had passed, and the hasty ride flanked by angered townsmen, his deepest desire was that the whole of Edinburgh was roused to hunt down the master of Somerled. But he was also cautious about losing Gavin's respect. If Gavin believed Tamhas had not protected Chloris during her time in Saint Andrews, their good dealings in commerce might cease to be.

Gavin frowned. "I can scarcely believe that they run amok in Saint Andrews, where pilgrims have traveled to worship for hundreds of years."

"That is the worst of it, isn't it? It is shameful. They seek to overthrow order with their spells and their heathen beliefs."

"How did it happen, and what has it to do with Chloris?" Gavin crossed to a wine table and poured out two glasses of claret while Tamhas related the tale.

"They gathered together as a coven close to Saint Andrews and under the protection of a wily leader. He gained them respectability, and trade. Meanwhile they dripped their poison. Sadly, they have influenced many in the burgh. They sought to be involved in matters of great import, to spread their wicked messages and their evildoings."

"They weren't ousted because of this?"

"Oh, I tried. I led the bailiff to them as soon as I had gathered evidence against them, but they had run, afraid for their lives, as well they should be."

"Good man," Gavin responded, and held out a glass.

Tamhas accepted the glass Gavin offered and swigged from it heavily, glad of the fortifier. Then he lowered his voice, lest the men who had traveled with him overheard what he said. They were waiting in the hallway outside while Tamhas spoke with Gavin in private. "My understanding is that Cousin Chloris went to them in order to try to become a more fruitful wife to you, Gavin."

He paused, allowing his words to be understood.

Gavin seemed most surprised. "How so?"

"They promised her their magic would make her fertile, and poor trusting innocent that she is, she believed them." He shook his head. "I quizzed her on the matter, and she said there were…rituals…"

Gavin's expression did not alter, but his eyes flickered. "Do you know what these 'rituals' did to her?"

"I sent her home as soon as I found out she had gone to them seeking advice." It was a slight deviation from the truth, but Tamhas had to manage this situation well. It was Lennox Fingal he wanted Gavin to be asking about, Fingal he wanted him to hunt down and obliterate.

A tap at the door interrupted their discussion.

A servant entered. "Sire, should I offer the men refreshment?"

Gavin nodded. As she was about to leave he called her back. "Where is Mistress Chloris?"

"She went out to pay calls."

"Did she say where she was going, or when she would return?"

The girl shook her head.

Where was Chloris? Tamhas wondered if Fingal had got to her already. Tamhas didn't say anything, but he and Gavin exchanged glances.

"Alert me as soon as she returns." Gavin shooed the girl out. When she shut the door, he returned his attention to Tamhas. "And you believe they have followed her here?"

"At least one. Perhaps more. Gavin, I fear they may have attempted to influence her with their evildoings. We need to be rid of them in order to protect her."

Gavin's eyes lit. "Influenced, yes. That would make sense of it, for she came back different, emboldened." His eyes narrowed and he glanced away. "She is no longer the woman that I married."

This was not the way Tamhas thought Gavin would react. "We must be rid of this vermin," Tamhas insisted again. "Then your good wife will return to you in body and soul."

Gavin grew silent and thoughtful. He paced up and down his study. His lips were pressed tightly together, his eyes flickering as he thought through what had been revealed.

Tamhas wondered what was going through his mind. A plan of action, he hoped. Gavin had many friends in high places in Edinburgh and could easily rouse expert witch finders, the ministers, the bailiff, soldiers and more, people who were willing to hunt this man down.

"We must protect Chloris from them," he repeated, willing Gavin to begin the witch hunt.

Gavin paused on his pacing and looked at Tamhas. "I fear we may be too late for that."

Tamhas frowned. "I do not understand your meaning."

"She is a changed woman, Tamhas. It is clear to me now that they have meddled with her soul." Gavin's mood was as self-assured as it was venomous. "If my wife has been influenced by these witches, and it seems that she has, then perhaps it would be better if she burned with them!"

Tamhas struggled to maintain his composure, for he was taken aback by Gavin's swift and harsh verdict on the situation. Did he really believe that was just, or did he perhaps see this as a convenient way to get rid of a wife who was no longer useful to him? Was it because she was barren? Tamhas worked through his thoughts quickly, trying to find the appropriate thing to say. He needed to gauge the depth of Gavin's conviction. "It would be a harsh thing, to oust her with them, but I suppose you have the burgh to think of. The capital must be protected."

Gavin nodded. "The people of Edinburgh will not respect me if my wife is in league with witches and I spare her."

Gavin's eyes were alight, as if he were excited by the uproar this might cause.

Tamhas wondered if he had judged the situation wrongly. He had not envisaged Gavin's fervor, nor his will to determine how involved Chloris had become. What worried him most of all was that he might be about to lose his most important agent in commerce. "However you decide to approach this, I will step behind you." He paused, stared at Gavin. "The good standing of our friendship and our business arrangements are foremost in my mind at this time."

Gavin looked at him with an assessing glance, his eyes shrewd and calculating. "You did well to come here so quickly, to warn me. I am indebted to you. You have always made good sense of how things are between us. If I must sacrifice my wife in order to protect Edinburgh, it will be done."

He walked over to a bureau against the far wall and opened a drawer, withdrawing a bundle wrapped in a cloth. He carried it back to Tamhas and placed it on a nearby table.

When Gavin unwrapped it Tamhas saw that the cloth covered a pistol.

"Our business arrangement will remain strong if the situation is dealt with quickly and tidily. If you understand my meaning." He polished the pistol with the rag it had been wrapped in, loaded it, and then set it down on the desk between them. "You have the evidence from Saint Andrews. I will send for the witch finder general and his men. You must point the finger. If Chloris attempts to deny it or escape, make sure it does not happen."

Tamhas stared down at the pistol. He did not need the weapon, for he had his own, but Gavin's message was clear. However, Tamhas suddenly found himself remembering those evenings back at Torquil House, when he had sat with her and lusted after her, and he wanted to back away and deny this bargain. He forced himself to be sensible about the matter. Chloris had gone to Fingal. Chloris had not come to him.

Besides, would it be so great a sacrifice to make if he was finally rid of Fingal?

There was a part of him that did not want to relinquish

his hold on his cousin, but if it meant he could smite Fingal that way, then perhaps Gavin was correct in his assumption.

For Gavin it appeared it was the only way. Gavin was set on it.

It was not the outcome Tamhas had hoped for, but if he had to sacrifice Cousin Chloris in order to be secure in his commerce, so be it.

"Mistress Chloris, you are home." When Mary opened the front door and took Chloris's cloak, Mary looked at Chloris with a disturbed expression in her eyes.

"What is it, Mary?"

"There are strange goings-on. Master Gavin has been asking for you."

"He is here?"

"In his study."

Chloris did not want to go in there again, but it seemed that she must. Perhaps he had come to his senses and was about to let her go, which would be a mercy. Then the sound of men's voices reached Chloris from beyond the stairs, where the scullery was. As Mary had indicated, something was amiss.

She knocked on the door and entered the study. When she saw who was in there with Gavin, she was staggered beyond belief.

Tamhas stared at her with a frown. The boots he wore were muddied. His clothes were dirty and he wore no hat or wig. He looked as if he had traveled hard and arrived here recently, as if he had not even had time to refresh himself.

The implications rushed in on her fast. Tamhas must have followed Lennox. There was no other conceivable reason for his hasty arrival so soon after Lennox. Chloris felt dizzy, suddenly sick to the gut. Tamhas had become so obsessed with Lennox that he had followed him here. What had he said to Gavin?

"Ah, and here she is." Gavin looked at her from hooded eyes. He pressed his lips together as if he were containing a smile.

"You know what this is about, I wager," Tamhas snapped at her.

Chloris held her head high. "No, I do not. Would you care to enlighten me?"

Tamhas looked enraged by that and he strode over to her, stepping between her and Gavin. When he glowered at her there was a warning in his eyes. "I know that Lennox Fingal has come here, and you would do well to reveal his whereabouts and quickly, lest you get dragged down to hell with him."

Chloris glared back at him. He could rant at her all he wanted, but she was not about to reveal Lennox's whereabouts.

"Speak out, Chloris," Tamhas urged when she did not respond. "Your husband has already summoned the witch finder general."

A rushing sound filled her ears and her mouth went dry, her heart hammering in her chest. The witch finder? Visions of what they might do if they found Lennox or Jessie filled her thoughts. It could not happen. She would not let them harm her lover or his sister. The very thought that they might get their hands on either one of them made her want to warn him and send him on his way. It was her fault that they had come here. She had to stand between them and their persecutors, there was no question about that. Chloris vowed she would because she loved him and it pained her deeply to think that he'd come here for her and put himself in such danger.

From behind Tamhas Gavin emerged, approaching her. "Tamhas has told me what happened to you in Saint Andrews. Now I understand why those dreadful changes I discovered in my wife have occurred. You've been consorting with witches, you have been subject to their evil ways." He looked her over with disgust. "I will hand you over to the witch finder general without a qualm, for I would rather forfeit my wife in order to have your soul redeemed."

Chloris fought the mad urge to laugh. How well this had played into his hands, she realized. He did not want her to leave him, for that would show him up, but he could play the martyr in front of the whole burgh if it suited him. People would talk about his brave sacrifice and his position would be maintained. "You can do what you want with me. I will never reveal his whereabouts."

"So it is true, you are in league with a witch." Gavin scrutinized her calmly. "Well, the witch finder will get the information from you. They have some canny tools for the task." He flashed her a brief smile. "Once he puts his thumbscrews on you, you will plead for mercy. When you get none, you will tell him everything he needs to know and then you will sign the confession with your bloodied and broken hand."

How he relished the prospect.

"I will die before I reveal anything," she replied.

Gavin inclined his head. "Your choice."

"Don't be a fool," Tamhas interjected, and raised his hands in a gesture of disbelief. "You cannot sacrifice yourself for one of the Devil's slaves. How could you even think this way?"

"They have stolen her soul," Gavin said, apparently delighted.

Chloris decided she hated him. She had never before hated anybody, but now she did.

"I told you to come back here for your own safety," Tamhas continued. "I warned you to stay away from them."

To her surprise, Tamhas looked aggrieved and disappointed. Could it be that her cousin cared more for her survival than did her husband? The reasons for that were manifold, but still it surprised her. It was ironic that she found out her value to them both now. Chloris felt strangely as if she wasn't really there, as if she were looking in on this room from far away. She wished it were so.

She looked away from their arrogant, aggressive faces in disgust.

It was then that she saw Gavin's pistol had been set out on a table and prepared for use. It was a fine French weapon he had bought several years earlier. She had only seen him use it once and that was on a game hunt, but she knew he would not bring it out now if he did not believe it would be needed.

Shocked that a weapon had been prepared, her blood began to boil. She turned to Tamhas. "You promised me you would leave the people of Somerled alone, and yet you have pursued their master here."

Tamhas lifted his brows. "He's clearly set on having you, and I could not let you fall into the hands of such a blackguard."

She was fast losing control of her tongue, but she could not help it. "How easily you judge something you do not understand."

It was Gavin who responded to that, and he fixed her with

a bright-eyed stare. "You really have consorted with these witches. Your soul is as black as the Devil's eyes."

Chloris could only offer her honest answer. "Believe what you want. They are decent people and I would rather be with them than you."

Gavin strode past her and slammed the door shut. Apparently he did not want the servants to hear that. "This 'he' that you speak of, you have given yourself into his hands?"

"I have, and it is the only happiness I have ever known since my parents perished." There was freedom in stating her truths, and Chloris felt almost light-headed with relief, as if a burden she had unwittingly been carrying had finally been taken from her.

The hatred she saw in Gavin's eyes grew fiercer. "I would rather see you dead than hear you speak to me that way again."

It was a warning, but she did not care anymore. "Of course you would, for that is what you have craved for some time, isn't it?"

Tamhas appeared shocked at that. He reached out for her and attempted to put his hand on her shoulder. "Think about what you're saying."

Chloris drew back. "It is too late for that. You initiated this, Tamhas. You came here to cause a disturbance. There is no way back for us now, but you will not get what you want, for I will not reveal his whereabouts."

Gavin stared her down. "Fool. When the witch finder arrives you will show him where they are hiding, and even if you don't, you know that I will have them hunted down."

He had the bloodlust now, and she feared he would be as hungry for the win as Tamhas. Her fear for Lennox grew.

"It'll be a fine show for Edinburgh," Gavin added, "a witch trial and a hanging."

Never. Chloris saw the image he craved and she darted to the table, snatched up the pistol and pointed it at them both.

Tamhas looked concerned but Gavin simply laughed. The sound held a cruel, dismissive note.

She turned the pistol fully on him.

"You are a weak woman. You don't have it in you to injure either of us."

When she pulled the trigger, she was not prepared for the violent start the weapon gave and she stumbled back, hitting up against the bureau.

Had she wounded him? She only knew for certain because his expression distorted, and his body jerked. Then a dot of red appeared on his shoulder and quickly grew larger, blood seeping across his waistcoat. He reached for the wound with his opposite hand and grunted heavily when he pressed upon it to stem the flow of blood.

Chloris threw the weapon to the floor.

"Seize her!" Gavin grunted.

Tamhas needed no further encouragement, for he already looked at her as if she had lost her mind. Arresting her, he pulled her hands together behind her back, holding her by the wrists.

She glared back at him. "I will die before I tell you anything."

Tamhas sneered at her. "You heard what your husband said. The witch finder general will find him, anyway. We will hunt him down and run him out of his lair."

Fear and anger tangled within her.

Gavin had staggered to the door, opened it and called for assistance.

Outside, she heard voices raised. When she glanced at the window she saw that the street outside was lit with torches. A mob had gathered.

"The finder is here," Tamhas told her. "You cannot protect him now."

Chloris didn't respond, for her mind worked frantically. She barely cared about the pain she felt or her own fate, and when Tamhas held her tightly by one arm and pulled her to face the angry crowd outside, she thought only of how much she loved Lennox.

Gavin had staggered down the hall, where the front door was open. "Call the surgeon," he shouted.

Men ran to his side.

Tamhas paused halfway down the hall, leaned close to her ear and whispered, "Reconsider, please. Save yourself."

She shook her head.

Tamhas growled low in his throat, then grabbed her shoulder and forced her on.

All she could think of was sending a message, but she did not know what to do.

She had to warn Lennox, but how? That's when she recalled the charm Jessie had given her. *Hold it to your heart. He will know.*

Would he? Would he sense her warning? It was her only chance.

Chloris fumbled for her pocket with her free hand, seeking the token.

When her fingers closed on it, she took it to her heart and willed Lennox to run.

chapter Twenty-Four

When he felt the tug at his heart, Lennox stood bolt upright.

Staring at Jessie, he quizzed her. "The charm I gave you?"

"I gave it to Chloris when she took her leave."

"You are a canny lass, sister." Lennox was most impressed.

Jessie rose to her feet. She had been trying to comfort him while he waited for Chloris, but now her eyes lit. "You feel something? Is she ready to join us?"

Lennox concentrated on the emotions that reached him. It was much darker than that, more immense, and Lennox feared for her. "I sense she is calling to me, but also that she is in danger, grave danger."

Jessie put her hand on his arm. "Hasten to her side. I will fetch Gregor. We will follow in case you need assistance."

"Thank you." He reached for his coat and pulled it on.

Jessie went out ahead of him.

Lennox ran down the stairs and out of the house.

Dusk was closing in. The skin on his back needled, the tension he felt building, his senses alert to the emotions that were spilling from Chloris now. Before he had reached the end of the street where they lodged, Jessie and Ramsay were on his heels.

As they approached the inn on the corner of the street the

sound of raised voices inside reached them. Lennox sensed there was trouble afoot. He glanced in and saw a man gesticulating, pointing out the door. After they had passed by the inn a group of men emerged behind him and ran in the same direction.

"I do not like the look of this," Ramsay commented.

"Neither do I," Lennox replied. Chloris's call grew more desperate.

He broke into a run.

When he turned the corner and saw what lay ahead, Lennox forced himself to halt and backed into the shadows, holding his hand up to stall those who followed. Ahead—outside the house they had located that very morning and identified as the Meldrum residence—a crowd had gathered. Several of the people had flaming torches held aloft. All around the gathering men held weapons—muskets, swords and bits of wood. At the center of the group he spied Keavey with Chloris. Behind them a man with a blood-soaked coat was being held up by two other men.

"Damn you, Tamhas Keavey," Lennox muttered. Seeing the man who had forced them from their home brought about a cold hard rage in Lennox. He was here in Edinburgh, and he had raised a mob.

There were shouts for justice, calls for a burning.

"Witch hunters," Jessie hissed, and she grabbed Lennox's arm, tugging at him. "Look at them. I have seen their kind before."

Lennox could only look at Chloris, his anger rising as he saw the way Keavey held her, dragging her along the ground like an animal.

"Hellfire," Ramsay said. "Let's away from here."

"No, Gregor, not without Lennox and Chloris," Jessie said. "My brother will need my assistance to fetch her."

Lennox turned to them. "Ramsay, go to the stables and retrieve the carriage. Take Jessie with you and keep her safe. I will join you as soon as I have Chloris."

"Lennox?" Jessie wore a frown and looked ready to argue.

"I need you to bring the carriage," he insisted. "Be ready for us, for we will need to hasten from this place, for good. We will make our escape, never fear, but I need the carriage to do so. Go as fast as you can and bring the carriage to this place, but no farther than the inn we just passed. I will send a sign for you to approach."

"A sign?" Ramsay asked with a dubious tone.

"You will know it when you see it."

Ramsay glanced at Jessie, then nodded.

"Now go, and be fast about it." Lennox rested a kiss on his sister's head and then shooed her on her way.

"Good luck," Ramsay said. "We will be ready for your sign."

Lennox locked his gaze. "If I do not signal within the hour, fly from this place. Keep Jessie safe."

Jessie stared at him. "Lennox, no."

"Do as I say! Promise me!"

"I promise." It was Ramsay who spoke. He nodded again and then grabbed Jessie by the arm and forced her to turn away.

Lennox could only be thankful his sister had such a determined protector.

Turning back to the scene ahead, he shut his eyes a moment in order to draw together every mote of power he had stoked for a time such as this. Then he stepped quickly along the street toward the gathering, his gaze on Chloris.

The simple blue gown she had on was torn, her hair loose.

He could only guess at what had occurred, but the nature of her position only made him more determined to pluck her from Keavey's grasp. He had the ability, he was sure of that, but—as usual—he needed a plan. He was still walking in the shadows and he assessed how much time he had before they saw him. Not long enough to make a plan, but still he strode on.

Chloris lifted her head. When she saw him, she shook her head vehemently.

She'd been trying to warn him. Oh, how he loved her and her brave heart.

That's when he saw the way.

Chanting his spell aloud, he stared at the fist she held to her chest.

With a startled cry she opened her palm and dropped the charm, which rolled across the street.

Lennox unleashed all the magic he had forced into it—and there was vitality aplenty. It had been done when he was an angry, thwarted young man, and the charm flared into life, flames as high as the rooftops soaring from it.

Screams issued from all around, the crowd shifting back quickly.

"She is a witch!" The fingers pointed at Chloris.

"I saw her throw the flame," shouted another. "Hang her, burn her body!"

"It was I who threw the flame," Lennox called, drawing their attention away from Chloris. "So it is me you will have to burn."

"He is the Witch Master," Tamhas Keavey informed them.

Several men charged at Lennox.

He darted away and changed direction, approaching the place where the charm blazed. "You want to see a witch burn?" he bellowed. "Then look and see!"

He lifted his arms, chanted the most ancient spell of all—that which created and sustained life—and stepped into the fire.

Screams issued from beyond and he heard Chloris's voice amongst the melee.

He turned, dousing himself in the radiant flames, arms outstretched.

When they saw that he did not burn, several of the gathered crowd turned and fled. Others spread out and circled him.

Keavey berated those who ran.

Chloris stared at him with wide eyes.

Lennox turned on the spot and drew a circle in the air with his fingertips. Pointing down at the ground he marked the place. The fire that surrounded him dropped to the ground, licked out across the mud track and then leaped high again in the circle he had drawn. He stood solid within the circle, staring through the flames.

As chaos erupted all around, he locked eyes with Chloris. "Come to me," he urged.

He nodded his head at her. "You will be safe."

Chloris looked about, but it seemed that no one had heard him call to her, only she heard the words. They were too busy trying to breach the circle of flames that surrounded him. No matter what they did, they could not get to him. Neither muskets nor pistols nor hurled wood broke through and reached him.

Trembling, she prayed she was not dreaming this.

Forgotten by the others in the panic, Gavin had collapsed and been left on the ground near to the steps of the house. The number of people gathered there had diminished, many having fled in fear. Tamhas and others paced about as if trying to work out how to break through to Lennox.

She felt as if she truly had lost her mind, for even though she had seen his magic before, she was shocked and afraid. When he walked into the flames she thought she would never breathe again, for she thought she had lost him forever, that he had sacrificed himself to save her. Then she recalled what he'd said that afternoon, the magic he had shown her then was nothing compared to what he felt for her. When she saw the way he reigned over the fire, controlling it, she was breathless with anticipation and hope that he would be able to find a way out of this.

"It is an illusion," Tamhas shouted, and darted over to one of the men who held a flaming torch aloft. Taking it from him, Tamhas hurled the torch in Lennox's direction. When the torch hit the flaming circle, its own fire was extinguished and it dropped in a pile of ashes. Smoke plumed from the place where the ashes fell on the ground.

Was it an illusion? Chloris tried to make sense of it. The flames looked real enough, but they stayed in the circle he had created, wavering high like ribbons all around him. Would he be able to keep the spell going, and what would happen if he could not? They would seize him and string him up.

Lennox beckoned to her.

"Come, Chloris, you will be safe, the flames will not harm you."

Could she do it? He had done it, but walking into the flames herself was another matter altogether, one that was far beyond her comprehension. She took a tentative step forward. He drew her to him with his gaze. The connection was so great, just as he had said, and he was leading her to him. Smoke rose all around her, and the smell of burned ground invaded her senses, frightening her.

"Come to me."

Chloris swallowed down her doubts and her fear, and let his voice guide her.

"The woman, he summons her," a voice cried out.

"Chloris, step away," Tamhas shouted, and he tried to drag her back. "Don't look at him, don't let him bewitch you."

Chloris shook him off.

Behind her she could hear shouts. Some issued warnings. Others called her a witch again. She was no witch, and if she was scorched to a cinder that fact would be revealed. She did not care. Even through the chaos it struck her that she was destined to be with them now, the Somerled people, and come what may it was where she wanted to be. Her legs were trembling under her and she could only take shallow breaths, but she forced herself onward.

As she grew closer, the heat from the flames convinced her it was real.

"Lennox," she cried out, then turned sideways and shielded her face with her raised arm. As she did so, something altered. It was as if a gateway opened. She stepped through a gap in the flames and found herself inside the circle, unharmed.

Trembling with relief, she swayed unsteadily.

Lennox put out his hand. When she took it, the flames at her back shot high again, closing them in. Inside the circle he had made, the heat seemed only comforting, and she was not afraid. Lennox drew her in against him, holding her to him with one arm around her.

Another shot rang out, but it hit neither of them.

She looked up at him.

"Hold tight to me," he whispered.

"Always."

"Don't be afraid."

She had already walked through fire to him, and now he tells her not to be afraid?

What was he about to do? Forcing down her nervousness, she looped her arms around his neck and kept her eyes trained on his face.

Lennox lifted one arm in the air, pointing skyward, and chanted in that strange tongue of his. A moment later the sky overhead lit up and a dazzling flash of lightning struck close by. He chanted again, and once again lightning bolts flashed all around. Chloris could hear screams, and through the flames she saw the shadowy figures outside the circle running in all directions.

Lennox glanced back over his shoulder.

From behind them a mighty thundering of hooves sounded, and a carriage approached at great speed.

"Are you able to run?"

She nodded.

He grasped her hand in his and held it tightly.

With his free hand he pointed at the flaming circle. "Be gone!"

In a heartbeat the fire disappeared. Only smoke remained, but it shielded them, rising from the charred ground in a thick cloud.

Holding tight to her hand he urged her to run. As they

approached the carriage the door was flung open. Lennox lifted her in.

Jessie was kneeling on the floor inside and she pulled Chloris close to where she huddled on the floor.

"Ramsay, strap yourself down, tightly," Lennox shouted up to where the coachman sat, then he clambered in.

Before the door was even closed, the carriage shunted off at great speed. Chloris's heart thundered in her chest, beating as hard and fast as the horses' hooves that carried them away. Her entire body shivered, shock, relief and gratitude making her senses swim.

The carriage rocked violently and Jessie clung to her side. They were on their way. Chloris could scarcely believe it. She stared across at her lover in awe. Lennox had drawn back the curtain and watched from the carriage seat where he perched, whispering beneath his breath, his arm out to shield the two women in case something was thrown. His eyes had that sheen in them that showed her he was still working magic, and then she felt as if the carriage moved faster still.

The carriage rattled and jolted and Chloris wondered how it was able to stay upright. They were traveling so fast she sensed they were already beyond the city walls.

"Oh, my belly." Jessie groaned.

Chloris wrapped the girl in her arms, holding tight to her.

Lennox turned to look at them, apparently satisfied they were on their way.

When he saw the way the two of them were huddled together, he shook his head and laughed. "We must find a way to cure you of this malady you have. No sister of mine should be afraid of anything."

Jessie lifted a hand in acknowledgment then buried her face in the curve of Chloris's neck.

"She cannot abide heights, and yet we are scarcely off the ground," Lennox explained.

"I will learn," Jessie mumbled.

Chloris felt for Jessie and hugged her tighter still.

She stared at Lennox in wonder. He was himself again.

Beyond him the curtain was still drawn back and everything appeared to shift fast outside, but he was still and solid and smiling at her.

He reached out his hand to her.

She rested her hand in his.

"I take it you were about to agree to come away with me anyway?"

Chloris laughed, and it let loose the tension she had held for so long. "Of course I was. I would have been back with you within the hour if Tamhas had not appeared and set panic loose in Edinburgh."

Lennox leaned over and drew her fingers to his lips. Kissing her tenderly on the back of her hand, he smiled. There was mischief in his eyes. "I just wanted to be sure I hadn't rescued you against your will."

She chuckled. "To be fair, you've done nothing to me against my will."

Lennox arched an eyebrow at her.

Memories flashed through her mind, intimate memories of all the times they had shared together. Now there would be more memories, and anticipation filled her as she thought about the days ahead. She would have to familiarize herself with his strange ways, his powers and beliefs, but she would work hard at that, to find their middle ground. "What you did there, your magic, it was astonishing."

His eyes twinkled. "My powers have been greatly forti-fied recently."

Jessie lifted her head and laughed softly. "It is because he loves you."

Chloris smiled. "And I love him."

chapter Twenty-Five

Lennox stared across the carriage at Chloris and felt a deep sense of contentment. She was finally his. It had taken some doing, but he had no regrets. He would have done whatever was needed to protect and win her.

Her tender beauty lit up his day. It had done, he now realized, since the moment he'd first seen her. He still recalled how dour his mood had been, as it often was back then, when she'd walked in to Somerled with the hawthorn blossom in her hair. The breath of spring she had carried was hers and hers alone. Thankfully he'd been there to welcome her, and thankfully he'd soon come to realize how ill-fated his plan to upset Tamhas Keavey had been. It was a mercy that they had finally left all of that behind.

Lennox would have been happier still if he had her beside him in the carriage, where he could hold her in his arms. However, because Jessie did not travel well Chloris had taken it upon herself to comfort Jessie and keep her from looking outside the carriage at the fast moving ground beneath the wheels. Chloris currently had Jessie tucked in against her, with Jessie's head upon her shoulder, soothing her with one arm around Jessie's back. Jessie dozed in reasonable contentment there.

At least the carriage was comfortable and well made, on a par with one built by his own craftsmen. Ramsay had insisted on spending a small fortune on it, as soon as they had the chance to offer for one at a staging post between Cupar and Edinburgh. It meant they could travel quicker without hiring a coachman and carriage at each town. He'd purchased a team of three horses, and Shadow led them. Shadow, who was used to his master's magic, kept the other horses in line when Lennox put wings beneath their hooves.

Gregor Ramsay had turned out to be a solid ally, and Lennox had now warmed to the man. Besides, he might not practice witchcraft, but he drove the carriage like a demon, and that had been most beneficial. No matter how rough the terrain, he sped them away from the Lowlands where the witch finders and their cohorts threatened their lives. Although Lennox knew he would miss the Lowlands, he would not miss the witch hunters who had stalked the people there for decades.

Lennox took his turn driving the horses and now, on day three of their journey, they were well on their way to Inverness. They would soon find his coven and then the Highlands were next. It would be good to see the place again, for it was that wild and powerful landscape that called to him most of all. It was so much more fitting to go there now, now that he'd gathered together his sister and his lover. Maisie still called to him. Once he had the women settled in the village where the Taskills had been born, he would have to return and continue his hunt for Maisie. But there was hope. If Jessie recalled the coat of arms upon the carriage that had taken her, he was sure that he would be able to pick up her trail. Once he'd found her as well, he would be thoroughly content.

Jessie grumbled in her doze. Chloris soothed her, then smiled across at him.

That simple action made him unerringly happy. Her eyes, so honest and open to him, had made him fall in love with her. Perhaps even from the moment she walked into his parlor asking for a magic favor, wearing that wide-eyed look that exposed her inner beauty. He vowed to cherish and protect her forever.

He glanced outside. The sun was getting low in the sky. "We will need to stop at the next inn."

Within the hour the carriage drew to a halt.

Jessie sat upright and yawned.

Lennox peered at the inn with caution. It was busy, far too well frequented for his liking. The women were tired and hungry, though, and it was too dark to head on. They had little choice in the matter. "Wait here and I will see if they have rooms."

Chloris grasped his hand and made him pause before he left the carriage. Her eyes were filled with affection as she looked at him, and it made him feel proud. "You worry so, and yet we are far away from Edinburgh and Saint Andrews now, my love."

"I will not be happy until we reach Inverness and reunite with the coven, then you will both be safe." Resting a hurried kiss upon her hand, he climbed out.

Ramsay leaped down from his perch and looked about. "What do you think of the place?"

Lennox frowned. "Perhaps it is better that it is busy, we will merge with the crowd. I will go and secure rooms if you want to deal with the stable hands."

Ramsay agreed.

Lennox paused. "There hasn't been a chance for me to thank you. I appreciate everything you have done, for me and Chloris, and for Jessie."

"Jessie was my savior. I would do anything for her."

"I see that now."

Lennox clasped the other man around the shoulder before turning back to the inn. The wariness between the two men had begun to fade after the events in Edinburgh, but this gesture was necessary and overdue.

The inn was crowded and raucous and it made Lennox wonder if they would have any rooms available, but luck was on their side once more and the landlord showed him two well-furnished rooms that he rented for the night. Requesting hot meals be served as soon as possible, he returned to the carriage.

A stable hand was already beside it. He had the door open and had put a wooden box beneath the carriage door for Chloris to step out upon. Immediately, Lennox felt possessive, protective. But it never had been any different. Once he'd had a taste of her he'd always felt that way. It was just that he now acknowledged it. She had forced him to embrace honesty, love and yes—it had brought greater power to his magic.

Chloris stepped out onto the box. One look at her face in the half light of dusk assured him that it would never be any different, he would always love this woman. He would accept his fate to be with her gladly, and with gratitude.

The stable hand was encouraging Chloris to jump across the muddy path to the stepping stones beyond. But from the doorway of the carriage he heard Jessie. She intervened, stumbling down from the carriage and assisting Chloris herself, instead of allowing the stable hand to do so.

Jessie shooed the stable boy away. "Take care, this woman is with child and must be treated gently."

With child? Lennox faltered.

He stared across at the woman he loved, and as he did he saw it in her smile. *How could I not have known?* Too busy he'd been claiming her for himself, to see what was there—and that which he would have spotted immediately had his emotions not been so entangled. Chloris was carrying his child.

Sharp pleasure and then confusion overcame him. How was it that Jessie knew when he did not? Women's ways. He was transported back in time to when their mother would round them up in the woods, and chastize young Jessie for her fae ways and her lack of fear or caution when it came to hiding her true nature. She was close to nature and sensed and sourced its most creative elements. She would have known instantly. Chloris, his precious love, was carrying his child.

Tearing his attention away from Chloris—which was doubly difficult now that he knew—he attempted to take in all that this meant. Kin, even more than he had imagined. His long search for his kin had resulted in so much, he felt blessed by nature, rewarded for surviving the hardships.

Jessie had dismissed the stable hand and now assisted Chloris, holding both her hands and smiling at her as they followed the stepping-stone path. Then Chloris met his gaze. For a long moment they stared at one another, and then Chloris drew her fingers to her mouth, her eyes misting.

He closed the gap between them in four strides and hugged her to him.

"I see by your expression that you heard what Jessie said?"

"Is it really true?"

She looked up at him. "I think so. I had my suspicions, but Jessie here said she knew."

"Let me look at you," he demanded as they drew apart, holding her at arm's length to study her again.

Lennox could tell that she was quelling her excitement, and yet all he could think of was wrapping her in a blanket and cherishing her. "You seem radiant and robust, but we must look after you well."

"You do look after me well." She beamed. "This is your doing." Laugher escaped her. "I meant the magic and the fertility, not the other…" Her cheeks flamed.

Her amusement triggered his own. "As I pointed out to you at the outset, I'm not entirely convinced the magic was needed, but I was very happy to assist with the other, as well."

Gregor emerged from the stables and waved his hand.

Together, the four of them went inside the inn.

"Where are we?" Chloris asked as they walked.

"Well on our way. We should reach Inverness within three days."

Inside, the crowd gathered in the inn showed little interest in them, which suited Lennox well. They were on a well-traveled route north now, having veered off it to begin with, in case they were followed. The inn was likely a busy passing point for strangers on the road. Soon, however, he would not have to double think everything they did, for soon they would be in the Highlands.

The landlord led them to a private dining room where tankards of ale and dishes of steaming stew had been put out on a rickety table. It was a simple but happy gathering, and Lennox kept his woman beside him, constantly reaching for her hand and staring into her eyes to reassure himself that this truly had come to pass.

After they had eaten, the landlord's wife brought a bottle of Port and stoked the fire. The conversation turned to their escape from Edinburgh.

"I warrant we are no longer welcome in the Lowlands after that show you put on," Gregor said. There was grudging admiration in his eyes.

"That is the truth, but it was necessary."

"Your magic is so powerful," Jessie said. "I have much to learn."

"Why does that sound like trouble to me?" Gregor said, and Jessie laughed.

"They would have burned me as a witch," Chloris commented. "They said so even before you arrived and showed your powers."

"Many bystanders have suffered," Lennox said, "as well as those who practice the old ways. People are too ready to judge and accuse, and the witch finders are able to finger whoever they want. I heard tell they put this mark upon people they suspect. They call it the Devil's mark, and then they force the victims to confess through torture."

He noticed that Chloris shuddered when he mentioned the confession.

"It will bring about a legacy of regret for Scotland," he added, "mark my words."

"It will be good to be at home in the Highlands," Jessie said.

"You drove that carriage like a demon, Gregor," Lennox commented, changing the subject.

Chloris nodded. "However did you stay upright when it was going at such speed?"

Gregor smiled. "When you have handled a ship on the high seas in rough weather, you get used to being cast about and keeping your wits about you."

Lennox was pleased to see the man less tense than he had appeared during their acquaintance thus far. But he knew the reason was because they were now on their way and talk of witch finders would soon grow more distant, as well.

"You have been aboard a ship?" Chloris asked.

She'd had time to become acquainted with Jessie's gentleman during his time resting in the carriage, while Lennox took the coachman's seat, but they obviously hadn't discussed his background to any great extent.

"I own a part share in a vessel, a ship I joined when I was a lad. It is called the *Libertas*. I traveled far and wide when I was away from Scotland." He turned to Jessie and smiled. "I believe I am thoroughly landlocked now, though."

"You will not go back to your ship?" Lennox asked, his curiosity kindled on the matter. He would hate to see Jessie disappointed and her heart broken if the sea beckoned to her lover once more.

"It is the new life that calls to me now, I am set on it. In fact I must soon think upon writing to Roderick, my partner, who is currently the captain. He will be expecting me to return to Dundee to meet the *Libertas* later in the year. I will need to send word to let him know my plans have changed, that I will be making my home in Scotland once again."

Lennox could see the man was devoted to Jessie, but Lennox was no longer wary of that, for he had put on a good show of defending her these past few days.

"There is a matter that I should discuss with you," Gregor said to Lennox. "Just before our paths crossed in Fife, I asked

Jessie to be my wife. Now that you and I have met, it is you that I should go to in order to request her hand in marriage. Will you agree to it?"

Lennox noticed there was a bit of tension in the man's expression. Was it because Gregor was not one of their kind? It no longer mattered. "If Jessie is happy, then I am happy."

Jessie, who had been listening carefully and with a serious expression, broke into a large smile. "You see," she said, "I told you there was nothing to worry about."

"Will you wed when we get to the Highlands?" Lennox asked, and as he did so he held Chloris's hand tightly in his. He could feel her mood alter. She was fretting. He would need to soothe her concerns when they were alone.

"If that suits us all," Gregor said.

Lennox nodded. "Glenna, the oldest and wisest woman in my coven, she has a gift for making a fine handfasting. She will enjoy taking on the task of binding you together."

His suggestion was greeted with good cheer all around.

Soon after, he said good-night to Jessie and Gregor and led Chloris away. They needed to speak on matters of their own.

When they were alone in the chamber he had secured for them, he lifted her in his arms and carried her to the bed, resting her down gently.

"Oh, this bed is nowt but boards and blankets, but it is still a fine blessing after our journey." She reached out her arms to him.

"I will secure you the best stuffed mattress in the Highlands, when we reach Fingal." He gazed down at her and sighed with contentment. Then he lay alongside her and held her in his arms. He'd never felt more grateful for the chance to be with her.

Chloris stared up at him, her eyes searching his.

"Don't fret."

"I cannot help it."

How he wanted to wash all those worries away. "Are you afraid I will not marry you?"

She stayed silent for the longest moment before she spoke. "I am married to another. We can never be the way that Jessie and Gregor are."

There was such sadness in her pretty hazel eyes and he did not like that. "We can, and we are."

She shook her head. "I will never be free of it, and you might...you might come to hate that and turn away from me and find love elsewhere."

He started. She thought he would wed another? "Chloris, we are bound together, ceremony or no ceremony. We both know that."

She looked at him and nodded. But she was sad still.

"Come now, things are very different in the Highlands. Clan life is closer to the heart and hearth. But things are fair and we will be treated as man and wife. Sometimes Highlands couples live together for a year before they wed, to be sure they are meant to be that way."

"Is that so?" She was fascinated, and now seemed eager for his opinion.

Lennox knew she had left her past life, but she was afraid he would think differently. All he wanted to do was reassure her. None of it mattered. They were meant to be together. "When you married it was in the Kirk?"

"Yes."

"Well, I have nothing against the Kirk and the people who believe in that way of life, but our way is different. If we were to handfast, it's a simple pledge to each other and it's made in nature's bower. It is an honest agreement between two people who wish to share their lives, and the life of their issue." He stroked his hand over her belly.

"You think we can handfast?" Her lower lip trembled.

He nodded. "The past is behind us."

"Oh, Lennox." She kissed him madly, his lips, his forehead, his cheeks. "The fact that you want me, it overwhelms me."

"Hush now. You should know how much I want you. I nigh on burned Edinburgh to the ground for you."

Chloris chuckled.

Lennox was much relieved that he had alleviated her concerns somewhat. There were things he still worried on, but he did not want Chloris fretting. He settled alongside her, with his fingertips trailing over her belly while they talked, reminding her that he was thinking of their precious union, too.

"There is a matter about which I am greatly curious," she said later.

"There is?"

"Our child, will it be magical?"

The question touched Lennox in a way he didn't think possible. The thought of a child with her had startled him and pleased him immensely. Now her question led him into a world to be explored—explored with her hand in his.

"The child will have the bloodline, and if the young one is brought up amongst those who understand and practice the craft there are great possibilities, even if both parents do not come from the line. My cousin Deirdra married a crofter who is not a witch and they had three mischievous bairns who are every bit as gifted as the other young ones in the clan."

Her eyes sparkled as she listened to him and he could see

how the possibilities of their life together invigorated her, as they did him.

"Will you still love the child if it does not have the powers that you have?"

Lennox was amused by her questions. "You have thought on this at great length."

"I had plenty of time to think on it during the carriage ride today, while I was nursing your sister. And when it was you that was sitting opposite me it helped to keep my mind upon the subject."

"You have nothing to fear. Even if we never had a child, I would be devoted to you. The child is a gift that we shall love and treasure together."

"It was meant to be," she whispered, as she looked up at him. "Just as you said." She rested her hand over his. "It was your magic that made this happen."

He saw how much she had thought upon this, how deeply she had engaged with the matter in her heart. "Perhaps." He studied her. "I told you I never believed you needed the fertility rituals. However the way you responded to my magic was so precious. It was something so unique to my experience. It revealed to me that we had a very deep connection."

She looked at him from under her lashes. "And it was just as magical without the magic."

"It pleases me that you think so." He chuckled and stroked her hair back from her forehead. The tresses were golden in the candlelight, and he hoped she would wear it loose more, when they were away from the formal life of the towns in the Lowlands.

She had stated her concerns, now it was time for his. "And

do you forgive me, for my misguided motivation at the out-set?"

"Yes."

"It was short-lived, believe me. You soon came to mean everything to me, much more than some festering feud."

That made her chuckle. "A festering feud, indeed it was. Tamhas grumbled at length about you, especially after you presented at council. The things he said. I didn't know where to look."

"Strangely enough, I can picture it."

"I confess I was shocked, but that was because I hadn't re-alized. With a little distance on it and time to think it fast fell into place." She meshed her hand with his. "I looked back, and I could see when it changed. When I wrote to you tell-ing you that I did not wish to continue with the rituals, you still sought me out. If you had just wanted to upset Tamhas, you could have revealed the matter to him then and moved on to some other conquest."

She looked deep into his eyes and Lennox felt her love shine within him.

"It was wrong of me, but I am happier that the truth is out. It will take me a while to believe you truly forgive me, but I will work hard for that." It was a promise he meant to keep.

Her lips parted softly, and he could do nothing other than kiss her.

Rolling her closer, he lifted her against him, joyous in their embrace.

Her lips parted, yielding to him. She was so soft and pre-cious in his arms he wanted to hold her like that forever, even if it meant carrying her all the way to the Highlands that way. He ached for her, every part of him attuned to her and her alone.

She sighed after they kissed. "Why is it that you love me? I still do not understand how this has occurred… You are all raw power and wildness, and I am not."

She was so bewildered looking that it amused him greatly. "Oh, well, the reason I love you should be obvious."

She waited for his reply.

"Because you told me you are not prone to melodrama."

She stared at him for a long moment, then burst into laughter. "And you believed me?"

"Of course I did." He nuzzled the soft skin behind her ear, kissing her there.

"You have made me so happy," she whispered.

"It is only the beginning."

"We do however have one problem," she added.

"We do?" Lennox did not like the sound of that.

"When you first came to my chamber at Torquil House, you said I could determine the amount of your fee if I was happy with the results of the rituals you undertook." She looked at him from under her lashes, a smile lifting the corners of her mouth. "Well, I am most pleased with the way it has turned out, but I do not think I have enough coins, nor will I ever have enough, for that is how happy I am with the results."

Lennox did not hesitate. "I will happily take you, in exchange for my fee."

"Are you sure that will be enough recompense?"

"Only if it is forever."

"In that case," she said, "I suppose I must agree."

★ ★ ★ ★ ★

Acknowledgments

I am indebted to Jody Allen for her knowledge on specific points about the history and culture of Lowlands Scotland. Thank you, Jody, for all your wisdom and guidance.

I am also indebted to the staff of the National Museum of Scotland, The Museum of Edinburgh and the People's Story Museum in Edinburgh, who upkeep terrific collections recreating the lives and history of everyday Scottish people, making research a joy and an inspiration.

Finally my thanks go to Portia Da Costa for her friendship, support and encouragement during the writing of this novel.

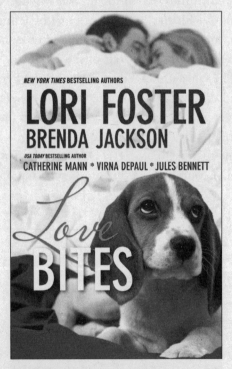

Harlequin More Than Words
Where Dreams Begin

Three bestselling authors
Three real-life heroines

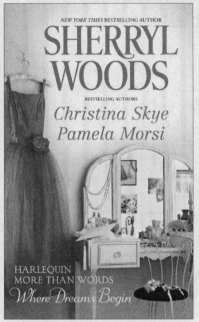

Each of us can effect change. In our own unique ways, we can all make the world a better place. We need only to take that first step, do that first good deed and the ripple effect will be life-changing to so many. Three extraordinary women who were compelled to take that first leap and make a difference have been chosen as recipients of **Harlequin's More Than Words** award. To celebrate their accomplishments, three bestselling authors have written short stories inspired by these real-life heroines.

SHERRYL WOODS captures the magic of pretty dresses and first dances in *Black Tie and Promises.*

CHRISTINA SKYE's *Safely Home* is the story of a woman determined to help the elderly in her newly adopted community.

PAMELA MORSI explores how literacy and the love of reading can enrich and indeed change lives in *Daffodils in Spring.*

*Thank you… Net proceeds from the sale of this book will be reinvested into the **Harlequin More Than Words** program to support causes that are of concern to women.*

Available wherever books are sold!

www.Harlequin.com

PHSWCKPM784TR

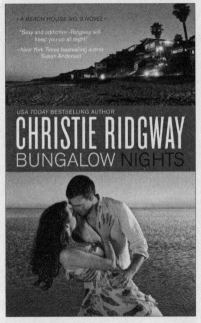

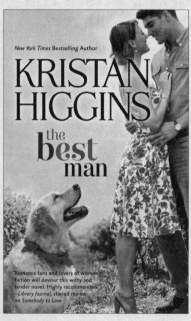